First Studies of Plant Life

This edition published 2024
by Living Book Press

ISBN: 978-1-76153-377-8 (hardcover)
978-1-76153-378-5 (softcover)

First published in 1901.

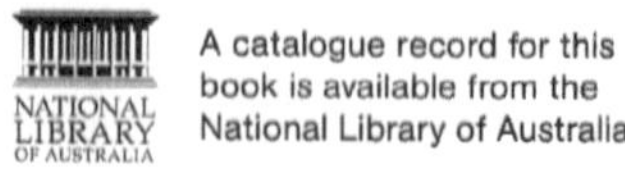

First Studies of Plant Life

by

George Francis Atkinson

Contents

Frontispiece.— A Congenial Plant Society, Minnesota
(Photograph, by H. E. Murdock)

INTRODUCTION

FOR a long time botanical science, in the popular mind, consisted chiefly of pulling flowers to pieces and finding their Latin names by the use of the analytical key. All the careful descriptions of the habits of plants in the classic books were viewed solely as conducive to accuracy in placing the proper label upon herbarium specimens. Long after the study of botany in the universities had become biological rather than purely systematic, the old régime held sway in our secondary schools; and perhaps some of us today know of high schools still working in the twilight of that first ray that pierced primeval darkness. However, this has practically passed away, and today life and its problems, its successes and its failures, absorb the attention of the botanist and zoölogist. The knowledge of the name of the plant or animal is simply a convenience for discrimination and reference. The systematic relations of a plant or animal are used in showing present anatomical affinities and past development. The absorbing themes of investigation and study are the life processes and the means by which the organisms living in the world today have climbed upward and placed themselves in the great realm of the "fit."

When the idea of nature study first dawned in the educational world, it was inevitably confused with the sciences on which it was based. Hence in earlier times we tried to teach the nature study of plants by making the children pull the flowers to pieces and learn the names of their different parts. This was as bad nature study as it was bad science, for we were violating the laws of the child's nature. The child cares very little about the forms of things; he is far more interested in what things do.

Today nature study and science, while they may deal with

the same objects, view them from opposite standpoints. Nature study is not synthetic; it takes for its central thought the child, and for its field work the child's natural environment. The child, through nature study, learns to know the life history of the violet growing in his own dooryard, and the fascinating story of the robin nesting in the cornice of his own porch. The differences of this violet and this robin from other violets and other robins in the world he considers not at all.

That the plant as well as the animal in nature study should be regarded a thing of life has long been recognized, and most of our nature study of plants begins with the planting and sprouting of the seed. Unfortunately, it mostly stops here; the life processes of the plant have seemed too complex to be brought within the comprehension of the child. There is much of chemistry in operations of plant growth, and we find very few things in chemistry that are simple enough to be properly a part of nature study.

First Studies of Plant Life has been written with the sole view of bringing the life processes of the plant within the reach of the child and, with the aid of the competent teacher, it will certainly be comprehensible to the pupil of even the lower grades. In this book the plant stands before the child as a living being with needs like his own. To live, the plant must be born, must be nourished, must breathe, must reproduce, and, after experiencing these things, must die. Each plant that is grown in the window box of a schoolroom should reveal to the child the secrets and the story of a whole life. He realizes that the young plant must be fed; it must grow; it is no longer a matter of commonplace; it is replete with interest, because it is the struggle of an individual to live. How does it get its food? How does it grow? It is of little moment whether its leaves are lanceolate or palmate; it is a question of what the leaves do for the plant; it is a matter of life or death.

When the child has once become acquainted with the conditions and necessities of plant life, how different will the world seem to him! Every glance at forest or field will tell him a new story. Every square foot of sod will be revealed to him as a battlefield in which he himself may count the victories in the struggle for existence, and he will walk henceforward in a world of miracle and of beauty,—the miracle of adjustment to circumstances, and the beauty of obedience to law.

ANNA BOTSFORD COMSTOCK.
BUREAU OF NATURE STUDY,
CORNELL UNIVERSITY.

AUTHOR'S PREFACE

IN presenting these *First Studies of Plant Life* the object has been to interest the child and pupil in the life and work of plants. The child, or young pupil, is primarily interested in life or something real and active, full of action, of play, or play-work. Things which are in action, which represent states of action, or which can be used by the child in imitating or "staging" various activities or realities, are those which appeal most directly to him and which are most forceful in impressing on his mind the fundamental things on which his sympathies or interests can be built up.

There is, perhaps, a too general feeling that young pupils should be taught things; that the time for reasoning out why a thing is so, or why it behaves as it does under certain conditions, belongs to a later period of life. We are apt to forget that during the first years of his existence the child is dependent largely on his own resources, his own activity of body and mind, in acquiring knowledge. He is preëminently an investigator, occupied with marvelous observations and explorations of his environment.

Why then should we not encourage a continuance of this kind of knowledge-seeking on the part of the child? The young pupil cannot, of course, be left entirely to himself in working out the relation and meaning of things. But opportunities often present themselves when the child should be encouraged to make the observations and from these learn why the result is so. No more excellent opportunities are afforded than in nature study. The topics most suitable are those which deal with the life, or work, or the conditions and states of formation.

To the child or young pupil a story, or the materials from

which a story can be constructed, is not only the most engaging theme, but offers the best opportunity for constructive thought and proper interpretation.

In the studies on the work of plants some of the topics will have to be presented entirely by the teacher, and will serve as reference matter for the pupil, as will all of the book on occasions. The chapter dealing with the chemical changes in the work of starch-making is recognized by the author as dealing with too technical a subject for young pupils, and is included chiefly to round out the part on the work of plants. Still it involves no difficult reasoning, and if young children can appreciate, as many of them do, the "Fairyland of Chemistry," the pupils may be able to get at least a general notion of what is involved in the changes outlined in this chapter.

The chapters on Life Stories of Plants the author has attempted to present in the form of biographies. They suggest that biographies are to be read from the plants themselves by the pupils. In fact, this feature of reading the stories which plants have to tell forms the leading theme which runs through the book. The plants talk by a "sign language," which the pupil is encouraged to read and interpret. This method lends itself in a happy manner as an appeal to the child's power of interpretation of the things which it sees.

Many older persons will, perhaps, be interested in some of these stories, especially in the Struggles of a White Pine.

The story on the companionship of plants also affords a topic of real interest to the pupil, suggesting social conditions and relations of plants which can be read and interpreted by the young.

Nearly all of the line drawings are original, and were made expressly for this book by Mr. Frank R. Rathbun, Auburn, N.Y. Figs. 64, 79, 215, 216, 260 were reproduced from Bergen's "Botany," and Fig. 84, from Circular 86, United States Department of Agriculture, by Mr. Chesnut. The author desires to acknowledge his indebtedness to the following persons, who have kindly contributed photographs: Mr. H. E. Murdock, for the Frontispiece; Prof. Conway MacMillan, University of Minnesota, for Figs. 220, 249, 257; Professor Gifford, Cornell University, for Figs. 87, 183, 285, 290, 293, 295; Mr. Gifford Pinchot, Division of Forestry, United States Department of Agriculture, for Figs. 280, 282, 289, 292; Prof. W. W. Rowlee, Cornell University, for Figs. 279, 281, 304; Miss A. V. Luther, for Figs. 200, 296, 302; Prof. P. H. Mell, for Fig. 278; Prof. William Trelease, Missouri Botanical Garden, for Fig. 307; Professor Tuomey, Yale University, for Fig. 306. Fig. 221 is reproduced from photographs by Mr. K. Miyake; Fig. 77, from photograph by Mr. H. Hasselbring; Figs. 76, 288, from photographs by Dr. W. A. Murrill. The remaining photographs were made by the author. Some of the text-figures were reproduced from the author's "Elementary Botany," while the photographs of mushrooms are from some of those published in Bulletins 138 and 168 of the Cornell University Agricultural Experiment Station, and from the author's "Mushrooms, Edible, Poisonous, etc."

GEO. F. ATKINSON.

CORNELL UNIVERSITY, March, 1901.

PART I.

THE GROWTH AND PARTS OF PLANTS

CHAPTER I.

How Seedlings Come up from the Ground

The life in a dry seed. For this study we shall use seeds of beans, peas, corn, pumpkin, sunflower, and buckwheat. You may use some other seeds if they are more convenient, but these are easy to get at feed stores or seed stores. If you did not know that they were seeds of plants, you would not believe that these dry and hard objects had any life in them. They show no signs of life while they are kept for weeks or months in the packet or bag in a dry room.

But plant the seeds in damp soil in the garden or field during the warm season, or plant them in a box or pot of damp soil kept in a warm room. For several days there is no sign that any change is taking place in the seeds. But in a few days or a week, if it is not too cold, some of the surface earth above the buried seeds is disturbed, lifted, or cracked. Rising through this opening in the surface soil there is a young green plant. We see that it has life now, because it grows and has the power to push its way through the soil. The dry seed was alive, but could not grow. The plant life was dormant in the dry seed. What made the plant life active when the seed was buried in the soil?

Fig. 1. Bean seedlings breaking through the soil.

How the corn seedling gets out of the ground. One should watch for the earliest appearance of the seedlings coming through the soil. The corn seedling seems to come up with little difficulty. It comes up straight, as a slender, pointed object which pierces through the soil easily, unless the earth is very hard, or a clod or stone lies above the seedling. It looks like a tender stem, but in a few days more it unrolls, or unwinds, and long, slender leaves appear, so that what we took for a stem was not a stem at all, but delicate leaves wrapped round each other so tightly as to push their way through the soil unharmed. What would have happened to the leaves if they had unfolded in the ground?

Fig. 2. Corn seedlings coming up.

How the bean behaves in coming out of the ground. When we look for the bean seedling as it is coming up we see that the stem is bent into a loop. This loop forces its way through the soil, dragging on one end the bean that was buried. Sometimes the outer coat of the seed clings to the bean as it comes from the ground, but usually this slips off and is left in the ground. Soon after the loop appears above ground it straightens out and lifts the bean several inches high. As the bean is being raised above ground the outer coat slips off. Now we see that the bean is split into two thick parts (*cot-y-le'dons*), which spread farther and farther apart, showing between them young green leaves, which soon expand into well-formed bean leaves.

Fig. 3. The "loop" of the bean seedling.

The pea seedling comes up in a different way. The stem of the pea also comes up in a loop. As it straightens up we look in vain for the pea on the end. There are small green leaves, but no

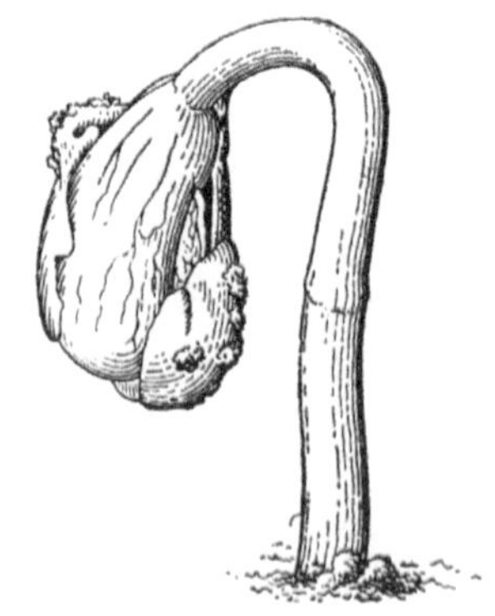

Fig. 4. Germinating bean shedding the seed coats.

thick part of the pea which was buried in the ground. This part of the pea, then, must have been left in the ground. When we have seen how the other seedlings come up, we can plant more seeds in such a way as to see just how each seed germinates, and learn the reason for the different behavior of the seedlings in coming from the ground.

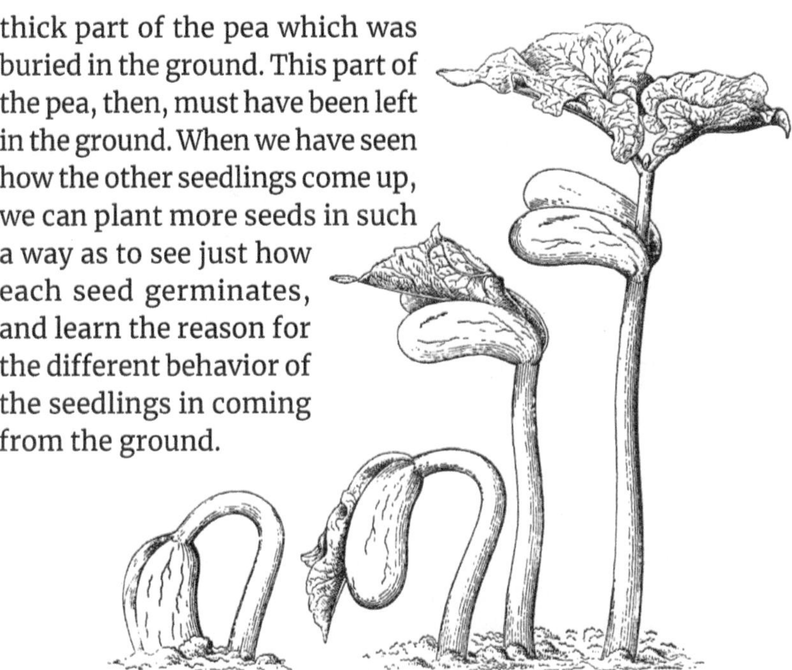

Fig. 5. Bean seedlings straightening up; the plumule and spreading leaves showing from between the cotyledons.

The pumpkin seedling also comes up in a loop, and on one end of the loop, as it is being lifted through the soil, we see two flat, rather thick parts. Together they are about the size of the pumpkin seed. By looking carefully we may sometimes find the old shell, or seed coat, still clinging to the tips of these parts of the seed; the shell is split part way down only, and so pinches tightly over the tips. Usually, however, it is left empty in the ground.

Fig. 6. Pea seedlings coming up.

It will be interesting later to see how this little pumpkin plant gets out of its shell. It usually escapes while still buried in the soil. As the loop straightens out, these two thick portions spread wide apart in the light and become green. There are little lines on them resembling the "veins" on some leaves. Are these two parts of the pumpkin seed real leaves? Look down between them where they join the stem. Very young leaves are growing out from between them.

The sunflower seedling. The sunflower seedling comes up with a loop, dragging the seed on one end. The shell, or seed coat, is sometimes left in the ground, because it splits farther through when the root wedges its way out. But often the seed coat clings to the tips of the cotyledons until the plant straightens. Then the cotyledons usually spread far apart. The seed coat of the pumpkin sometimes clings to the tips of the cotyledons until the sunlight pries them apart.

Fig. 7. Pumpkin seedlings coming from the ground, showing loop and opening cotyledons.

Fig. 8. Loop on stem of sunflower as it comes from the ground.

The buckwheat seedling. This also comes up with a loop, and we begin to see that this way of coming up is very common among seedlings. The seed coat of the buckwheat is often lifted above ground on one end of the loop. It is split nearly across. Through the split in the seed we can see that there are leaves packed inside very differently from the way in which the cotyledons of the pumpkin and sunflower lie. The buckwheat

Fig. 9. Seedlings of sunflower casting seed coats as cotyledons open.

Fig. 10. Loop of buckwheat seedlings coming through the surface of the soil.

cotyledons are twisted or rolled round each other. As the seedling straightens up they untwist, and in doing this help to throw off the coat.

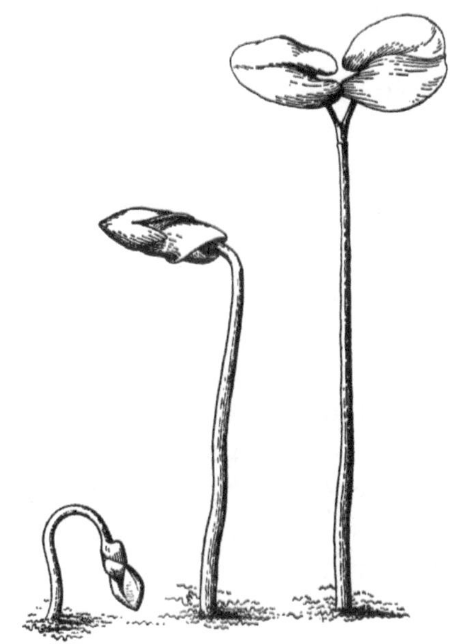

Fig. 11. Cotyledons of buckwheat seedling untwisting and casting seed coats.

CHAPTER II.

How the Seeds Behave When Germinating

To prepare the seeds for observation. We could not see how the seeds planted in the ground behaved while they were germinating, for they were hidden from sight. To watch the behavior of the different kinds, the seeds are put where there is warmth and moisture under glass, or they are covered with damp paper or moss, which may be lifted at any time to see what is going on. They may be grown in tumblers, or in shallow vessels covered with glass, with wet moss or paper inside. The best way to plant them for easy observation is to put them in a lamp chimney filled with wet peat moss or sawdust, as shown in Fig. 12. Or a box may be made with glass doors on the side. This may be filled with wet moss or sawdust, the seeds put in place, and the door then closed. If desired, some soft manila paper may be placed on the moss or sawdust, and the seed placed between this and the glass. If the lamp chimney is used, roll the paper into a tube smaller than the chimney and slip it in. Now put the peat moss inside, not very tight. The seeds may be started between the glass and paper, and with a blunt wire may be pushed into any position desired.

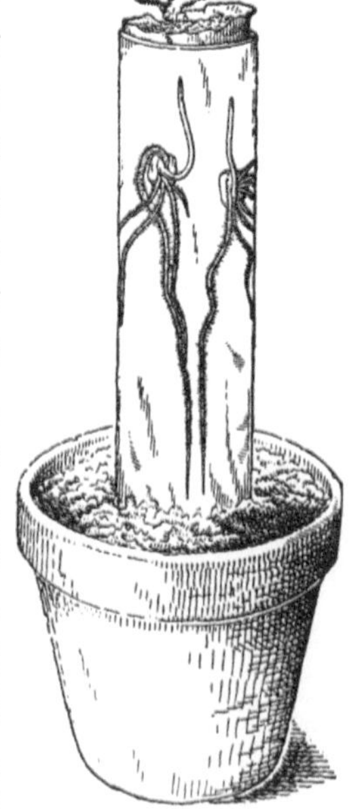

Fig. 12. Corn seedlings growing in lamp chimney.

The seeds first absorb water and swell. Before the seeds

Fig. 14. Box with glass door on side for growing seedlings.

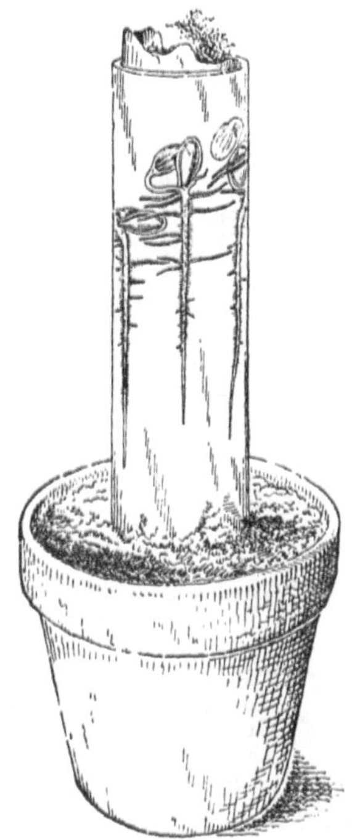

Fig. 13. Pumpkin seedlings growing in lamp chimney.

are planted for this study they should be soaked from twelve to twenty-four hours in water. Then they may be placed in the germinator for observation. Look at the seeds in the water several times during the day, and see what changes take place in them. All of them become larger. After they have been in the water for a day, cut one, and also try to cut one of the dry seeds. The seeds that have been soaked in water are softer and larger than the dry seed. Why is this so? It must be that they have taken in water, or have absorbed water, as we say. This has increased their size, made them wet inside, and soft.

How the pea and bean seeds swell. The pea and bean swell in a curious way, as can be seen by looking at them at short intervals after they have been placed in the water. The water is taken in at first more rapidly by the coat of the seed than by the other parts. The coat becomes much wrinkled then, as if it were too big for the seed. First the wrinkles begin to appear round one edge.

Fig. 15. Bean seed before soaking in water.

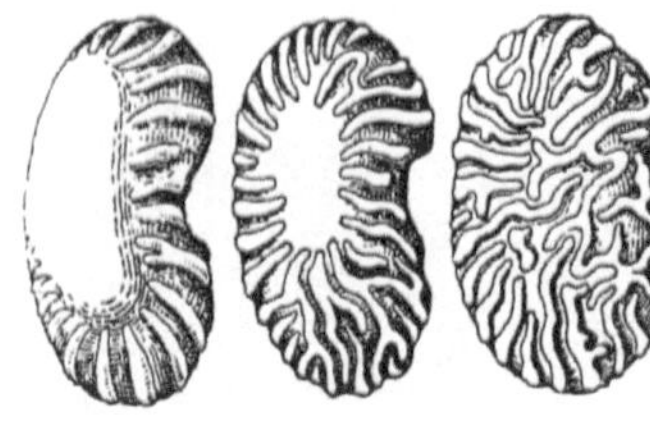

Fig. 16. Bean seeds with coats wrinkling as they soak in water.

Fig. 17. Bean seed after soaking in water, larger, and now smooth.

Then they become more numerous, and extend farther over the surface, until the entire coat is strongly wrinkled, as shown in Fig. 16. This loosens the coat from the bulk of the seed, and perhaps is one reason why this coat slips off so easily while the loop of the stem is pulling the inside of the seed out of the ground. Finally the inside parts swell as they take up water. They fill out the coat again so that it is smooth, as shown in Fig. 17.

Fig. 18. Corn seeds germinating under glass, the left-hand seed upside down.

The first sign of the seedling. In a very few days, now that the seeds are thoroughly soaked with water, the signs of life begin to appear. The root grows out of the seed as a small, white, slender, pointed object. It comes from the same spot in every seed of one kind. In the sunflower, pumpkin, buckwheat, and corn it comes from the smaller end of the seed. In the bean it comes out from the hollowed, or concave, side. As soon as the root comes out it grows directly downward, no matter which way the seed happens to lie.

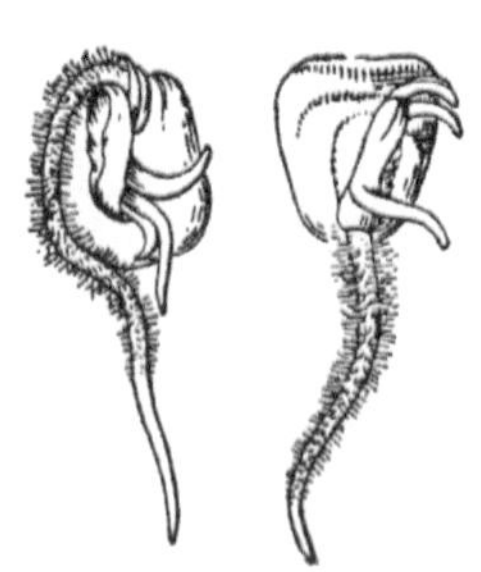

Fig. 19. Later stage of Fig. 18.

When the seeds are placed in the lamp chimney, or in a box with a glass side, they can be easily held in any position desired. It will be interesting to watch seeds that have been placed in different positions. When the roots have grown an inch or more in length,

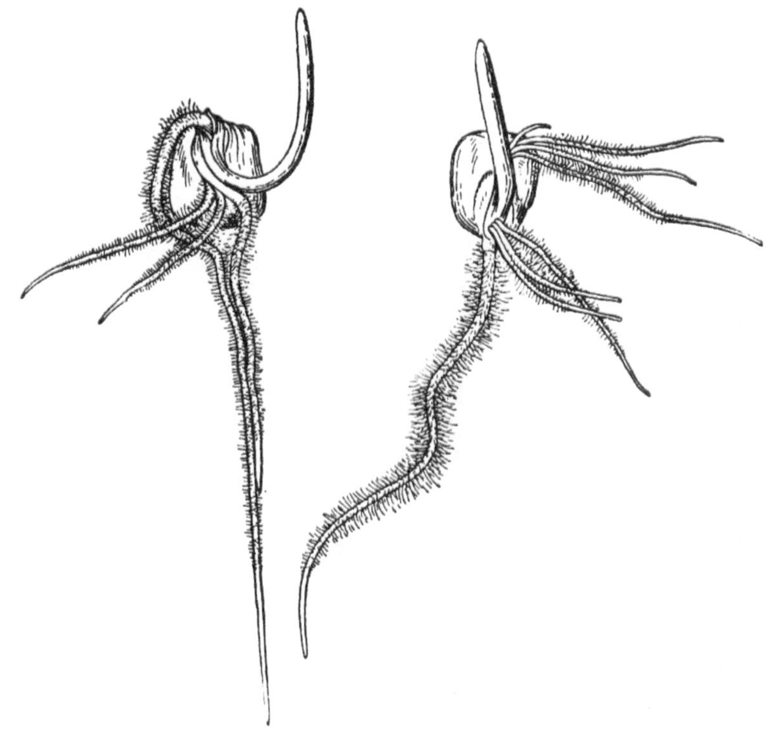

Fig. 20. Still later stage of Fig. 18.

sketch some of the different positions. Is there any advantage to the plant in having this first root grow downward?

How the pumpkin plant gets out of the seed coat. As the root grows out of the small end of the seed, it acts like a wedge and often splits the shell or seed coat part way, but not enough for the rest of the plant to escape. The little plant develops a curious contrivance to assist it in getting out. There is formed on one side of the stem a "peg" or "heel." This is formed on the underside of the stem, when the seed is lying on its side, at the point in the opening of the seed. This peg presses against the end and helps to split the seed coat further open. The stem now elongates above this peg, presses against the other half

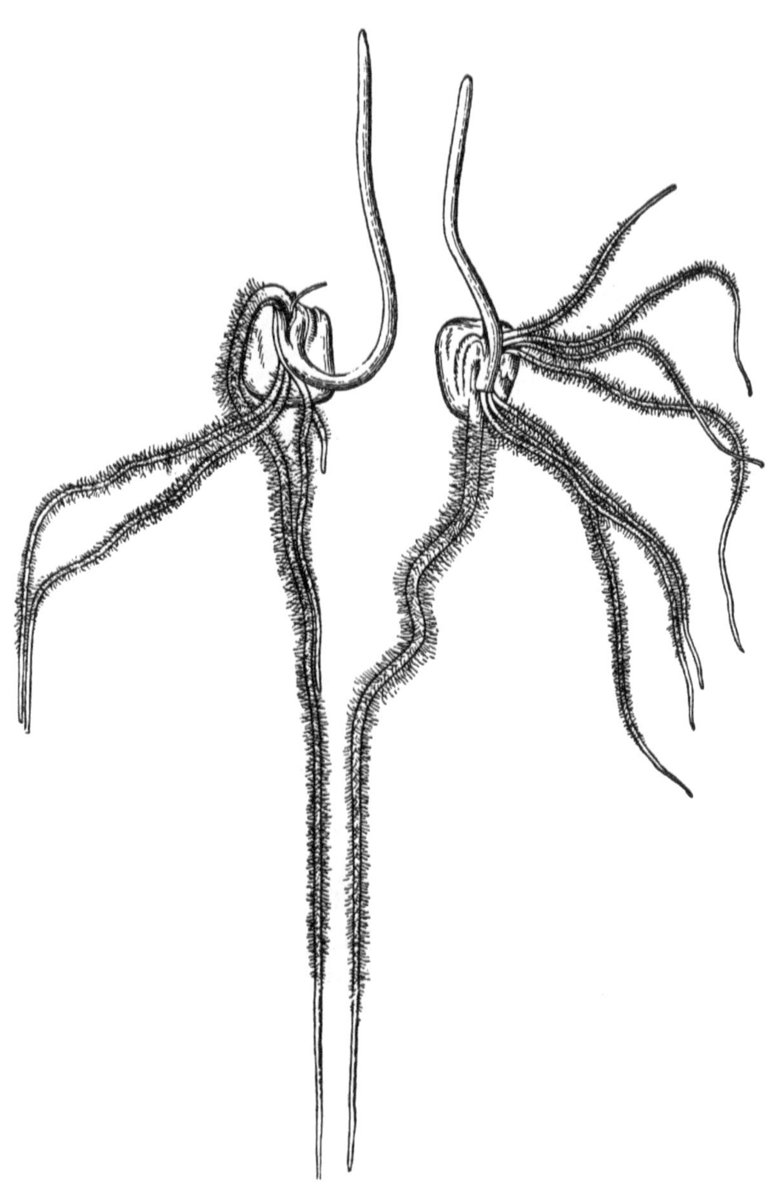

Fig. 21. Still later stage of Fig. 18. Note root hairs in all.

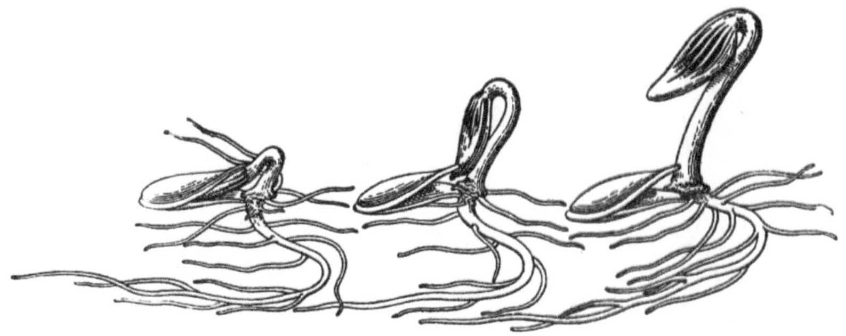

Fig. 22. Pumpkin seedlings casting the seed coats (note the "peg").

of the seed coat, and pries the two halves far apart so that the plant readily slips out, as shown in Fig. 22.

Germination of the bean. After the root comes out of the bean on the concave side, the two halves of the bean swell so that the outer coat is cracked and begins to slip off. We can then see that the stem is a continuation above from the root, joined to one end of the two thick parts or cotyledons. This part of the stem now grows rapidly, arches up in a loop, and lifts the bean upward.

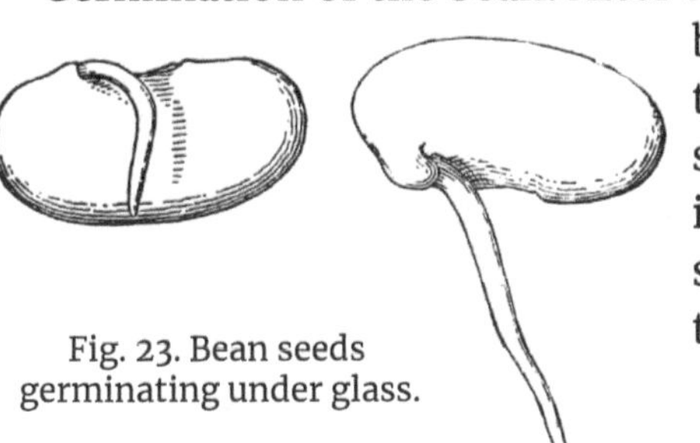

Fig. 23. Bean seeds germinating under glass.

Fig. 24. Pea germinating under glass.

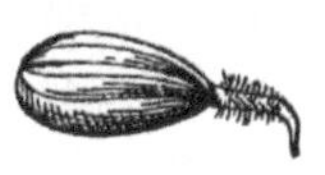

Fig. 25. Sunflower seed germinating.

The pea. The pea germinates in a different way. After the root begins to grow the pea swells, so that the thin coat is cracked. The stem, just as in the bean, is joined at one side to the two thick cotyledons of the pea. But this part of

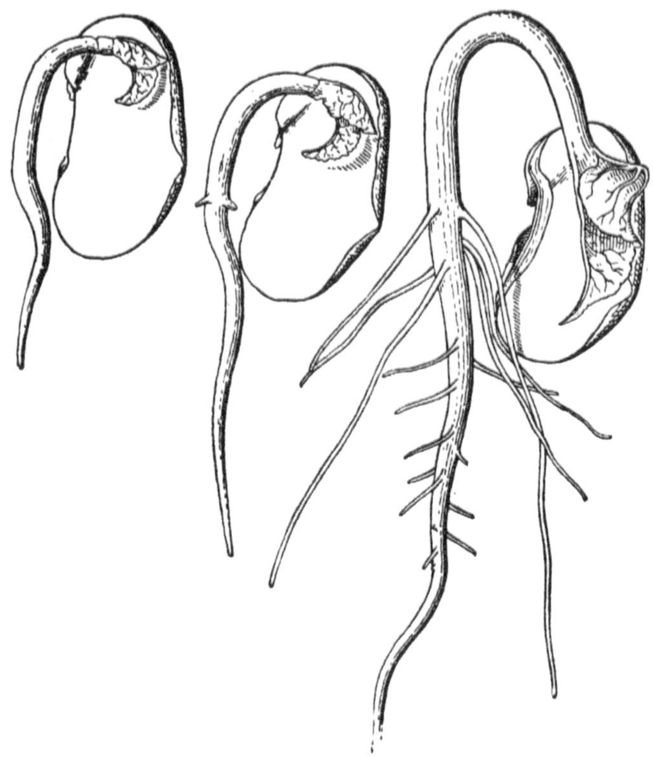

Fig. 26. Beans with one cotyledon removed to see how the cotyledons are raised up from the ground.

the stem of the pea does not grow longer, so the pea is left in position in the ground. The stem grows on from between the two thick cotyledons, arches up in a loop, pulls out the young and tender leaves from the ground, and then straightens up.

To compare the germination of the bean with that of the pea. This can be done very easily by first soaking beans and peas for twenty-four hours in water. With the finger or with the knife split the bean along the line of the convex side and pull the halves apart. The young embryo plant lies attached to one of these halves, having broken away from the other. Split several beans in the same way and place the half which has the embryo bean plant under glass, in position as shown in Fig. 26.

Take one of the peas and, by a slight rubbing pressure between the fingers, remove the thin outer coat. The split between the halves is now seen. Carefully break away one of these halves and split several more peas in the same way; those pieces which have the embryo attached should be planted under glass near the beans, in position as shown in Fig. 27. From day to day observe the growth in each case. That part of the bean stem below the cotyledon can be seen to elongate, while in the pea it is the stem above the attachment of the cotyledon which grows.

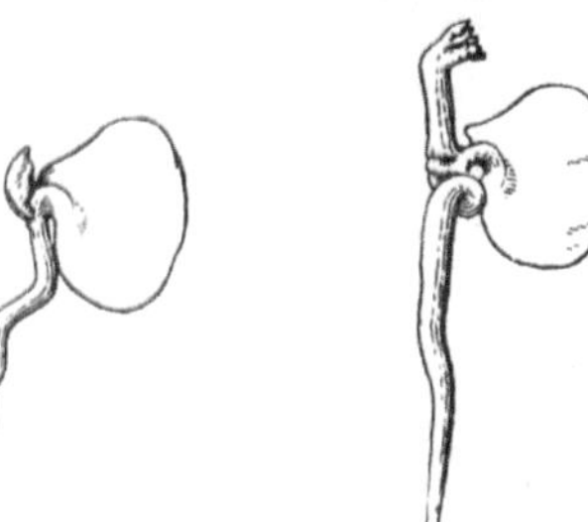

Fig. 27. Peas with one cotyledon removed to see how the cotyledons are left in the ground.

The oak seedling. The young oak plant comes out of the acorn in a curious way. It is easy to get the acorns to see how they behave. Visit a white oak tree in late October several weeks after the acorns have been falling from the tree. If the tree is situated by the roadside, or in a field where there is some loose earth which is damp and shaded, many of the acorns will be partially buried in the soil. Or you may collect the acorns and half bury them in a cool, damp soil, which should be watered from time to time.

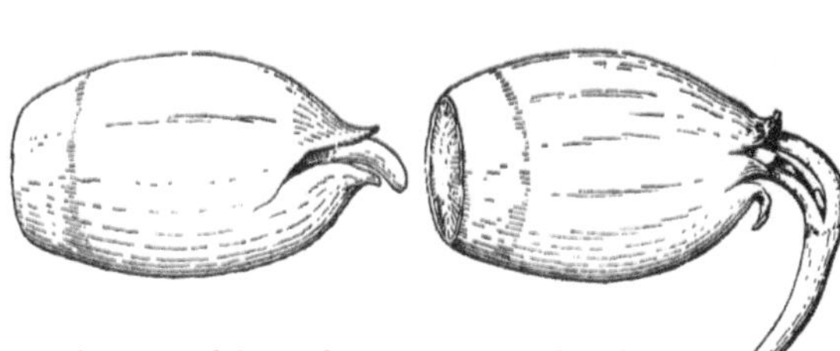

Fig. 28. White oak acorns germinating.

The root is the first to appear,

Fig. 29. Pumpkin seeds germinating under glass, turned in different positions.

and it comes out of the small end of the acorn, splitting the short point on the end of the seed in a star-shaped fashion. The root immediately turns downward, so that if the acorn is not buried the root will soon reach the soil. This can be seen in Fig. 28.

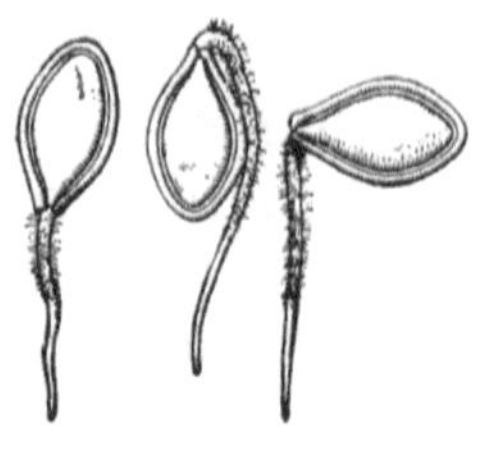

Fig. 30. Same as Fig. 29, but later stage.

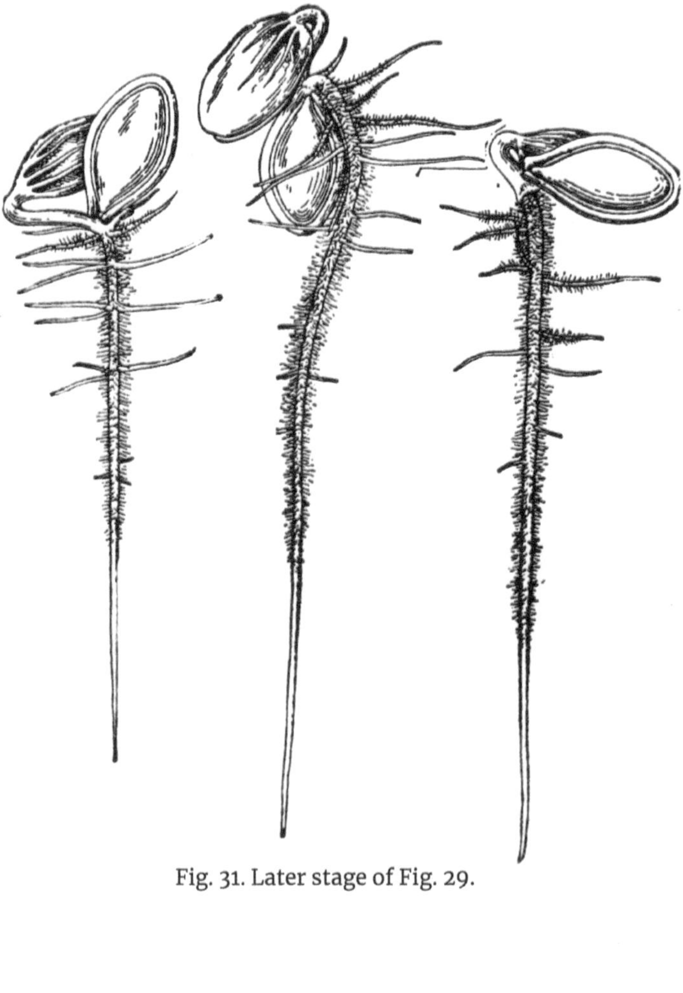

Fig. 31. Later stage of Fig. 29.

How the oak seedling escapes from the acorn. If you look for sprouted acorns, you will find them in different stages of growth. Some with the root just emerging will be found, and others with the "tail" an inch or more long. In these larger ones we can see that the part next the acorn is split into two parts. As it curves, this split often widens, so that we can see in between. In such cases a tiny bud may be seen lying close in the fork of the two parts. This bud is the growing end of the stem, and we now see that the tiny plant backed out of the acorn.

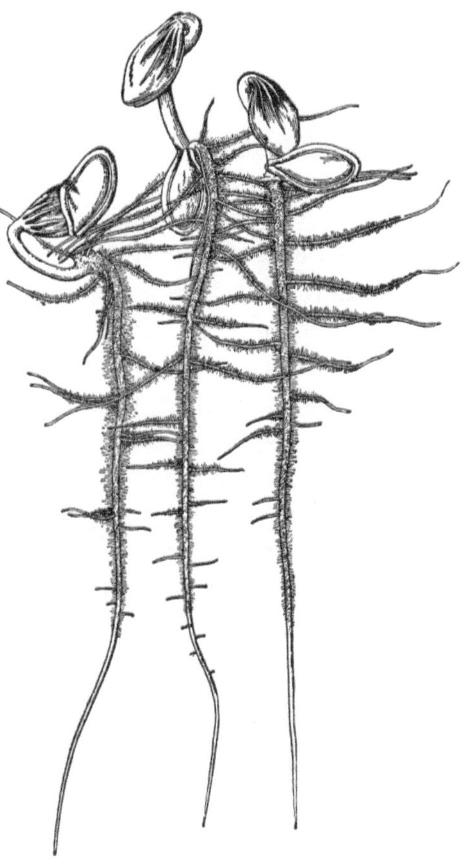

Fig. 32. Still later stage of Fig. 29.

The root hairs. In this study of the seedlings grown under a glass, or in a box or vessel where there is no soil for the root to bury itself, you will see that the root soon becomes covered, a little distance back of the tip, with a dense white woolly or fuzzy growth. You will see that these are like very tiny hairs, and that the root bristles all around with them. They are the *root hairs*. They help the root to do its work, as we shall see in a later study.

CHAPTER III.

The Parts of the Seed

Are the parts of the seedling present in the seed? Since the root comes from the seed so soon after planting, when the soil is moist and the weather warm, and the other parts quickly follow, one begins to suspect that these parts are already formed in the dry seed. We are curious to know if this is so. We are eager to examine the seeds and see. The dry seeds might be examined, but they are easier to open if they are first soaked in water from twelve to twenty-four hours. When they are ready, let us open them and read their story.

The parts of the bean seed. The bean seed can be split, as described on p20, into halves by cutting through the thin coat along the ridge on the rounded or convex side. Spread the two parts out flat and study them. The two large white fleshy objects which are now exposed we recognize as the two cotyledons which were lifted from the soil by the loop. The thin coat which enclosed them is the *seed coat*. Lying along the edge near the end of one of the cotyledons is a small object which looks like a tiny plant. Is this the *embryo* of the bean plant? The pointed end is the root, and we see that it lies in such a position that when it begins to grow it will come through the seed coat near the scar on the bean.

Fig. 33. Bean showing scar.

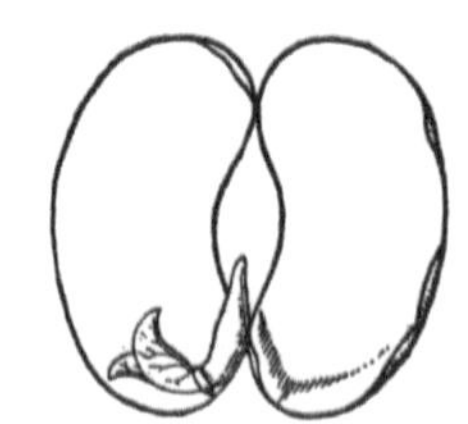

Fig. 34. Bean seed split open to show plantlet.

At the other end of the plantlet are two tiny leaves, pointed, and set something like the letter V. We know that they are leaves because there are veins on them like the veins on the leaf. Between these leaves and the pointed end or root lies the stem. It is short and stout, and there is no *distinct dividing line between it and the root. Root and stem in the embryo are called the* **cau-li-cle**. The upper end of the stem just below the tiny leaves is joined to the cotyledon, one cotyledon breaking away as the bean was split open. *The part of the stem below the cotyledons, that is, the part between them and the root, is called the* **hy'po-cot-yl**.

Fig. 35. Cross section of bean showing situation of plantlet.

The parts of the pea seed. The position of the plantlet can be seen on one side of the rounded pea, below the scar, after the pea has been soaked in water. By a slight rubbing pressure between the thumb and finger the thin seed coat can be slipped off. The two thick cotyledons can now be separated. If this is done carefully, the embryo plant remains attached to one of them. Sketch this, as well as the embryo of the bean; compare them and indicate in the drawings the names of the parts.

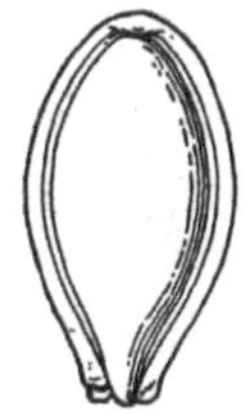

Fig. 36. Pumpkin seed.

The parts of the pumpkin seed. The scar on the pumpkin seed is found on the smaller end. The seed coat can split by cutting carefully part way around the edge of the flattened seed and then prying it open. The "meat" inside is covered with a very thin *papery layer*. The pointed end of the meat is the *caulicle (root and stem)*. It lies, as we see, in the small pointed end of the seed coat. The meat is in halves, as shown by a "split" which runs through to the point where they seem to be joined.

Fig. 37. Pumpkin seed split open in right-hand half the papery covering shown which surround the "meat."

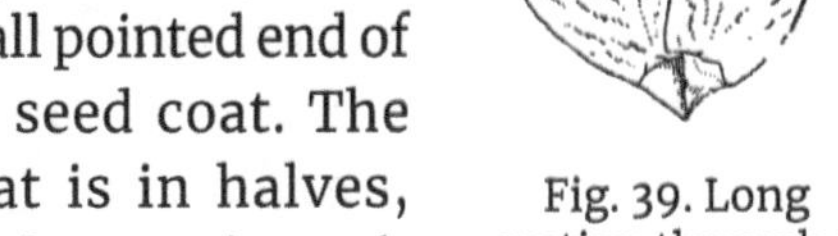

Fig. 39. Long section through a pumpkin seed.

Fig. 38. "Meat," the embryo, with one cotyledon turned to one side.

These halves of the meat are the **cotyledons** *of the pumpkin.* Pry them apart so that one is broken free. At this junction of the cotyledons will be found a tiny bud on the end of the stem attached to one cotyledon after the other is broken off. The stem is very short in the pumpkin plantlet. We have found in the pea and bean that it lies between the cotyledon and the root. So it does in the pumpkin. Is it so in all seeds?

Cut a pumpkin seed through the cotyledons, but lengthwise of the seed. Make a sketch of one part showing the seed coat, the position of the *papery lining*, the cotyledons as well as the short root and stem. Cut a seed in two, crosswise, and sketch, showing all the parts.

Fig. 40. Cross section of pumpkin seed.

The sunflower seed. The sunflower seed can be split open to remove the seed coat in the same way as the pumpkin seed.

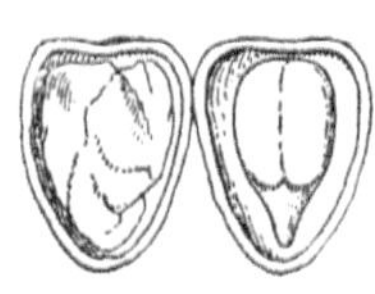

Fig. 41. Sunflower seed split open showing "meat," the embryo in right and papery covering in left half of seed coat.

The meat occupies much the same position, and is covered with a papery layer. While the proportions are different, the general shape of the plantlet reminds one of that of the pumpkin or squash. The root and stem are more prominent. There are two flat cotyledons. As we spread them apart we see that they are joined to the end of the stem; we can also see between them the tiny bud. If we cut the seed in two, as we did the pumpkin seed, we shall see that the relation of the parts is much the same.

Fig. 42. Embryo of sunflower with one cotyledon removed.

Structure of the corn seed. In the germination of the corn we have seen that the root comes out at the small end of the kernel in the groove on one side, while the leaves first appear on the same side at the other end of this groove.

Fig. 43. Cross section of sunflower seed at left; at right, side view of embryo taken from seed.

If the tiny plant is present in the seed, then it should be found in the groove. Split the soft kernel lengthwise through this groove. Just underneath the seed coat at the small end will be seen the end of the root and stem (caulicle). Near the other end of the groove there may be seen several converging lines running as Shown in Fig. 44. These lines represent several leaves cut lengthwise while they are rolled round each other. The stem lies between the leaves and root; it is now very short, and cannot be distinguished from the root. On the opposite side of the stem from the groove is a small curved object. *This is the* **cotyledon** *cut through. There is only* **one** *cotyledon in the corn seed, while in the other seeds studied there are* **two**.

Fig. 44. Section of corn seed; at upper right of each is a plantlet, next the cotyledon, at left the endosperm.

The meat in the corn seed. In the pea, bean, pumpkin, and sunflower seeds the cotyledons form nearly all the meat inside the seed coats. In fact, *the whole seed inside the seed coat in these plants, except the papery lining, is the* **embryo, for the cotyledons, being the first leaves, are part of the tiny embryo plant.** We have found something very different in the corn. *The embryo is only a small part of the inside of the seed.* After the seed has germinated, the *food substance* is still there. Did you ever examine a kernel of corn after the seedling had been growing some time? There is scarcely anything left but the old and darkened seed coat. It is nearly hollow within. *The meat which formed most of the inside of the kernel has disappeared.* What has become of it? I think every one who has examined the corn in this way can tell. *It has*

Fig. 45. Long section of buckwheat seed showing one view of embryo surrounded by the endosperm.

gone to form **food** *for the young corn plant. The substance which is used by the embryo for food is called* **endosperm.**

Fig. 46. Another section showing another view of embryo of buckwheat in seed.

Is there endosperm in the seeds of the pumpkin, the bean, the pea, and the sunflower? That is perhaps a hard question for you to answer. It is a difficult matter to explain without taking a good deal of time. But I will ask a few more questions, and then perhaps you can guess. Where does the germinating pumpkin, sunflower, bean, or pea seedling find its food before it can get a sufficient amount from the soil? If from the cotyledons, or first leaves, where did they obtain the food to become so big in the seed? What about the papery lining in the squash and sunflower seed?

Fig. 47. Cross section of buckwheat seed showing coiled cotyledons.

CHAPTER IV.

Growth of the Root and Stem

The part of the root which lengthens. One of the interesting things about the root is the way it grows in length. We know that as the root becomes longer the tip moves along. But does this take place by a constant lengthening of the extreme tip of the root? Or is the tip pushed along through the soil by the growth or stretching of some other part of the root? We can answer this if we examine the seedlings which are growing in germinators, as in the lamp chimney, where the roots are not covered with soil.

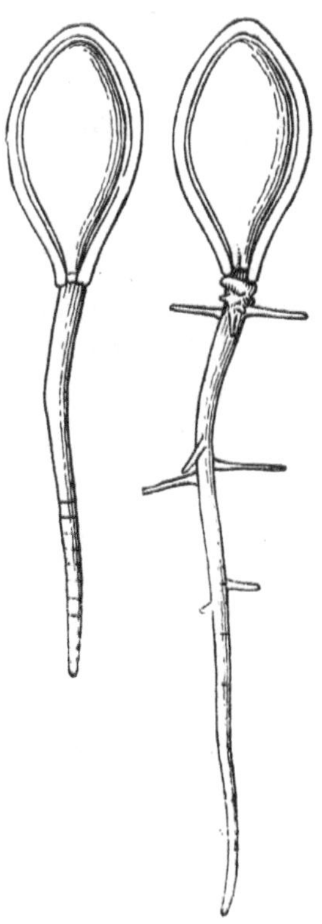

Fig. 48. Pumpkin seedlings, the root marked in left. Right one showing where growth took place in twenty-four hours.

To tell where the root elongates. Take a fine pen and some indelible or water-proof ink. Beginning at the tip of the root, mark off on one side very short spaces, as close together as possible, the first 1 mm. from the tip, and the others 1 mm. apart, as shown in Fig. 48. Now place the seedling back in the germinator in position, the root pointing downward. In twenty-four hours see the result. The spaces between the marks are no longer equal, showing that stretching of the root takes place over a limited area. Figs. 48 and 49 show the result with corn and pumpkin seedlings. The root has not grown perceptibly at the tip, for the space marked off by the first line does not appear to be any greater than it was twenty-four hours ago. *Growth in length occurs in a region a short distance back of the tip.* The spaces between the marks back of the tip, especially those between the third, fourth, fifth, and sixth marks, are much wider. This is the place, then, where the root stretches or grows in length. The stretching is greatest in the middle of this region.

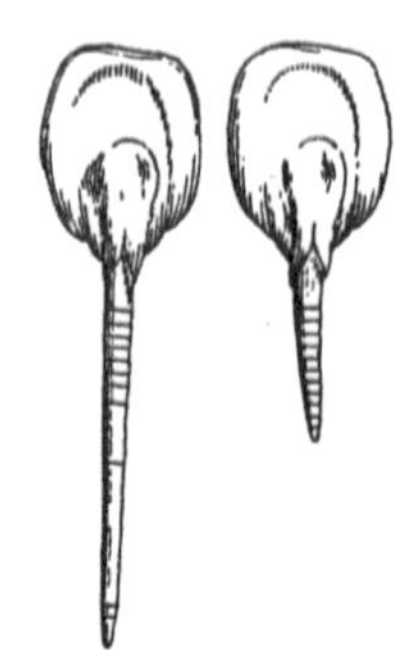

Fig. 49. Corn seedlings marked to show where growth takes place in the roots.

Direction of the roots of seedlings. The first root from the seedling grows downward, as we have seen. In the germinating seed, what advantage is there to the plant in this downward direction of the first root? The roots which grow out from this first or primary root are called lateral roots. What direction do they take? What advantage is there to the plant in the direction which the lateral roots take? Look at the root system, as a whole, of the seedling when well developed. What are the advantages to the plant of the distribution the roots which you observe?

Fig. 50. Stems of bean marked to show where growth takes place in stem.

Growth of the stem. In a similar way the region over which growth extends in the stem may be shown. As soon as the seedlings come above the ground, or as soon as a new portion of the shoot begins to elongate above the leaves, mark off the stem with cross lines. The lines on the stem may be placed farther apart than those on the root. They may be put as indicated in Fig. 50. A rule may be used to locate the marks on the stem, and then, after several days, if the rule is placed by the side of the stem, the amount of growth will be determined.

CHAPTER V.

Direction of Growth of Root and Stem

In our studies of the seedlings we cannot fail to observe that the *first root grows downward* and the *stem upward.* No matter which way the seed is turned, as soon as the root comes out it turns downward. It grows toward the earth, or if it is in the ground it grows toward the center of the earth. So we say that the root grows toward the earth, while the stem grows away from the earth, or upward. It is interesting to notice how persistently the root and stem grow in these directions. To see how persistent they are in this, change the positions of the seedlings after they have begun to grow.

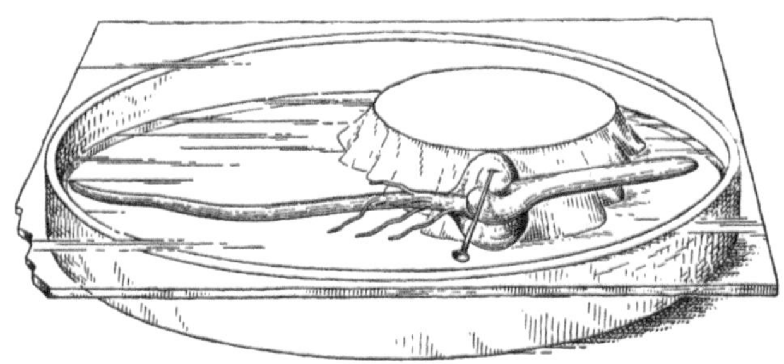

Fig. 51. Corn seedling pinned in a horizontal position.

Downward growth of the root. Take any one of the seedlings germinated in moss or sawdust or behind glass. Place it in a horizontal position. This may be done behind a pane of glass in a box, or a pin may be thrust through the kernel into a cork which is then placed as in Fig. 51, with a little water in the bottom of the vessel to keep the air moist. In several hours, or on the following day, observe the position of the root. The greater part of it remains in a horizontal position, but the end of the root has turned straight downward again.

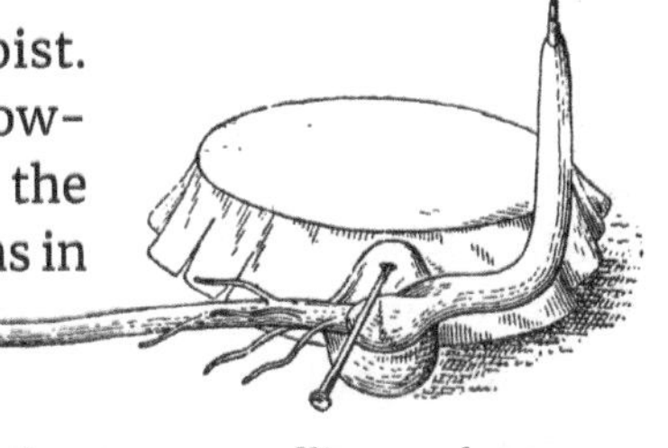

Fig. 52. Same corn seedling as shown in Fig. 51., twenty-four hours later.

What part of the root bends when it turns from the horizontal position? We should now determine what part of the root it is which bends when it grows downward in this fashion. To do this the root of another seedling should be marked and placed in a horizontal position. With a fine pen and India ink, mark spaces as close together as possible, about 1 mm. apart, beginning at the tip of the root. Mark off ten such spaces, as shown in Fig. 53, and leave the root in a horizontal position for a day. Now observe where the curve has taken place. It has not taken place at the tip, for the mark made near the tip is still there. The curve has taken place back from the tip, in the region of mark 3, 4, or 5, probably, if the marks were close together at first. These marks on the bent region of the root are now far apart.

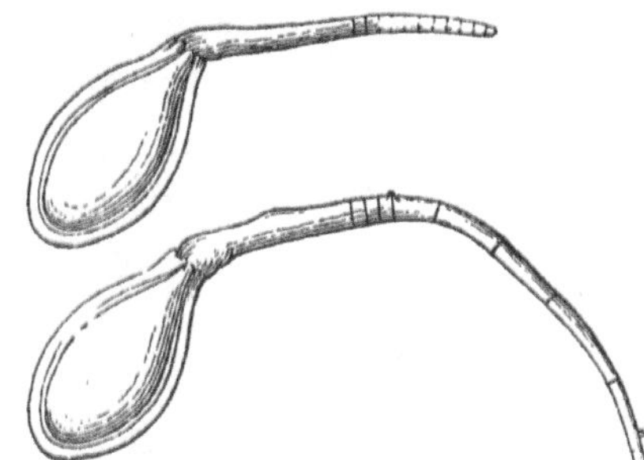

Fig.53. Pumpkin seedling placed horizontally and marked to show where the root bends when turning downward.

You remember that when the root was measured to see where growth in length took place, we found that the root grew in this same region, just back of the tip. This is an interesting observation, and I think you can understand why the root can bend easier in the region where it is stretching than in the region where elongation has ceased. The region of elongation is called the *motor zone*, because this is where the root moves.

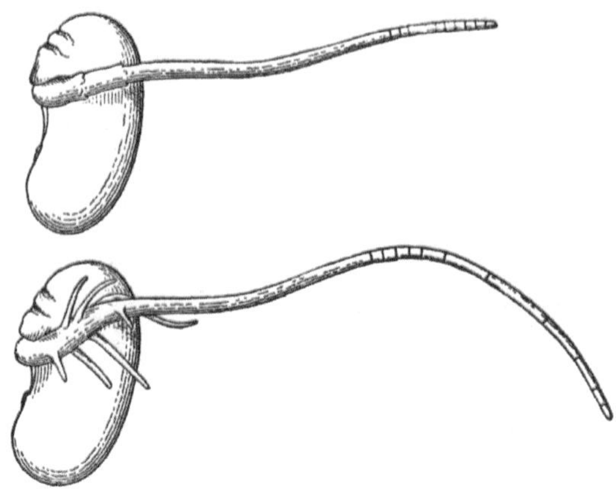

Fig. 54. Bean seedling placed horizontally and marked to show where the root bends.

What causes the root to turn downward? This is a question that is difficult, perhaps, to demonstrate to your satisfaction. It can be shown, however, that gravity influences the root to turn toward the earth. Gravity, you know, is the force which pulls an apple or a stone toward the earth when either is let fall. We must bear in mind, however, that gravity does not pull the root down in the same way in which it acts on the stone or apple. It only influences or stimulates, we say, the root to turn. (If desirable the teacher can explain or demonstrate for the pupils, that when the influence of gravity is neutralized, the root does not turn downward but continues to grow in the direction in which it was placed. This may be demonstrated by the well-known experiment of fastening, in different positions, several seedlings on a perpendicular wheel or disk which revolves slowly. The position of the root with reference to the earth is constantly altered, and the influence of gravity is neutralized.)

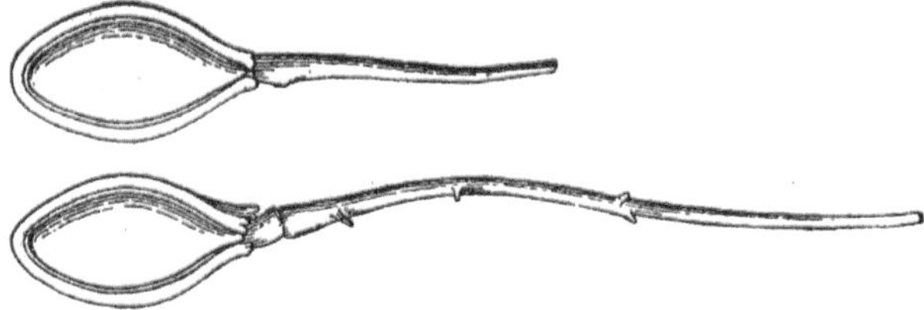

Fig. 55. Pumpkin seedling placed horizontally and root tip cut off to show that without the root tip the root will not bend.

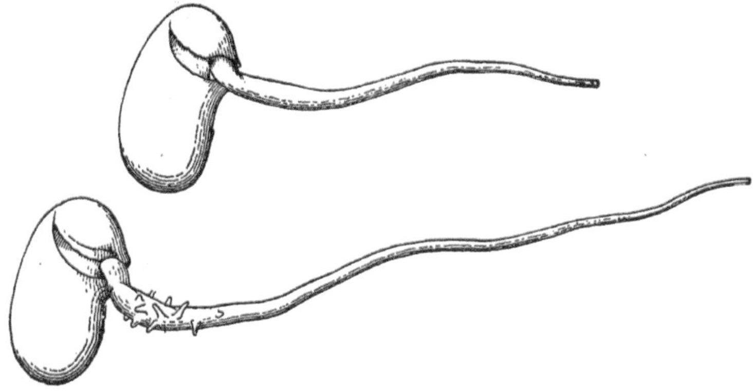

Fig. 56. Bean seedling treated as the pumpkin seedling in Fig. 55.

If the tip is removed, will the root turn? Now place some more seedlings with the roots in a horizontal position, or, if you choose, this experiment can be carried on along with the others. With sharp scissors, or a very sharp knife, cut off the extreme tip of the root. In twenty-four hours afterwards observe the roots. *They have elongated*, but they have not turned downward. They have continued to grow in the horizontal position in which they were placed, although the motor zone was not cut away. Why is this? It must be that the tip of the root is the part which is sensitive to the influence or stimulus of gravity. For this reason the tip of the root is called the *perceptive zone*.

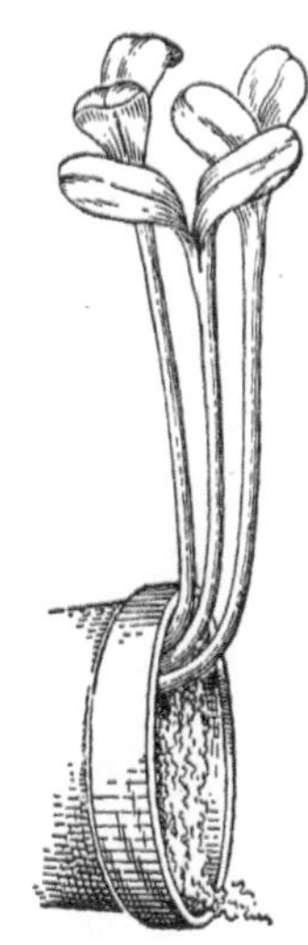

Fig. 57. Sunflower seedlings turning upward.

The upward growth of the stem. If the stem is well developed in any of the seedlings placed in a horizontal position, we see that the stem turns up while the root turns down. The corn seedling shows this well in Fig. 52. It is more convenient in studying stems to take seedlings grown in pots. Squash, pumpkins, corn, bean, sunflower, etc., are excellent for this study. Place the

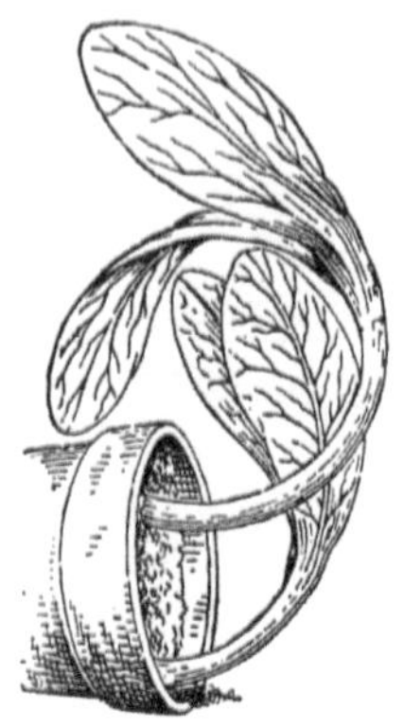

Fig. 58. Pumpkin seedlings turning upward.

pot on its side. In twenty-four hours observe the plants. They have turned straight upward again, as shown in Figs. 57 and 58. In the case of the stems the part which turns is at a much greater distance from the end than in the root. This is because the *region of elongation or motor zone in the stem is farther from the tip than in the root.*

How gravity influences the stem. It may seem remarkable that gravity, which influences the root to grow downward, also influences the stem to grow upward. It is nevertheless true. The lateral roots and lateral stems are influenced differently. What are the advantages to germinating seeds from this influence of gravity on root and stem?

Behavior of the roots toward moisture. Test this by planting seeds in a long box, keeping the soil in one end dry and in the other end moist. The root grows toward moist places in the soil. If the soil is too wet, the roots of many plants grow away from it. Sometimes they grow out on the surface of the soil where they can get air, which they cannot get if the soil is too wet.

CHAPTER VI.

Buds and Winter Shoots

Do buds have life? When the leaves have fallen from the trees and shrubs in the fall the forest looks bare and dead, except for the pines, spruces, cedars, and other evergreens. The bare tree or shrub in the yard looks dead in winter. But examine it. The slender tips of the branches are fresh and green. If we cut or break a twig, it is not dry like a dead stick. It is moist. It seems just as much alive as in the summer, when the trees are covered with green leaves. But look at the tip of the twigs, and on the sides, just above where the leaves were! What do the buds mean? Do they have life?

Fig. 59. Winter condition of trees and shrubs.

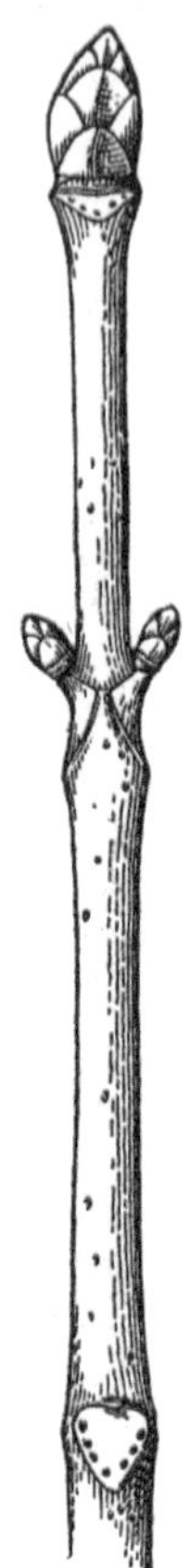

Fig. 60. Shoot of horse-chestnut.

Fig. 61. Shoot of lilac.

How the buds look inside. On the shoot of the horse-chestnut see the overlapping "scales" on the bud. Take a pin and remove them one after another. Observe how they are seated in the bud. On this side is one, and on the opposite side is another. How are the next two seated? And the next? They are not very easy to remove, and our hands are "stuck up" if we handle them. This sticky substance helps to hold the scales close together and keeps out water.

When the brown scales are removed, see the thin chaff-like ones! Then come scales covered with long woolly hairs. These scales are green in color, and in shape are like miniature leaves! They are alive even in the fall or winter! How are they kept from being killed? The long woolly hairs are folded round them like a scarf, and all are packed so tightly and snugly under the close-fitting brown scales that they are well protected from loss of water during dry or cold weather, or after freezing. They lie "asleep," as it were, all winter. In spring we know they awake!

How the bud looks when split. With a sharp knife we will split the bud down through the end of the stem.

Fig. 62. Opening bud of hickory.

We see how closely all the scales fit. Near the center they become smaller and smaller, until there is the soft end of the stem, which seems to be as much alive as in the summer, but it is resting now. The leaves in the bud are winter leaves. How convenient it is for the tree or shrub that in the fall it can put on this armor of brown scales and wax to protect the tender end of the stem!

The lateral buds. There are several large buds on the side of the shoot, larger near the terminal bud. If we examine these, we find that they look the same inside as the terminal bud. The lateral buds are smaller, perhaps. Where are the buds seated on the shoot? The lateral buds are seated just above the scar left by the falling leaf. We say that they are in the axils of the leaves, for they began to form here in

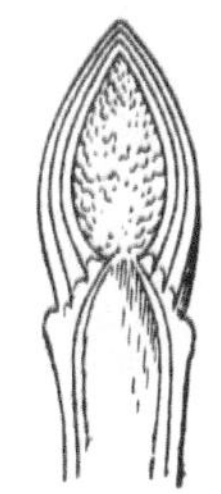
Fig. 63. Long section of horse-chestnut bud— scales and woolly scale leaves inside.

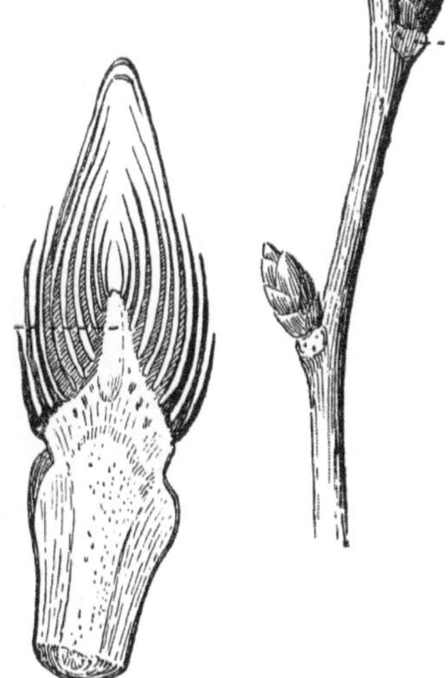
Fig. 64. Bud of European elm in section, showing overlapping of scales.

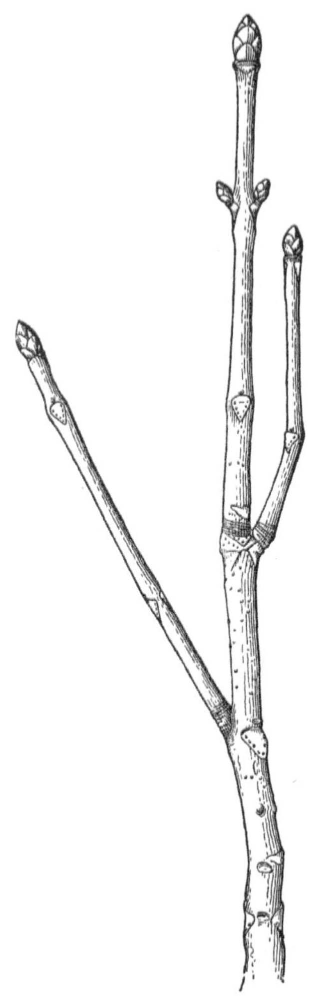
Fig. 65. Shoot and buds of horse-chestnut.

the summer, before the leaves fell. Are there buds in the axils of all the leaves of the shoot which you have? Which buds will form branches next spring? What will the terminal bud do? Why is the terminal bud larger than the lateral buds?

The winter shoot. You should have a shoot two or three feet long, branched, if possible. See how it is marked. *The leaf scars.* These are very large, and are in pairs opposite each other, just as the scales are seated in the bud, only the different pairs are farther apart on the stem. Who can tell what the row of pin holes in the scar means? Perhaps you can tell better later on. What else do you see on the shoot? *There are the scale scars, or girdle scars.* What do they mean? When the bud begins to grow in the spring, the winter scales

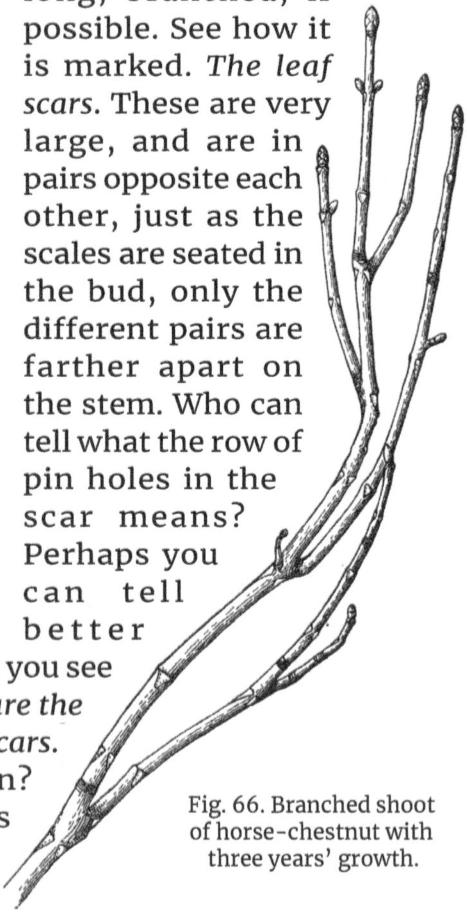

Fig. 66. Branched shoot of horse-chestnut with three years' growth.

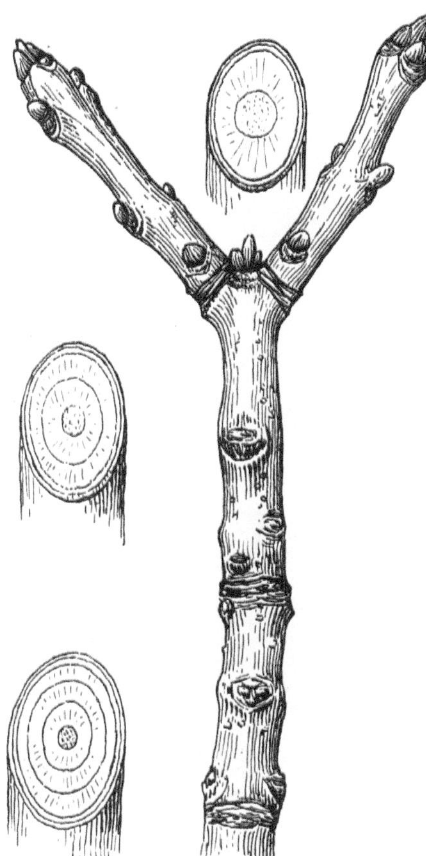

Fig. 67. Shoot and ash three years old, and section showing annual rings.

and leaves are thrown off. Each tiny scale and winter leaf leaves a scar on the shoot just as the large summer leaves do, only it is a tiny scar. But there are many scars close together all round the shoot, for, as we have seen, the winter scales and leaves are seated so in the bud. Each year, then, a girdle of scale scars is formed on the shoot. How old is the branch you have? Get a shoot which has several girdle scars on it. Cut it through, between the girdle scars. How many rings show in the cut surface of the wood? What does this mean?

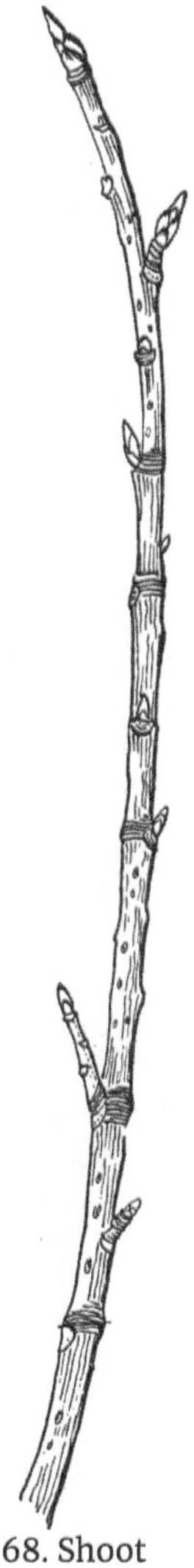

Other buds and shoots. Gather other shoots and study the buds, the leaf scars, and their arrangement. Good ones to study are the

Fig. 68. Shoot of butternut showing leaf scars and buds.

Fig. 69. Shoot of butternut showing leaf scars, axillary buds, and adventitious buds (buds coming from above the axils).
Fig. 70. Shoot and bud of white oak.
Fig. 71. Two-year old shoot of white oak showing where the greater number of branches arises.

ash, ailanthus, walnut or butternut, oak, elm, birch, dogwood, peach, apple, willow, poplar, etc.

Some buds may be made to open in the winter. Bring in shoots of dogwood, willow, poplar, ash, oak, etc. Rest the cut ends in water and see what will happen after several weeks or months.

CHAPTER VII.

The Full-Grown Plant and Its Parts

I. The plant

The plant has different parts. The seedling has roots, stem, and leaves. The full-grown plant has the same parts. But the roots, of course, are larger, longer, and much more branched. There are many more leaves also, and the stem is often very much branched. Are there any other parts? There are the flowers, you say, and the fruit, and some plants have thorns, spines, hairs, and tendrils. Yes, but many plants have just the root, stem, leaves, flowers, and fruit. And how different they are in different plants! Did you ever notice that the form of the stem, and the shape and arrangement of the leaves and flowers mark the different kinds of plants so that you can tell them apart? The form of the entire plant we call its *appearance* or *habit. The seeds of each kind of plant make new plants of the same kind and shape.*

Tall, erect plants. The sunflower is tall and slender. At first there is a simple, straight, tall, shaft-like stem, and large, spreading leaves pointing in different directions. At the top of the stem the first and largest flower head is formed, and others come on later from short branches in the axils of the upper leaves. The full-grown plant has a golden crown of flower heads held up by the tall stem shaft.

The mullein is also tall and slender, with rough, woolly leaves and a long spike of yellow flowers. The plants are tall and slender because the main stem is so prominent and branches not at all, or but little. In the sunflower and mullein the habit is *cylindrical*.

Tall larches, spruces, and pines. These trees branch very much. But observe how small the branches are compared with the main shaft, which extends straight through to the top. The habit is like that of a *cone*.

The oaks and birches have a more or less oval habit. The elms have a spreading habit, and so on. Is a pine, or oak, or other tree different in form when it grows alone in a field from what it is when grown in a forest? Can you tell why?

Prostrate plants. The strawberry, trailing arbutus, and others are prostrate or creeping. You can find other plants which show all forms between the prostrate and the erect habit.

Fig. 72. Cylindrical stem of mullein.

THE DURATION OF PLANTS

Annuals. Many of the flowers and weeds of the field and garden start from seeds in the springtime and ripen a new crop of seeds in late spring, in summer, or in autumn. Then the plant dies. It must be very clear to us that a plant which starts from the tiny embryo in the seed, forms the full-grown plant, flowers, ripens its seed in a single growing season, and then dies, has spent its life for the main purpose of forming the seed. The seed can dry without harming the young plantlet within.

Do you know that the seeds of many plants lie in the frozen

Fig. 73. White oak, oval type.

ground all winter without killing the embryo? These plants live and grow, therefore, to form seed, so that their kind may be perpetuated from year to year. Plants which live for a single season we call *annuals.* Beans, peas, corn, buckwheat, wheat, morning-glory, ragweed, etc., are annuals.

Biennials. When you plant seeds of the turnip, radish, beet, carrot, cabbage, etc., a very short stem is formed the first season, with a large rosette of leaves close to the ground. No flowers or seeds are formed the first season. But if these plants are protected from the cold of the winter, the following season tall, branched stems are formed which bear flowers and seed. Then the plants die. The purpose of these plants, also, is to form seed and perpetuate their kind. It takes two seasons, however, to form the seed. Such a plant we call a *biennial.* The mullein is a biennial. The short stem and the roots live during the first winter.

Perennials. We know that trees and shrubs grow for a number of years. All but the evergreens shed their leaves in the autumn, or the leaves die. But new leaves come forth in the spring. Some of the herbs, like trillium, golden-rod, aster, Indian turnip, etc., produce flowers and seed each season. The part of the stem above ground dies down at the close of the season, but the short stem under ground, or at the surface of the ground, lives on from year to year. When the seed germinates, the plant is so small at first, and even for several seasons, that for the first few years no flowers and seed are formed. Those herbs which live for several years, as well as the trees and the shrubs, we call *perennial* plants. In these plants, also, so far as we know, the main purpose of the plant, from the plant's point of view, is to form seed and perpetuate its kind. Plants like the cotton, castor-oil bean, etc., are *perennial in the tropics* but become *annual in temperate zones*, because the cold weather kills them; they produce one crop of seed the first season.

Woody plants and herbaceous plants. The stems and roots of trees and shrubs are mostly of a hard substance which we call wood. They are often called woody plants, while the herbs, whether annual, biennial, or perennial, are herbaceous plants.

CHAPTER VIII.

The Full-Grown Plant, Etc. (Continued)

Fig. 74. Sunflower, cylindrical type.

II. The stem

What are some of the different kinds of stems that you can find in the field or wood, in the garden or greenhouse? There are many forms and shapes. *The stem of the sunflower is long and straight.* There are short branches at the top where the plant bears a cluster of large flower heads, the largest one on the end of the main stem. Did you ever see a sunflower plant with only one flower head? Can you tell why there is only one flower head sometimes? *The corn plant and the bamboo are good examples of tall and slender stems.* The corn tassel is a tuft of branches bearing the stamen flowers. The silken ear is another branch which bears the pistil flowers, and later the fruit. Are other branches of the Indian corn ever developed? *Wheat and oats, also, have tall and slender stems.* Perhaps all these plants have formed the habit of long stems because they often grow in large, crowded masses, and take this means of lifting themselves above other plants in search of light and air.

In the pines, spruces, and larches the main stem rises like a great shaft from the ground

Fig. 75. Conical type of larch.

straight through the branches to the top. The highest part is the end of this straight shaft. These trees have many branches reaching out in graceful curves, but the main stem remains distinct. *A stem which continues or runs through to the top is said to be* **excurrent**. Have you ever been on the top of a mountain surrounded by a forest of oaks, maples, beeches, pines, and spruces? You remember how the tall, slender pines or spruces towered above the oaks or beeches.

How is it with the oak stem? The branches are larger in proportion to the main stem, so that the main trunk is often lost or disappears. Compare the oak tree or pine tree which has grown in the open field with those grown in the forest. How should you account for the difference?

The trunk of the elm tree and its branches. Study carefully the way the branches of the elm are formed and you will see why the main stem is soon lost. *Such a stem is said to be* **deliquescent**, because it seems to be dissolved. Compare large elms grown in the forest with those grown in the field. Why are they so different? Compare pines, spruces, and larches grown in the field with those grown in the woods. What are the points of difference and why? Why do the pines and spruces still have so different a habit from the oaks, elms, apple trees, and some others?

The strawberry, dewberry, and other prostrate stems creep or trail on the ground. *We call them* **creeping** *or* **trailing** *stems.* The strawberry vine takes root here and there and sends up a tuft of leaves and erect flower stems. The creeping water fern

Fig. 76. Diffuse type of elm.

(*marsilia*) is a beautiful plant, the stem usually creeping on the bottom of shallow ponds or borders of streams, and the pretty leaves with four leaflets floating like bits of mosaic on the surface.

Fig. 77. Prostrate type of the water fern (*marsilia*).

The pea, the Japanese ivy or Boston ivy, the morning-glory, and similar stems cling to other plants, or places of support. *They are* **climbing stems**. Then there are many stems which neither climb nor creep, nor do they stand erect, but are between erect and prostrate stems. Some *ascend*; that is, the end of the stem arises somewhat from the ground, although the rest of it may be prostrate. *These are* **ascending stems**. Others topple over so that the end is turned toward the ground. *They are downward bent* (**decumbent**).

Burrowing stems. Then there are stems which *burrow*, as it were. They creep along under the surface of the ground, the bud pushing or burrowing along as the stem grows. The mandrake, Solomon's seal, and the common bracken fern are well-known examples. The mandrake and Solomon's seal, and some others, as you know, form each year erect stems which rise above the ground. *Stems which burrow along under the surface of the ground are called* **rootstocks,** *or* **rhizomes,** *which means* **root form.** They are known from roots because they have buds and scale leaves, though the rhizome of the bracken fern, the sensitive fern (see Fig. 93), and some others have large green leaves which rise above the ground. The trillium has a short, thick rhizome.

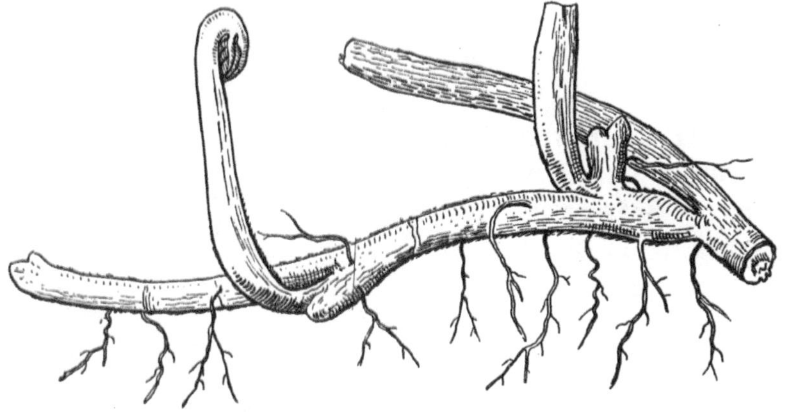

Fig. 78. Burrowing type, the mandrake, a "rhizome."

STEMS AS STOREHOUSES FOR FOOD

Bulbs are familiar to all of us. They are short stems covered with numerous overlapping thick scale leaves, as in the onion, the lily, or the tulip. Some bulbs, like the Easter lily, have a single stem. Some have several stems, like the Chinese lily, or the "multiplier onion." Quantities of food are stored up in the thick scale leaves, to be used by the plant as the flower and fruit stalk are being formed. In the Chinese lily there is so much food in these leaves that the bulb will grow if it is placed in a warm room with the lower surface resting on broken bits of crockery immersed in a vessel of water, so that the fibrous roots can furnish moisture. The lily will develop green leaves, flower stem, and flowers from the food in the scale leaves alone. These Chinese lily bulbs can be obtained from the florist and grown in the schoolroom or home.

Fig. 79. Bulb of hyacinth.

Another kind of food reservoir for plants is the tuber. The most common and well-known tuber is the potato. It is a very much thickened stem. The "eyes" are buds on the stem. Do you know what develops from these "eyes" when the potato is planted in the warm ground? Place several tubers in cups of water so that one end will be out of the water, and set them in the window of a

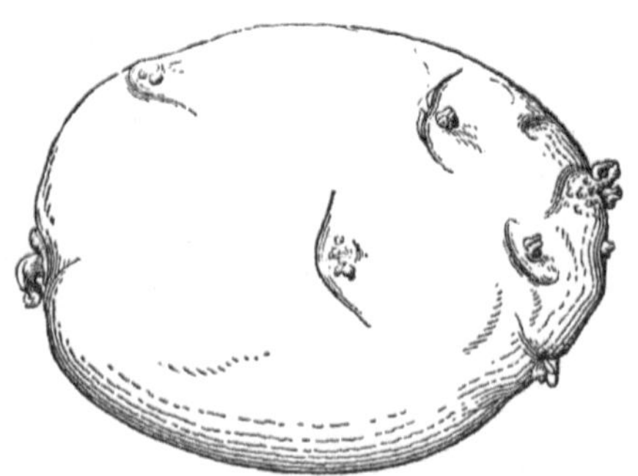

Fig. 80. Tuber of Irish potato.

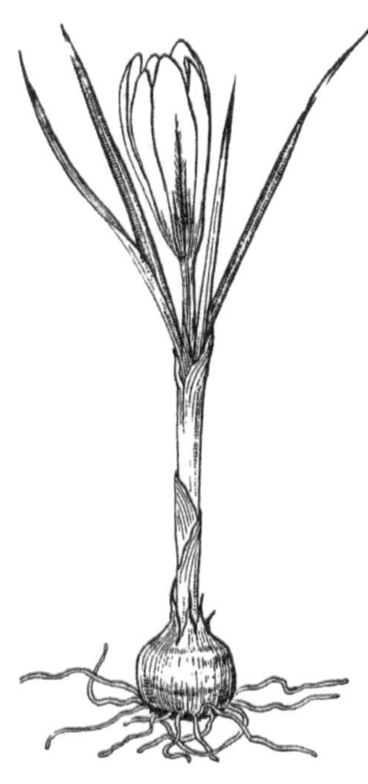

Fig. 81. Corm of Jack-in-the-pulpit.

warm room. Place some in a dark drawer where they will not freeze in winter; leave them for about a year and see what will happen.

The potato is filled with starch grains. It is an underground stem. If you dig away the soil carefully from a "hill" of potatoes, you will see that there are underground stems more slender often than the erect ones, which have buds and scale leaves on them. On the end there is often a potato tuber. The starch is stored here for the good of the potato. New plants can be started from the tuber. They grow more rapidly and vigorously than from the seed of the potato. Man and other animals make use of the potato for food.

The short, flattened underground stem of the Jack-in-the-pulpit is called a corm. This lives from year to year. Every spring it sends up a leafy flower stem which dies down in the autumn. Young corms are formed as buds on the upper surface of the larger one, probably in the axils of older leaves which have disappeared. These become free and form new plants. *Other corms are the* **crocus**, **gladiolus**, etc. To see how corms differ from bulbs, cut one open. It is a solid, fleshy stem, sometimes with loose, scale-like leaves on the outside.

Storehouses which are partly stem, partly root, are found in the parsnip, beet, turnip, radish, etc. The upper part, where the crown of leaves arises, is the stem, and the lower part is root. *Such a tuber is sometimes called a* **crown tuber**.

Food is stored in rootstocks, or rhizomes, also, and

in the stems of trees and shrubs. But the kinds enumerated above show some of the results which the plants have gained in forming special reservoirs for food. Most seeds, as we have seen from the few studied, are reservoirs of food so situated that the little plantlet can feed on it as soon as it begins to germinate.

CHAPTER IX.

The Full-Grown Plant, Etc. (Continued)

III. The root

Taproots. In the seedlings studied we found that the first root grows downward, no matter in what position the seed is planted. This habit of downward growth in the first root is of the greatest importance to the plant to insure a hold in the soil where it must obtain a large part of its food and all its water. It also puts the root in a position to send out numerous lateral roots in search of food, and serves to bind the plant more firmly to the ground. In some plants the first root, or the one which grows directly downward, maintains this direction, and grows to a large size as compared with the lateral roots. *Such a root is called a* **taproot**. The taproot is a leader. You see it continues through the root system

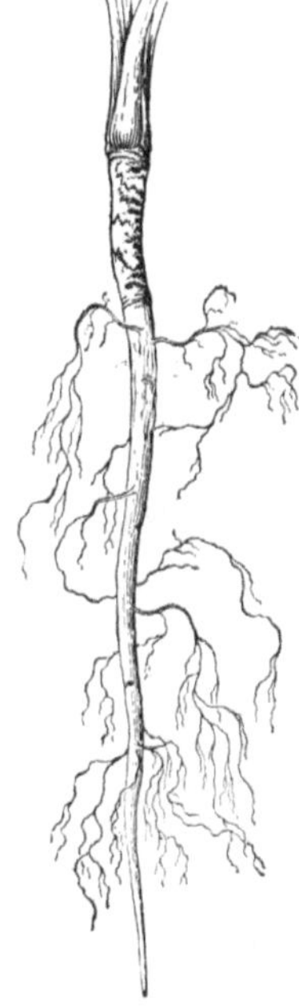

Fig. 82. Taproot of dandelion.

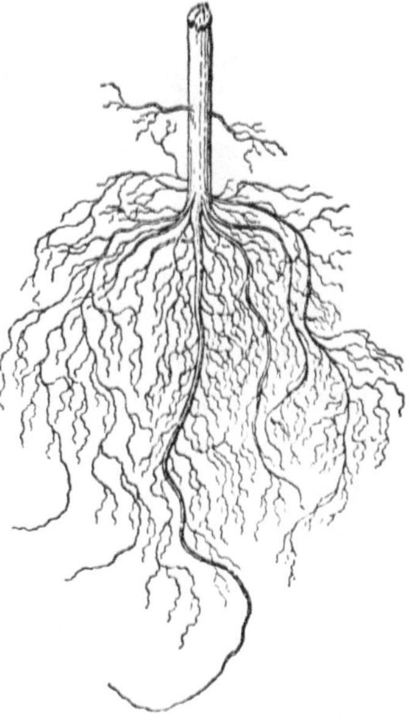

Fig. 83. Fibrous roots of bean.

somewhat as the main stems of pines, spruces, etc., do through the branches, only it goes downward. The dandelion is a good example. The turnip, carrot, and beet also have taproots.

The root system. The roots of a plant, with all their branches, form the root system of that plant. Where the roots are many and all more or less slender, the system is *fibrous*, or the plant is said to have *fibrous roots*, as in the clover, the corn, wheat, grasses, etc. Where one or more of the roots are stout and fleshy, the system is *fleshy*, or the plant is said to have *fleshy roots*. Examples are found in the sweet potato, the carrot, beet, turnip, etc. In the carrot, beet, and turnip the root is part stem (see reference page) and is called also a crown tuber. The fleshy roots of the sweet potato are sometimes called root tubers, because they are capable of sprouting and

Fig. 84. Air roots of poison ivy.

Fig. 85. Bracing roots of Indian corn.

Fig. 86. Bracing roots of screw pine.

forming new potatoes. Examine roots of a number of plants to see if they are fibrous or fleshy.

Air roots. Most roots with which we are familiar are soil roots, since they grow in the soil. Some plants have also air roots (called *aërial roots*). Examine the air roots of the climbing poison ivy, but be careful not to touch the leaves unless you know that it will not poison you. One side of the stem is literally covered with these roots. They grow away from the light toward the tree on which the ivy twines, and fasten it quite firmly to the tree.

Fig. 87. Buttresses of silk-cotton tree, Nassau.

Air roots or braces are formed in the Indian corn, the screw pine, etc. Air roots grow from the branches of the banyan tree of India, and striking into the ground brace the wide branching system of the stems.

Buttresses are formed partly of root and partly of stem at the base of the tree trunks where root and stem join.

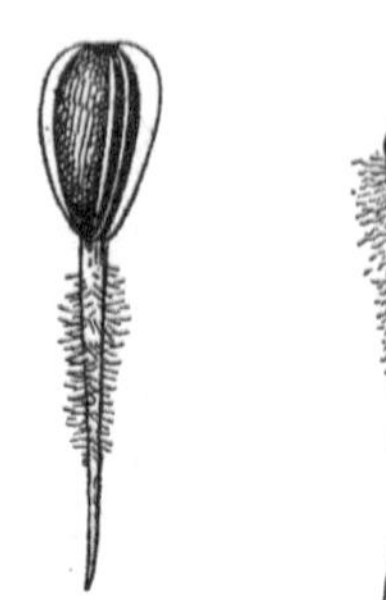

Fig. 88. Root hairs of sunflower seedling.

Fig. 89. Root hairs of radish seedling.

The work of roots. The roots do several kinds of work for the plant. They serve to anchor plants to the soil, or in the case of certain climbing plants to fasten them to some object of support. They aid also in supporting the plant and in holding the trunk or stem upright. Another important work is the taking up of water and of food solutions from the soil. In the absorption of water from the soil the root hairs of plants play a very active part. Pull up some of the seedlings growing in the soil and rinse the roots in water. If the smaller roots have not been broken off pulling up the plant, particles of earth will be clinging to them which cannot be washed off. This is because the root hairs cling so firmly to the soil particles. This is seen in Fig. 91. When the soil is only moist the water in it forms a very thin film, as thin as the film of a soap bubble, which lies on the surface of the soil particles. It is necessary then for the root hairs to fix themselves very closely and tightly against the soil particles, so that they may come in close contact with this film of water.

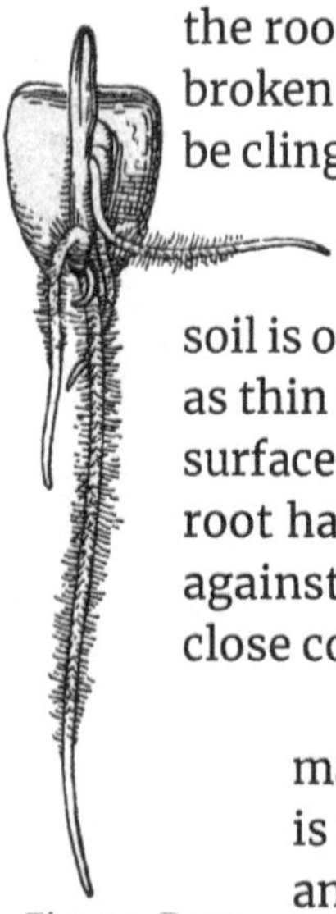

Fig. 90. Root hairs of corn seedling grown under glass.

While plants need a great deal of water a great many kinds can thrive much better where the soil is moist, not wet. Most of the cultivated plants and many flowers and trees do better in well-drained land. Perhaps you have seen how small and yellow patches of corn or wheat look in the low and wet parts of a field. This is because there is too much water in soil and not enough air. On the other hand, there are a few trees and many other plants which thrive better in wet soil, or even in the water. It has been the habit of the parents and forefathers of such plants to live in these places, so they naturally follow in this habit.

How the roots and root hairs do the work of absorbing the water from the soil can be understood by the study of Chapters XI and XII.

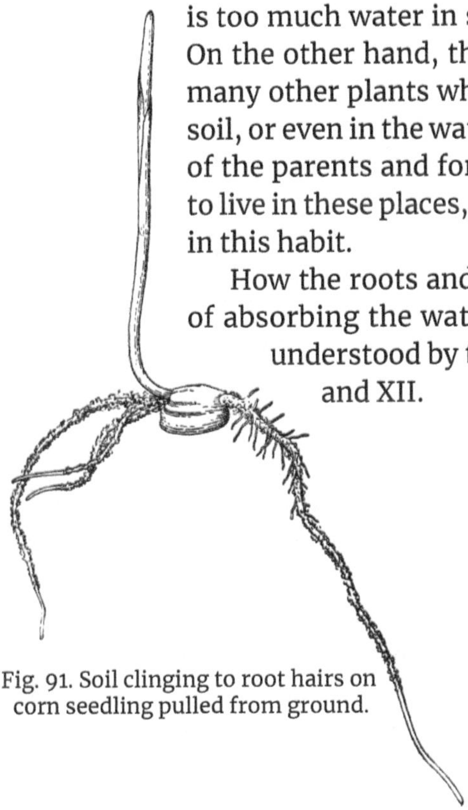

Fig. 91. Soil clinging to root hairs on corn seedling pulled from ground.

CHAPTER X.

The Full-Grown Plant, Etc. (Continued)

IV. Leaves

The color of leaves. In the spring and summer gather leaves of different plants in the garden, field, and woods. Examine those of many more. In the autumn or winter, plants in greenhouses or those grown in the room will furnish leaves for observation. What colors do the different leaves have? The oak, hickory, maple, elm, strawberry, dandelion, corn, bean, pea are all green in color.

Do you think that all leaves are green? Look further. Maybe you will see in some yard a copper beech, or birch, with leaves that are copper colored or brown, especially those that are on the ends of the new shoots. They are not so bright when they get older. They then show shades of brown and green. In the garden or in the greenhouse you may see leaves that are red, brown, or partly green and partly white. The coleus plant has variegated leaves, part of the leaf being green, and the middle

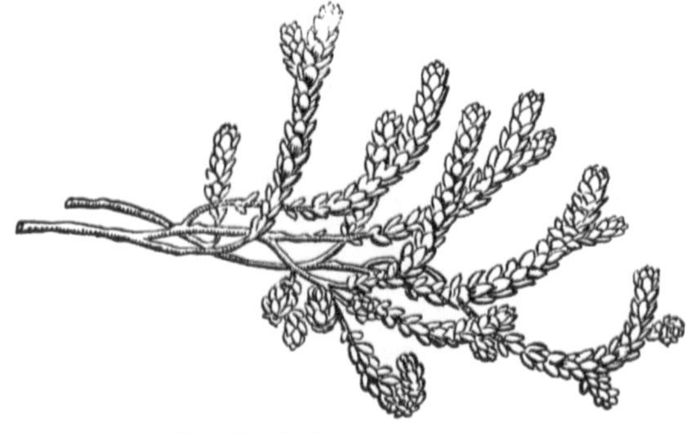

Fig. 92. Purslane or "pusley" showing small thick leaves.

part white (see Fig. 148). Many of you know the ribbon grass, striped white and green. Why are leaves differing in color from the common green leaf usually found in the flower garden or greenhouse? Plants which grow in the fields and woods occasionally have variegated leaves, but they are rare.

If you should happen to find the Indian-pipe plant, or ghost plant, you would see that the leaves are white, or sometimes pink, but never green. They are very small. Has the dodder leaves? Yes, but they are yellowish white, not green. They, too, are very small. Do you know any other plants which always have white leaves? Are the leaves of such plants always small?

The green leaf, compared with white ones. [1] Compare the green leaves with the white ones. You see that nearly all the green leaves you have gathered, such as those of the oak, elm, maple, apple, bean, pea, and corn, are broad and thin. The grass leaves are long and narrow, but they are thin. If you have gathered some pine leaves, or leaves of the spruce, balsam, fir, hemlock, or larch, you see how very different they are from the other leaves. Perhaps you have never heard of leaves on the pine, for they are often called pine needles, because of their needle-like shape. They are not so thin as most other leaves, and they are stiff. Did you ever see the purslane, or, as some people call it, "pusley"? Its leaves are not very large, and they are thick. So we find that while most green leaves are broad and thin, some are not. You see how quickly the thin leaves wilt and dry after they are picked. But the purslane leaves do not wilt so easily. On hot days, during a long "spell of dry weather," did you ever notice how many of the plants with green leaves wilt and suffer for want of water? At such times how is it with the purslane?

NOTE.—During late summer and autumn the leaves of many trees take on bright colors, such as red, yellow, etc., of varying shades. The pupils interested in gathering leaves will be attracted by this brilliant

1 The leaves of plants grown in the dark are often white. This comparison should be made between leaves grown in the light.

foliage. The beautiful coloring is the expression of certain changes going on inside the leaf during its decline at the close of the season. The causes of these colors form too difficult a subject for discussion here. But it should be understood that the "autumn colors" of leaves are not necessarily due to the action of frost, since many of the changes occur before the frosts come.

THE FORM OF LEAVES

Stalked leaves and sessile leaves. Most leaves are green. Most green leaves are broad and thin. You have seen this by looking at different kinds of leaves. Have you noticed the shapes of leaves? Yes, of course. You see the larger number of them have a little stalk (*petiole*) where they are joined to the stem which holds out the broad part (*blade*). In some of the water-lilies the stalk is long and large. In many ferns the stalk is also large and is sometimes taken for the stem (Fig. 93). But in many other leaves there is no stalk, and the blade is seated on the stem; such leaves are *sessile*. In some plants the stem appears to grow through the leaf, but in reality the leaf grows all round the stem; sometimes there is one leaf only at one point on the stem, and in other cases two leaves which are opposite have their bases grown together round the stem.

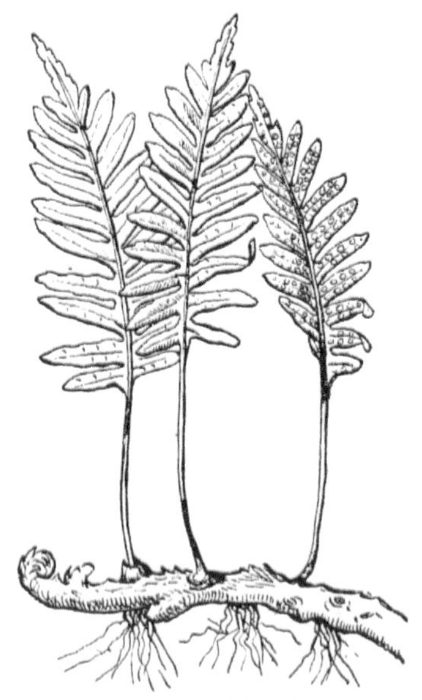

Fig. 93. Sensitive fern showing large leaves and the rhizome or rootstock which runs underground.

Simple leaves and compound leaves. How many different pieces are there in the blade of a leaf? Look at the elm, the oak, the lilac, and the sunflower leaf. You see the blade is all in one piece, although the elm leaf is notched on the edge, and the scarlet oak leaf is deeply

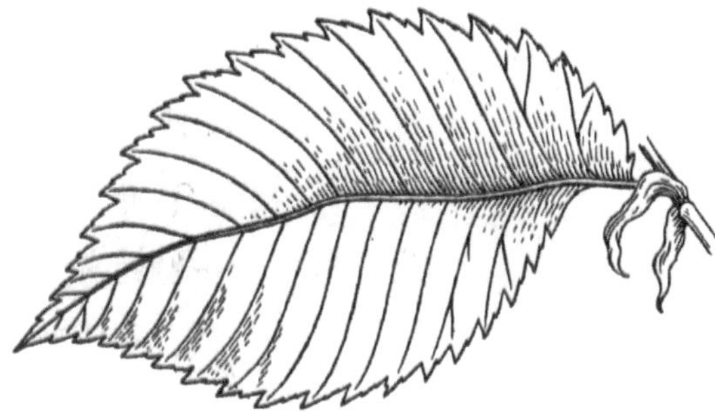
Fig. 94. Elm leaf (stipules where the leaf is joined to stem).

scalloped. Where the blade of the leaf is in one piece it is called a *simple leaf*.

How many pieces are there in the blade of a bean leaf? a clover leaf? of the oxalis, pea, ash, hickory, and ailanthus leaves? If you do not find all these plants, you may find others which have leaves somewhat like them. Perhaps you thought each one of the pieces of the blade was the entire leaf. But see where the stalk of the leaf joins the stem. *The leaf stalk and all that it supports is one leaf.* We call such leaves as these *compound*. Do you know a compound fern leaf? The pieces of each compound leaf are called *leaflets*. Each leaflet is supported on the leaf stalk by a *stalklet*. If you can find some of the different kinds of compound leaves, make drawings to show the shape, and where the leaflets are attached to the leafstalk. The bean leaf, as well as that of the pea, ash, etc., is *once compound*. The

Fig. 95. Compound leaf of ash.

Fig. 96. Scales, leaves and young summer leaves in opening bud of ailanthus tree.

leaves of the sensitive plant, of the honey locust and some others, are *twice compound*, and so on.

LEAVES WEARING A MASK

Masks on the pea leaf. Some of the leaves which you have seen may have puzzled you because they have parts which are not leaf-like. The pea, for example, has curled, thread-like outgrowths on the end, which we call *tendrils*. These tendrils cling to objects and hold the pea vine upright. Now see where these tendrils are joined to the leaf. They are in pairs, in the same positions as the leaflets. *Are they not leaflets which have changed in form to do a certain kind of work for the plant? Has the leaflet here given up its thin part and kept the midrib, or vein, to do this new work?* This part of the pea leaf is then *under a mask; it is disguised.*

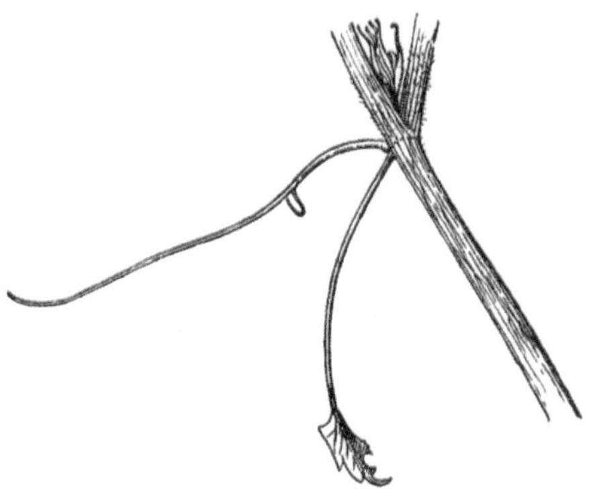

Fig. 97. Tendril of squash partly turned to leaf.

Fig. 98. Awl-shaped leaves of Russian thistle.

Masked leaves of the squash or pumpkin. Examine the tendrils on a squash or pumpkin vine, or some one of their near relatives. Draw a cluster of tendrils and show how they are attached to the vine. Make a drawing of a leaf. Compare the two. Do the tendrils correspond to the large veins of the leaf?

Did you ever find one of these which was part leaf and part tendril? Such leaves tell a very interesting story. Can you tell it?

Spine-like leaves. If there are barberry bushes growing in the yard, examine them. What position do the spines occupy? See the short, leafy branches which arise in the axil between the spines and stem. Is not the spine a mask under which some of the barberry leaves appear?

Not all spines, however, are masked leaves. Where do the spines or thorns occur on the hawthorn? Have you ever seen them on the Russian thistle, or on the amarantus, or pigweed, as it is sometimes called? What are the spines on a cactus? What are the spines on a thistle, like the Canada thistle or common thistle?

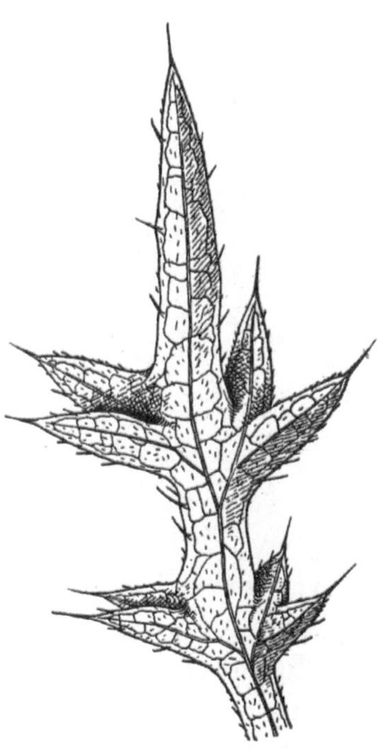

Fig. 99. Spines on edge of common thistle leaf.

THE POSITION OF LEAVES

The plants in the field, forest, and garden, as well as those grown in the house, can tell some interesting stories about the positions of their leaves on the stem. The plants speak in a very quiet way. We cannot hear them, because they speak in a sign language. Now you know what this means, so you must look at the plants and see how the leaves are arranged. *The position of the leaves on the plant is the sign.* You are to act as the interpreter does, and put what the leaves tell into your own words. One of the plainest signs which the green leaves make can be understood if you compare a geranium plant grown in the window with one grown out of doors, or in a glass house where the light comes in from above as well as from one

Fig. 100. Garden-balsam plant showing leaves near ends of branches.

side. The leaf wants to face the light, to be in such a position on the plant that it can get light easily and directly on the upper surface.

In the corn plant, the sunflower, or the mullein, with erect and usually unbranched stems, the leaves stand out horizontally, so that they get light from the sky where it is strongest (see Fig. 72). You see also that in most cases one leaf is not directly over another. They are set so that they do not shade one another. If two leaves are in the same perpendicular line, one is so much above the other on the stem that the slanting light can easily reach the lower one.

The garden-balsam plant, or the wild "touch-me-not," tells the same story and more. You see the stem is branched, and in an old plant all the leaves are near the ends of the branches, and on top. As the branch grew in length the leaves reaching out all around cut off much light from the center of the plant, and the leaves here, which were formed when the plant was younger, became so shaded that they died and fell away. Can you read this story in other plants?

The leaves of many trees tell a similar story. When

Fig. 101. "Feather down," elm.

the trees are in leaf observe how the leaves are arranged on the oaks, maples, elms, etc. You will see that the position of the leaves varies somewhat in different trees of the same kind. The oak, or elm, or apple tree, which has a great many branches, will have nearly all its leaves on the outside. These allow so little light to get to the inside of the tree that few leaves are formed there. Have you seen trees of this kind on which there were many leaves all through the tree and down its large branches? What story is told by a tree which has a great many leaves in its center? Did you ever see a tall tree standing alone in a field or a yard, with a great many leaves standing out from its trunk on young branches? What story do they tell?

The story that leaves of forest trees tell. In the deep forest all the leaves of the larger trees are at the top. When these were very young trees, the leaves were near the ground. The young trees had branches also near the ground. Now the old forest

Fig. 102. Mosaic of leaves of Fittonia, showing veins of the leaf. The leaves present a beautiful broad side to the light.

trees show no branches except near the top. They have long, straight, bare trunks. The great mass of leaves in the top of the forest tell us that they shaded the lower branches so much that few or no leaves could grow on them, and the branches died and dropped off. A little light comes in here and there, so that the young trees in the forest have some leaves on them. But do you see so many leaves on young maples, pines, oaks, and other trees in a deep forest, as you do on trees of the same size growing in an open field? The forest also tells us that there are some plants which like to grow in its shade; for we find them doing well there, while they cannot grow well in the open field.

The duration of leaves. The leaves of most plants live but a single season. Most trees and shrubs shed their leaves in the autumn. Evergreen trees form a crop of leaves each season, but these leaves remain on the tree for more than a year, in some trees for several years, so that the trees are green during winter as well as summer.

The veins of leaves. If you examine carefully the leaves which you have gathered while learning the stories of their color and form, you will see that all of them have *veins*, as we call them. These show especially on the underside of the leaf as prominent raised lines where the leaf substance is thicker. There are large veins and small ones. The midrib of the leaf is the largest vein. The smaller veins branch out from the larger ones, or arise at the base of the leaf. If you look carefully at the leaves of some plants (*Fittonia,* for example, Fig. 102), you will see that the smallest veins form a fine network. The entire system of veins in a leaf forms the skeleton of the leaf. Where the veins form a network the leaf is said to be *net-veined*. Where the veins run in parallel lines through the leaf the leaf is *parallel-veined*.

You have observed the germination of the corn, and that it has *one cotyledon*. How do the veins in the leaves of the corn run? In germinating beans, peas, pumpkin, sunflower, oak, etc., you found *two cotyledons*. How do the veins in the leaves of these plants run?

The work of leaves. Leaves do a great deal of work. They do several kinds of work. They work together to make plant food, and to do other work which we shall learn later.

PART II.

THE WORK OF PLANTS

CHAPTER XI.

How the Living Plant Uses Water to Remain Firm

To restore firmness in wilted plants. We all know how soon flowers or plants wilt after being picked, unless they are kept where the air is moist. Many times we restore wilted flowers or plants to a fresh or firm condition by putting the cut stems or roots in water for a time. By a simple experiment one can show how to hasten the return of firmness or rigidity in the wilted plant.

Cut off several of the seedlings growing in the soil. Allow them to lie on the table for several minutes until they droop. Put the stem of one in a glass of water and place over this a fruit jar. Leave another stem in a glass of water uncovered. The covered one should revive sooner than the uncovered one.

How beet slices remain rigid. A beet freshly dug from the soil is quite firm. Cut out slices from the beet 4 to 5 cm.[2] 2 long, 2 to 3 cm. broad, and about 4 to 5 mm. thick. Hold them between the thumb and finger and try to bend them. They yield but little to pressure. They are firm or rigid.

Place some of the slices of beet in a five per cent salt solution,[3] and some in fresh water. After a half hour or so, test the slices in the fresh water by trying to bend them between the thumb and finger. They remain rigid as before. Now test those which

2 2½ cm. = 1 inch. 25 mm. = 1 inch.

3 Dissolve a rounded tablespoonful of table salt in a tumbler of water. The solution will be nearly a five per cent one.

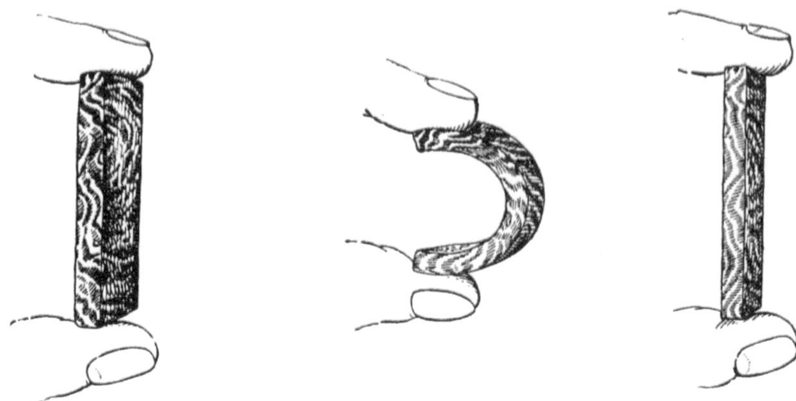

Fig. 103. Beet slices; at left fresh one, middle one after lying in salt solution, right-hand one taken from salt water and placed in fresh water.

have been lying in the salt solution. They are limp and flabby and bend easily under pressure.

Now remove the slices from the salt solution and place them in fresh water. After an hour or so test them again. They have regained their rigidity. Instead of being limp and flabby they are firm and plump. It appears from this that they have regained their firmness by taking in or absorbing water. The slice of beet, like all parts of plants, is made up of a great many *cells*, as they are called. These cells are like tiny boxes packed close together. Each one absorbs water and becomes firm. Perhaps the following experiment will help us to understand how this takes place.

A make-believe plant cell. Fill a small, wide-mouthed vial with a sugar solution made by dissolving a heaping teaspoonful of sugar in a half cup of water. Over the mouth tie firmly a piece of a bladder membrane. (The footnote, see reference page, tells how to

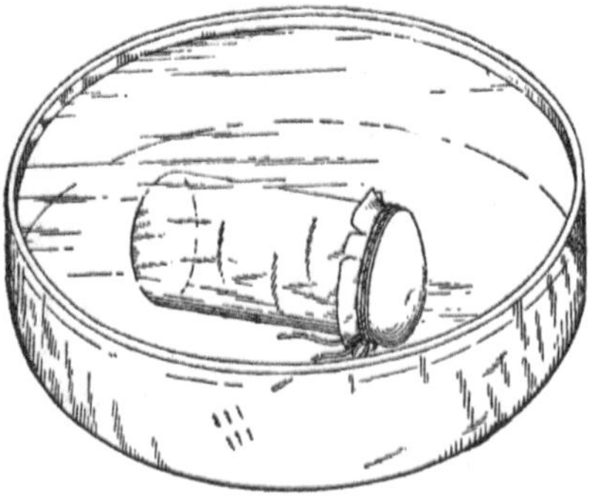

Fig. 104. Make-believe cell, with sugar solution inside, lying in water.

get a bladder membrane.) Be sure that, as the membrane is tied over the open end of the vial, the sugar solution fills it. Sink the vial in a vessel of fresh water and allow it to remain twenty-four hours. Then take it out and set it on the table. The membrane which was straight across at first is now bulged out because of inside pressure.

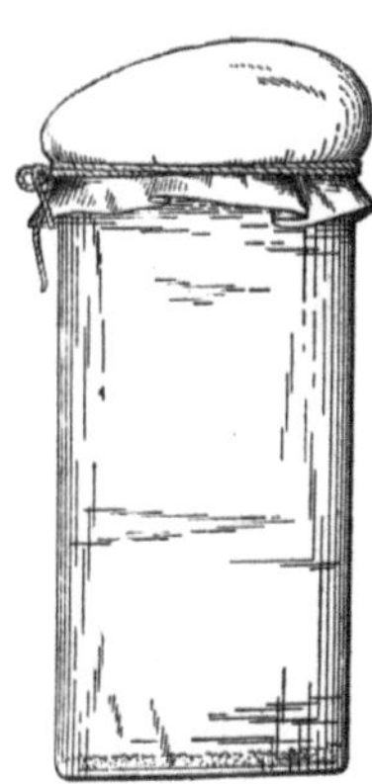

Fig. 105. Make-believe cell after taking in water.

Now sink the vial in a very strong sugar solution for several hours. There should be so much sugar in the water that all of it will not dissolve. The membrane has become straight across again because the inside pressure is removed. Now sink it in fresh water again. The inside pressure returns, and the membrane bulges again. Thrust a sharp needle through the membrane when it is arched or bulged, and quickly pull it out again. The liquid spurts out because of the inside pressure.

What is it that causes the inside pressure? Why is the

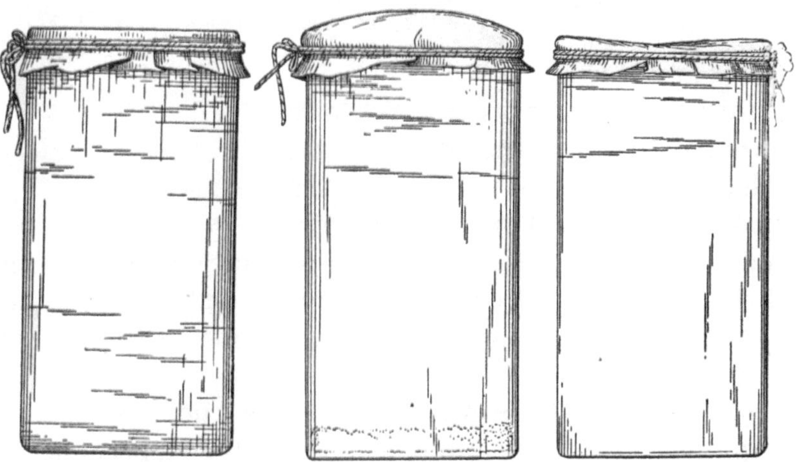

Fig. 106. Make-believe cell, at left before placing in water, middle one after lying in water has inside pressure, one at right after lying in very strong sugar solution has collapsed or become flabby.

inside pressure removed when the vial is immersed in the stronger solution?

Movement of water through membranes. This experiment illustrates the well-known behavior of water and solutions of different kinds when separated by a membrane. Water moves quite readily through the membrane, but the substance in solution moves through with difficulty. Also the water will move more readily in the direction of the stronger solution. The fresh water has no substance, or but little, in solution. The sugar solution is stronger than the water, so the water moves readily through the membrane into it.

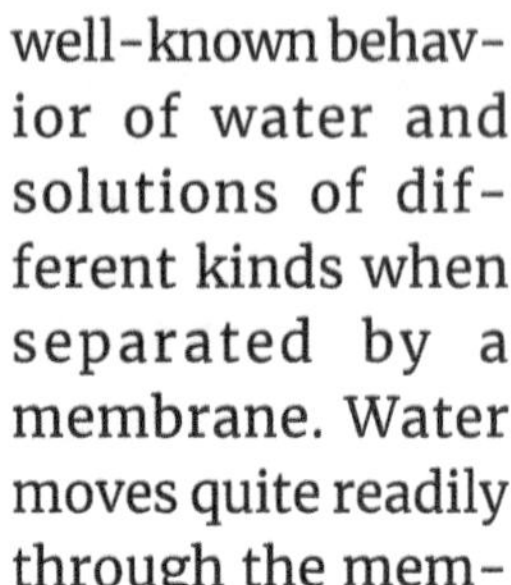

Fig. 107. Puncturing a make-believe cell after it has been lying in water.

Now when the vial containing the sugar solution is immersed in fresh water, some of the water flows through the membrane into the sugar solution, because this is stronger. This increases the bulk of the sugar solution and it presses against the membrane, making it tight and firm, or rigid. When it is placed in the stronger solution, this draws some of the water out, and the membrane, losing its firmness, becomes flat again.

Fig. 108. same as Fig. 107, after needle is removed.

How the beet slice works. The beet slice is not like a bladder membrane, but some of the substances in the beet act like the sugar solution inside the vial. In fact, there are certain sugars and salts in solution in the beet, and it is the "pull" which these exert on the water outside that makes the beet rigid. While these sugars and salts in the beet draw the water inside, what is there in the beet which acts like the bladder membrane through which the water is "pulled," and which holds

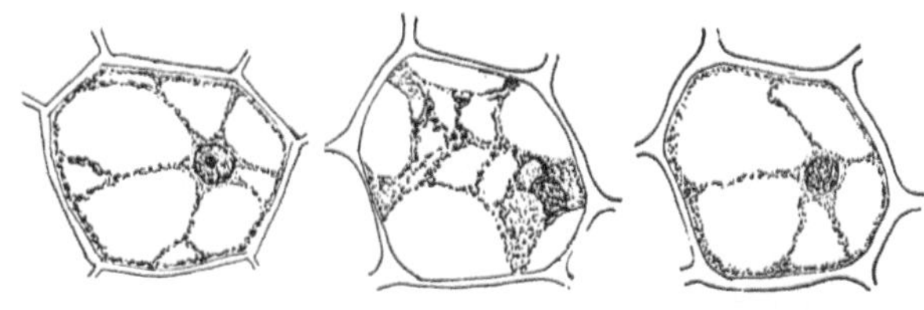

Fig. 109. Picture of a real plant cell, at left it is in natural condition, middle one after lying in a salt solution, one at right after being taken from salt and placed in water.

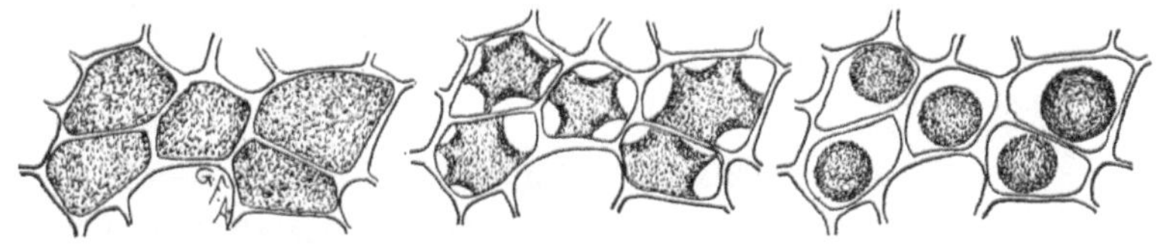

Fig. 110. Cells of beet slice, at left fresh, middle ones just placed in salt water, ones at right after lying in salt water a few moments.

it from flowing quickly out again? *In the beet slices there are thousands of tiny membranes of a slimy substance in the form of rounded sacs, each lining a tiny box. Every one of these forms a plant cell, and acts like the bladder membrane in the make-believe cell.* Inside these tiny membranes the sugars and salts of the beet are in solution. When the cells are full and plump they press against each other and make the entire mass of the beet firm and plump. They are too tiny to be seen without the use of a microscope, but we can look at some pictures of them.

A dead beet slice cannot work. Place some of the fresh slices of beet in boiling water for a few moments, or in water near the boiling point. Then test them with pressure. They are flabby and bend easily. Place them in fresh cold water, and in about an hour test them again. They are still limp and do not again become firm. Why is this? *It is because the hot water killed all the tiny membranes in the beet, so that they cannot longer do the work. In the living plant, then, these tiny membranes are alive.* Yes, they are alive; and *really, they are the living substance of the*

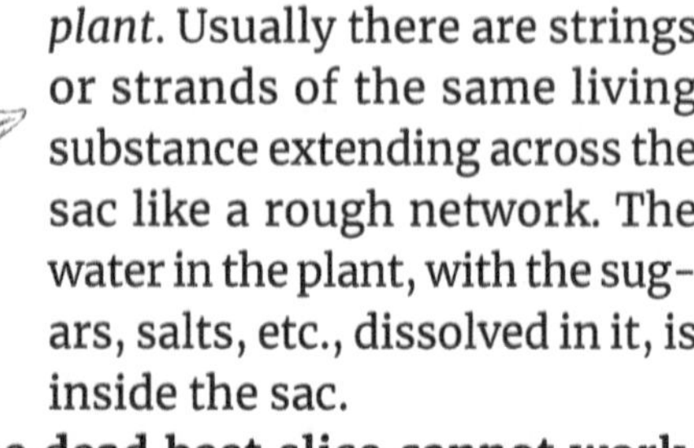

plant. Usually there are strings or strands of the same living substance extending across the sac like a rough network. The water in the plant, with the sugars, salts, etc., dissolved in it, is inside the sac.

Why the dead beet slice cannot work. When the living substance is killed the tiny membranes can no longer hold the sugars, salts, etc., inside them. These escape and filter through into the water outside. In the case of the beet this is well shown by the behavior of the red coloring matter, which is also in the water, inside the tiny living membrane. When the living beet slice is placed in cold water the red coloring matter does not escape and color the water. Nor does the salt solution pull it out when we place the slice in salt water, although some of the water is pulled out. But when the beet slice is killed in hot water the red color escapes.

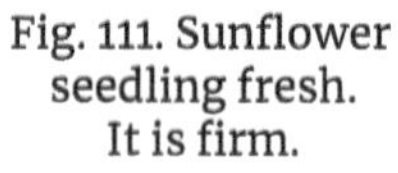

Fig. 111. Sunflower seedling fresh. It is firm.

How other plant parts behave in salt solution and in water. Pull up a sunflower seedling or some other plant. It is firm and rigid as we hold it in the hand, and the leaves stand out well, as shown in Fig. 111. Immerse the leaves and most of the stem in a five per cent salt solution for fifteen minutes. Now hold it in the hand. It is limp and flabby, as shown in Fig. 113. Immerse the seedling in fresh water for half an hour and test it again. It has

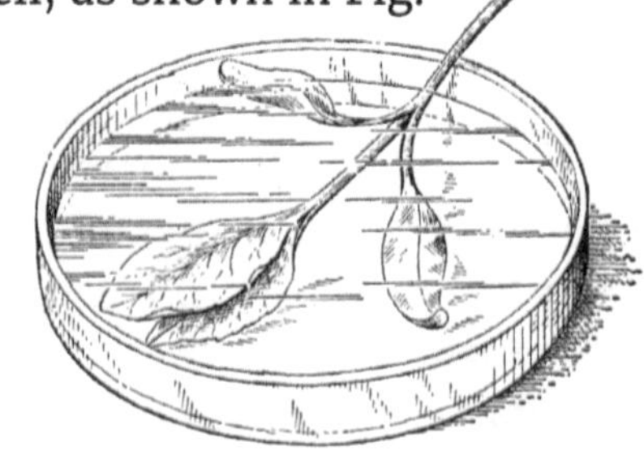

Fig. 112. Same seedling as shown in Fig. 111 lying in salt water.

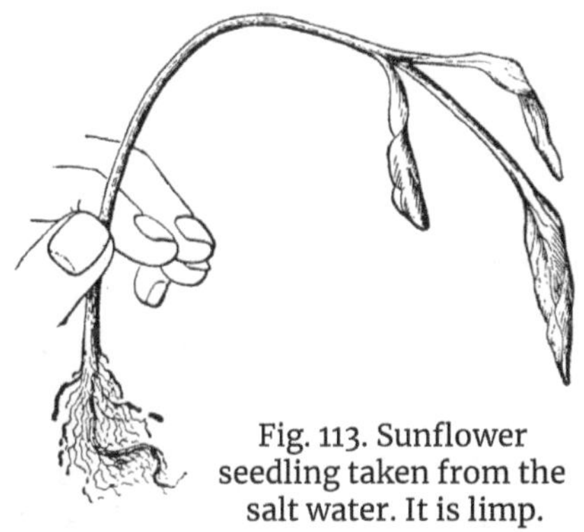
Fig. 113. Sunflower seedling taken from the salt water. It is limp.

regained its former firmness, as shown in Fig. 114. Can you account for the behavior of the seedling under these conditions? How would it behave if we should immerse it in boiling water for a few moments? Why? Immerse it in alcohol for fifteen minutes. What effect has the alcohol had on it? Immerse a red beet slice in alcohol. Describe the results.

Fig. 114. Sunflower seedling taken from salt solution and placed in water. It becomes firm again.

Other plant parts may be treated in the same way, if it is desired to multiply these experiments.

The effect of too strong food solutions in the soil. Some of the plant foods are in the form of salts in the soil. If the salts are too abundant in the soil, the food solutions are so strong that the plant cannot take them up. In fact, too strong solutions will draw water from the plants so that they will become limp and will fall down, as shown in Fig. 115, where a ten per cent salt

Fig. 115. Sunflower seedlings after salt solution was poured in soil.

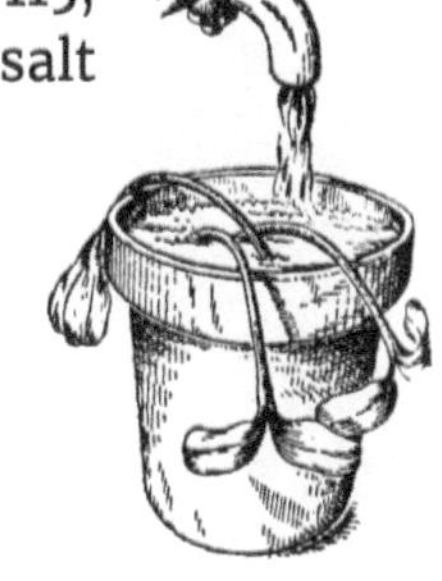
Fig. 116. Washing the salt out of the soil.

solution was poured into the soil. After these plants had collapsed, tap water was allowed to run through the soil overnight, as shown in Fig. 116. In the morning the plants had straightened up again, as shown in Fig. 117, because the excess of salt was washed out of the soil and the root hairs could then absorb water.

Fig. 117. After the surplus salt has been washed out of the soil the plants revive.

How some stems and petioles remain firm. Did you ever think how strong some stems and petioles must be to hold up so much weight as they often do? The pie plant or rhubarb leaf is very large, broad, and heavy. The leafstalk, or *petiole*, as we call it, is quite soft, yet it stands up firm with the great weight of the leaf blade on the end. If you shave off one or two thin strips from the side, it weakens the leafstalk greatly. Why does the leafstalk become so weak when so little of the surface is removed?

Cut a piece from a fresh leafstalk[4] six or eight inches long. Cut the ends squarely. With a knife remove a strip from one side, the entire length of the piece. Try to put it in place again. It is shorter than it was before. Remove another strip and another, until the entire outer surface has been removed.

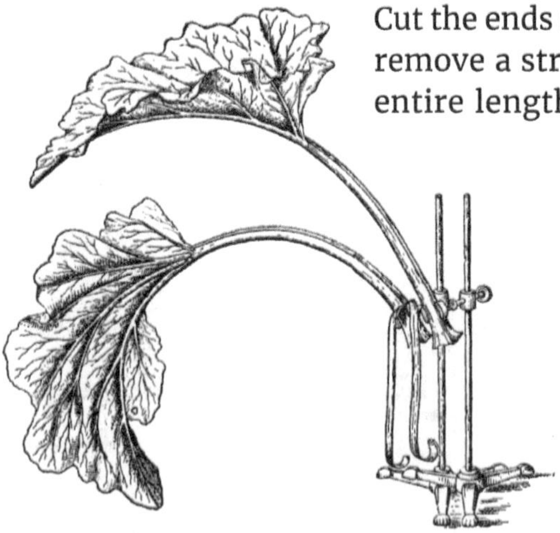

Fig. 118. Leaf of pie (rhubarb) before and after shaving off two narrow strips from the leafstalk.

4 If pie plant cannot be obtained, the plant known as Caladium in greenhouses is excellent. In early summer the young soft shoots of elder are good for the experiment.

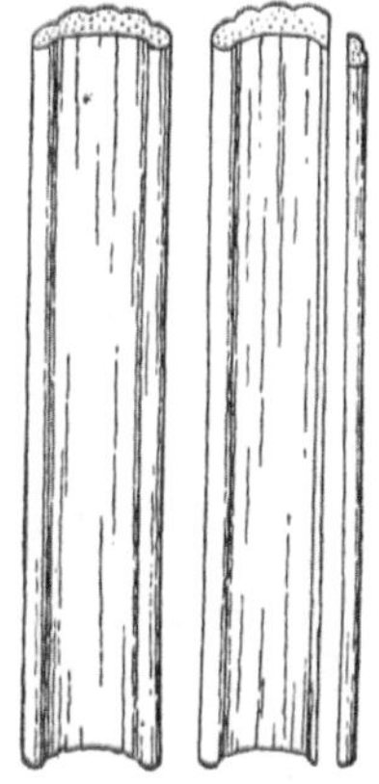

Fig. 119. Portion of leafstalk of pie plant with one strip removed.

Now try to put one of the outside strips in place again. It is now shorter than before as compared with the center piece.

You see when the outside strip was removed it shortened up. When all the outside strips were removed the center piece lengthened out. I think now you can tell why it is that the leafstalk was so firm. Of course it must have plenty of water in it to make the cells firm. But the center piece alone, with plenty of water, is limp. You see when it is covered with the outside strips, as it is when undisturbed, the outside part is pulling to shorten the stalk and the center is pushing to lengthen it. *This lengthwise pull between the inside and outside parts makes the stalk firm.*

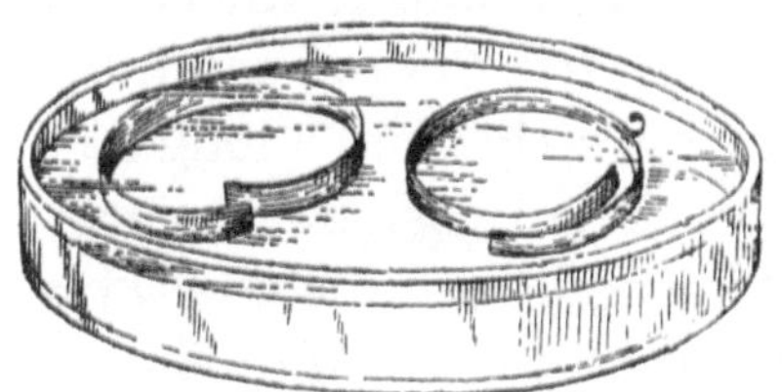

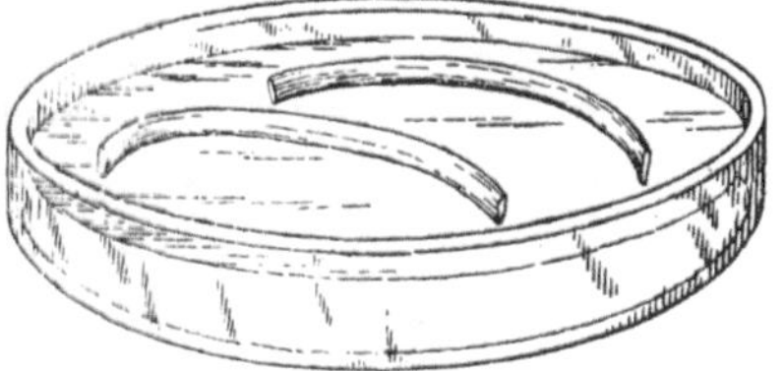

Fig. 120. Strips from outside of leafstalk of pie plant placed in water, at left they coil up, at right in salt water they uncoil.

Why the dandelion stem curls. Did you ever break off a dandelion stem, press one end against your tongue, and make it coil up into beautiful curls as it splits? Do you know why it does so? Even when you split a stem with a knife or with your fingers it will curl a little. The inside part is trying to lengthen, and the outside part is trying to shorten. So when it is split it curls around toward the outside part.

Split a stem and place it in a vessel of fresh water. Watch it. It begins to curl more and more and more, until it makes a very close coil of several rings. *The life substance in the tiny*

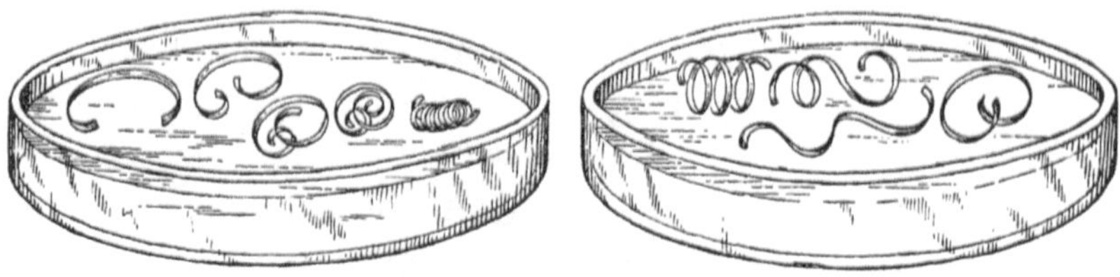

Fig. 121. Strip from dandelion stem in water, at left it gradually coils up, in salt water at right it uncoils.

cells takes in more water and swells so, that all together they push harder than they did before. To prove this, put the strips from the dandelion stem in salt water. They begin to uncoil and finally become nearly straight and quite limp. We know this is because the salt "pulls" water out of the cells, just as it does in the beet slice. Now place the strips from the salt water back into fresh water. They become firm and coil up again.

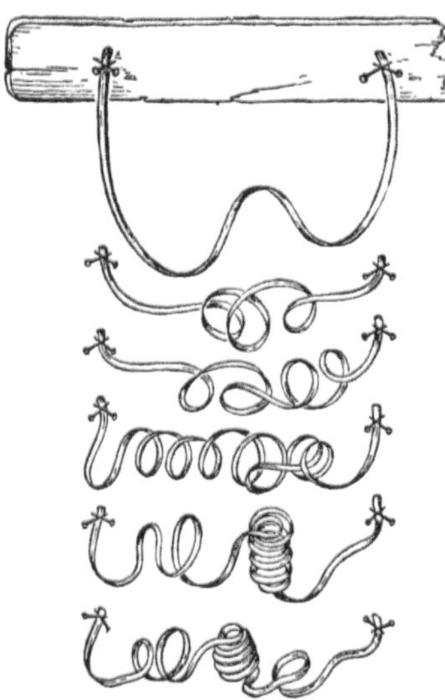

Fig. 122. Strip from dandelion stem made to imitate a plant tendril.

How to imitate the coiling of a tendril. Cut out carefully a narrow strip from a long dandelion stem. Fasten to a piece of soft wood, with the ends close together, as shown in Fig. 122. Now place it in fresh water and watch it coil. Part of it coils one way and part another way, just as a tendril does after the free end has caught hold of some place for support.

CHAPTER XII.

How the Root Lifts Water in the Plant

Root pressure in seedlings. To see this we may use the seedlings which are growing vigorously—sunflower, bean, pumpkin, buckwheat, and others. With a sharp knife cut off the stem near the upper end. In a few minutes a drop of water will be seen forming on the cut end of the stem. This increases in size until a large, round drop is formed. We know that water would not flow upward out of the stem unless there was some pressure from below. This pressure comes from the absorptive power of the roots. The roots, as we have found in our previous study, take up water from the soil through the root hairs so forcibly as to produce an inside pressure which makes the tissue firm. This water is passed inward in the root by a similar process until it reaches minute vessels or tubes which are continuous with similar tubes in the stem. The continued pressure which is formed in the roots lifts the water up and forces it out through the cut end of the stem. (The bleeding of cut stems in winter or early spring is due to changes in the expansion of the air, because of the great differences in temperature.)

Fig. 123. Drop of water pressed out of cut end of stem of sunflower seedling by work of roots.

ROOT PRESSURE IN A GARDEN BALSAM

The materials necessary for the study. Select a vigorously growing potted garden-balsam plant. If this is not at hand, use a coleus plant, geranium, or other plant. Select a piece of glass tubing several feet long and about the same diameter as that of the stem of the plant to be used. Next prepare a short piece of rubber tubing which will slip over the end of the glass tube. Then have ready some wrapping cord, a small quantity of water, a tall stake, and a sharp knife.

Fig. 124. Cutting off stem of balsam plant.

To start the experiment to show root pressure. With the knife cut off the stem squarely near the ground, as shown in Fig. 124. Slip one end of the rubber tubing over the end of the stem and tie it tightly with the wrapping cord. Then pour in a small quantity of water to keep the end of the stem moist at the start. Insert one end of the glass tubing in the other end of the rubber tube, tie it tightly, and then bind the glass tubing to the stake to hold it upright. The experiment must be made in a room in which the temperature is suitable for growth.

The result of the experiment. In a few hours the water will be seen rising in the glass tube. This will continue for a day or two, and perhaps for a longer time. The soil in the pot should be watered just as if the entire plant were growing.

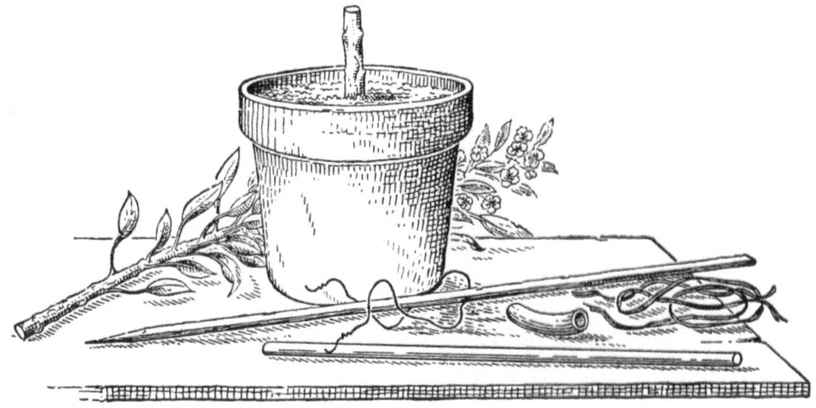

Fig. 125. The materials for setting up the apparatus to show root pressure.

Observations on the height of the water in the tube should be made several times a day for several days. It will be found that the column rises and falls, showing that there is some fluctuation in the pressure from the roots.

Thus we see that the roots by their absorptive power are capable, not only of taking in water from the soil with considerable force, but also of lifting it up to a considerable height in the stem. Root pressure, however, cannot lift the water to the tops of tall trees. It has been found that the root pressure of the birch can lift water 84.7 feet high, the grapevine 36.5 feet, and the nettle 15 feet.

A simple experiment to illustrate how root pressure works. Here is an experiment, easy to perform, which illustrates very well the way the root works in lifting water. Take a thistle tube (Fig. 127) and fill with a strong sugar solution. Tie tightly over the large open end a piece of a bladder 5[5] membrane, after soaking it to make it pliant. Pour out from the small end enough of the solution so that it will stand but a short distance above the bulb in the narrow part of the tube. Invert this in a bottle

5 Get one sheep's bladder, or several, at the butcher's and remove the surplus meat. Inflate, tie the open end, and place where it will dry. From these dried bladders a membrane can be cut whenever wanted. Soak in water before using.

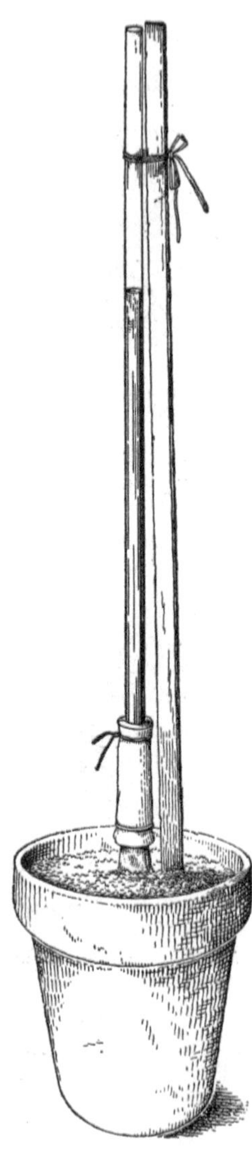
Fig. 126. The experiment in operation showing water rising in the glass tube.

partly filled with water, pass a perforated cork down the tube and into the mouth of the bottle to hold the tube in position, and bring the tube so that the sugar solution in the tube is at the same level as the water in the bottle. Allow this to rest for several hours.

If the experiment has been set up properly, the sugar solution now stands higher in the tube than the level of the water. Because the water in the tube has sugar dissolved in it, it is a stronger solution; that is, of a stronger concentration than the water in the bottle. In such cases, where the two liquids are separated by a membrane, more water always goes through into the stronger solution. The bulk of the sugar solution is thus increased, and it is forced higher up in the tube.

Fig. 127. A "thistle" tube.

The root acts much in the same way, except that each of the tiny root-hair cells and the tiny cells of the root act as the thistle tube and sugar solutions do, or as the make-believe cell did. The sap in the cells is a solution of certain sugars and salts. The life substance (protoplasm) in each cell lines the cell wall and acts like the bladder membrane. The water in the soil is

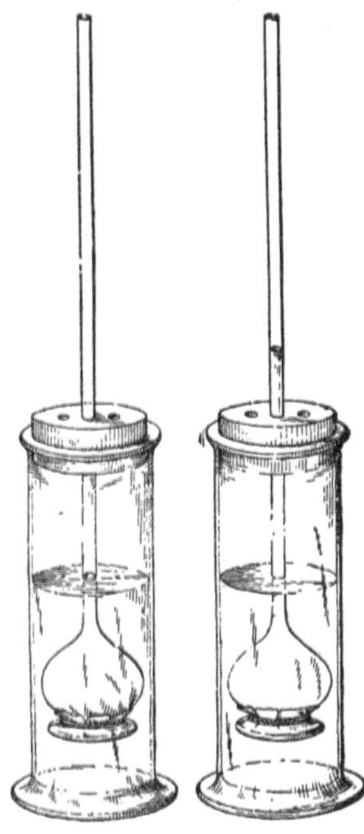

Fig. 128. Apparatus with thistle tube, bladder membrane, and sugar solution to imitate root pressure.

outside the roots, but comes in touch with the life membrane because it filters easily through the cell walls. So all the tiny cells work together, and the result of their combined work is like that of the thistle-tube experiment.

A potato tube may be used to represent the work of a single root hair, or of the root. Cut out a cylindrical piece from a potato tuber. Bore a hole nearly through it, forming a tube closed at one end. Place in the bottom of this tube a quantity of sugar and rest the tube in a shallow vessel of water. Observe how the sugar becomes wet from the water which is drawn through the potato tube. Does the water rise in this tube above the line of the water in the vessel outside? Why?

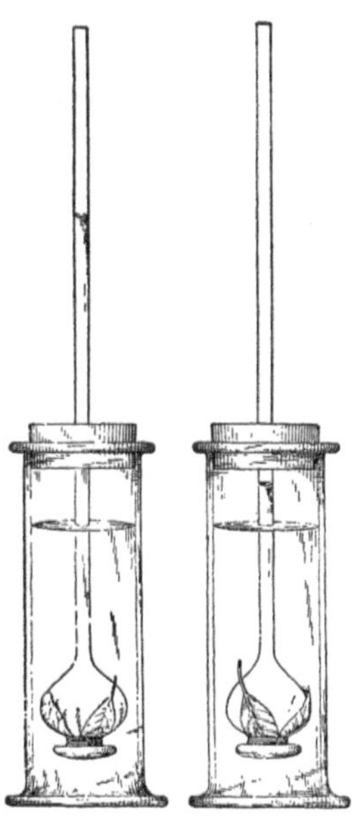

Fig. 129. The same apparatus as shown in Fig. 128, but a leaf of a plant takes the place of the bladder membrane.

NOTE.—**A living leaf of a plant may take the place of the bladder membrane.** In the experiment illustrated in Fig. 129 the leaf of the jewel weed, or wild touch-me-not (*Impatiens*), was used instead of the bladder membrane. It is necessary to select a leaf which is free from any puncture, and it must be tied on carefully with a soft cord. In this experiment the sugar solution rose two or three inches in a day, and then rose no further. The thistle tube was then carefully lifted out, and the leaf was allowed to come in contact with boiling water to kill it. The tube was then replaced in the bottle of water. Strange as it may seem, the dead leaf worked much better as a membrane than the living leaf, and the sugar solution rose to near the top of the tube in two or three days.

CHAPTER XIII.

How Plants Give off Water

What becomes of the water taken up by the plant? We have learned that the food which the plants take from the soil is taken up along with the water in which it is dissolved. We know that the solutions of plant food must be weak, or the plant is not able to absorb them. A large amount of water, then, is taken up by the plant in order to obtain even a small amount of food. We know also that water is taken up by the roots of the plant independent of the food solutions in it. It is of great interest, then, to know what becomes of the large amount of water absorbed by the plant. Some of the water is used as food by the plant, but it would be impossible for a plant to use for food all the water which it takes from the soil.

Loss of water by living leaves. Take a handful of leaves, or several leafy shoots from fresh plants. Place them on the table and cover them with a fruit jar, as in Fig. 130. Place another jar by its side, but put no leaves under it. Be sure that the leaves have no free water on them and that the jars are dry. In the

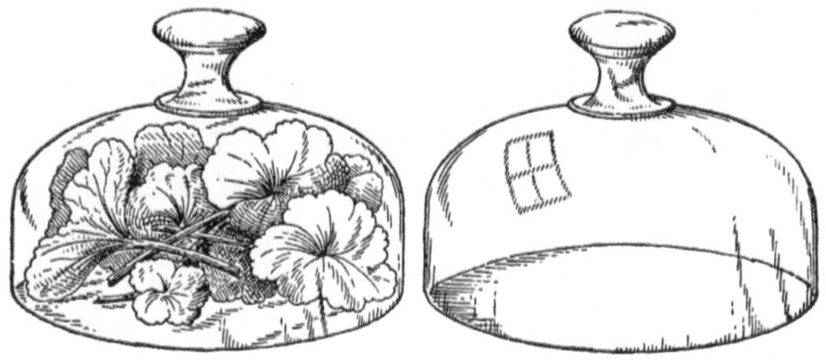

Fig. 130. To show loss of water from leaves the leaves just covered.

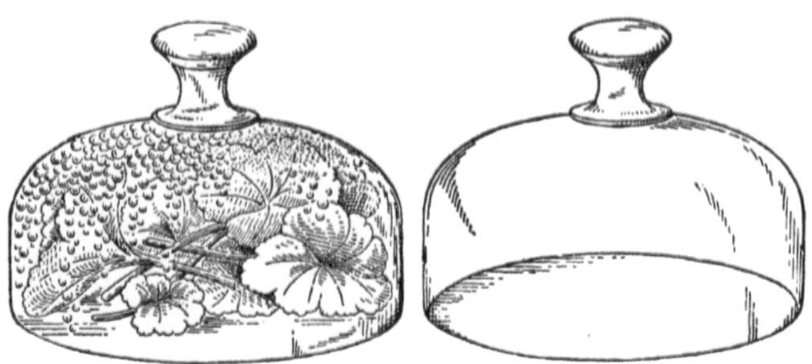

Fig. 131. After a few hours drops of water have accumulated on the inside of the jar covering the leaves.

course of fifteen or twenty minutes you can see a thin film on the inner surface of the jar covering the leaves. In fifteen or twenty minutes more it will be seen that this is water, for it is accumulating in small drops which become larger as the experiment continues. The other jar is dry. The water, then, which first formed the moisture film, and later the drops, on the inner surface of the jar covering the leaves must come from the leaves. We see that it is not only on the sides of the jar, but also on the top above the leaves. So the water did not run off the leaves.

Further, we cannot see any sign of water until we see it accumulating on the jar, so that it must pass off from the leaves in a very light form, so light that it can float in the air like dust without being visible. When water is in this form in the air we call it *vapor. The water passes of from the leaves in the form of* **water vapor.**

Loss of water from living plants. In the above experiment the leaves were removed from the plant. It is not certain from this experiment whether the water passes off from the surfaces of the leaf or from the broken or cut ends of the petioles. We are going to test the living plant in a similar way. To do this, place a potted plant under a tall bell jar, or invert a fruit jar over the plant, after having covered the pot and soil with a flexible oilcloth or sheet rubber, or several layers of oiled paper.

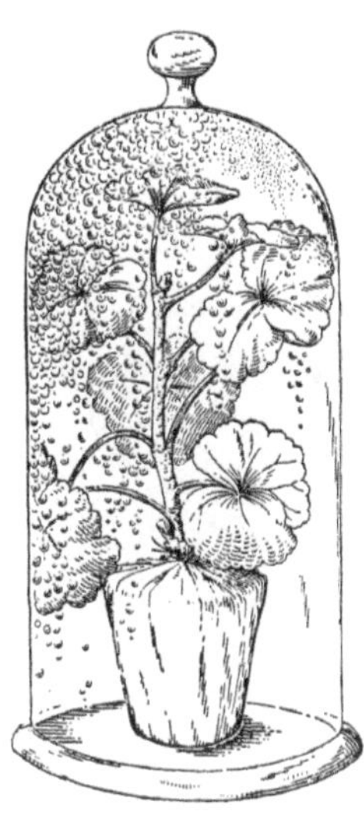

Fig. 132. Water is given off by the leaves when attached to the living plant.

Tie the paper close around the stem of the plant to prevent the evaporation of water from the soil or pot. During several hours the moisture film can be seen forming on the inside of the glass vessel. Gradually it accumulates until numerous drops are formed, some of which in time may trickle down the side of the jar. The accumulation of the moisture may often be hastened or increased at certain places on the jar by holding a piece of ice near the jar outside. The cold glass condenses the water vapor into water again, in the same way that the cold air above condenses the water vapor as it arises from the earth, first forming clouds and later raindrops. *The living plant, then, loses water through its surface in the form of* **water vapor**.

A delicate test for the escape of water vapor from plants. A very pretty and delicate test for the escape of water vapor from living plants can be made in this way. Make a solution of a substance known as cobalt chloride in water. Saturate several pieces of filter paper with it. Allow them to dry, and then dry them still more thoroughly by holding them near a lamp or gas jet, or in a warm oven. You will observe that the water solution of cobalt chloride is red. *The wet or moist paper is also red, but when it is thoroughly dry it is blue. It is so sensitive to moisture that the moisture of the air is often sufficient to redden the paper.*

Take two bell jars, as shown in Fig. 133. In one jar place a potted plant, the pot and earth being covered as described on see reference page. Or cover the plant with a fruit jar. Pin to a stake in the pot a piece of the dried cobalt paper, and at the same time pin to a stake, in another jar covering no plant, another piece of cobalt paper. They should be dried and entirely blue when they are put into the jars, and both should be put under the jars at the same time. In a few moments the paper in the jar with the plant will begin to redden. In a short time, ten or fifteen minutes, probably, it will be entirely red, while the paper under the other jar will remain blue, or be only slightly reddened. *The water vapor passing of from the living plant comes in contact with the sensitive cobalt chloride in the paper and reddens it before there is sufficient vapor present to condense as a film of moisture on the surface of the jar.*

Fig. 133. A good way to show that the water passes off from the leaves in the form of water vapor.

The loss of water from plants. This is similar to evaporation, except that from a given area of leaf surface less water evaporates than from an equal area of water surface. It further differs from evaporation in that the living plant is enabled to retard or hold back the loss of water. This may be shown in the following way. Pull up several seedlings of beans, sunflowers, etc., and take some leaves of geranium or other plants. Divide them into two lots, having in the lots an equal number of the various kinds. Immerse one lot in boiling water for a few moments to kill the plants. Immerse the other lot in cool water, in order to have the living plants also wet at the beginning of the experiment. Spread both lots out on a table to dry. In twenty-four hours examine them. Those which were killed have lost much more water than the living plants. Some of them may be dried so that they are crisp. The living plants are enabled to retard the loss of water, so that the process of evaporation is hindered, not only by the action of the life substance within the plant, but also by a regulating apparatus of the leaves. *The loss of water from plants under these conditions we call* **transpiration.**

Does transpiration take place equally on both surfaces of the leaf? This can be shown very prettily by using the cobalt chloride paper. Since this paper can be kept from year to year and used repeatedly, it is a very simple matter to make these experiments. Provide two pieces of glass (discarded glass negatives, cleaned, are excellent), two pieces of cobalt chloride paper, and some geranium leaves entirely free from surface water. Dry the paper until it is blue. Place one piece of the paper on a glass plate; place the geranium leaf with the underside on the paper. On the upper side of the leaf now place the other cobalt paper, and next the second piece of glass. On the pile place a light weight to keep the parts well in contact. In fifteen or twenty minutes open and examine. *The paper next the underside of the geranium leaf is red where it lies under the leaf. The paper on the upper side is only slightly reddened.* **The greater loss of water, then, is through the underside of the geranium leaf.** This is true of a great many leaves, as tests which you can make will show. But it is not true of all.

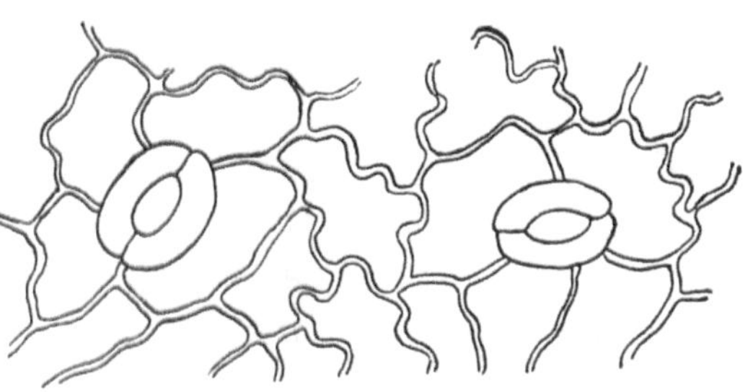

Fig. 134. The holes (stomates) in the leaf bordered by the guard cells.

Why do many leaves lose more water through the underside? You will not be able to see with your eyes the mechanism in the leaf by which it can, to some extent, control the escape of the water vapor. It is too tiny. It can only be seen by using a microscope to look through pieces of the skin, or *epidermis*, of the leaf which we can strip off. Perhaps it will be just

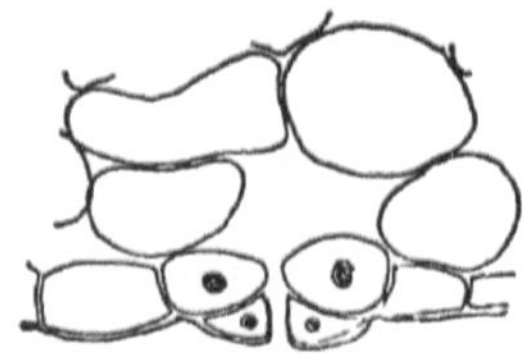

Fig. 135. The stomate open.

as well for the present if you look at a picture of it made from the leaf. Fig. 134 shows little holes through the epidermis. These open into spaces between the cells inside the leaf. Two cells, each shaped like a crescent, if you take a surface view, fit in such a way around the opening that they stand guard over it. We call them *guard cells.*

During the day the guard cells are filled tightly with water and press back against the other cells and keep the little holes (*stomates*) open. At night they lose some of their water, so they are not so tight. They then collapse a little, so that their inner edges come together and close the opening. *The water vapor cannot escape so fast when the stomates are closed.*

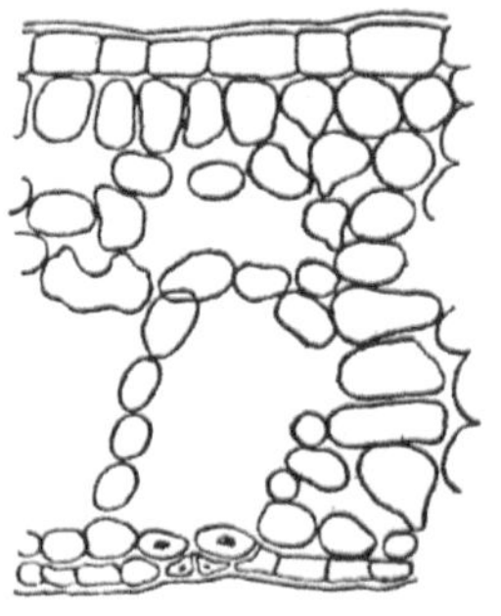

Fig. 136. The stomate closed; the air spaces in the leaf can also be seen.

On very sunny days during dry weather, if the roots cannot give the plant enough water, the guard cells lose some of their water, so that they close up and prevent such a large escape of water as would take place should they remain open. Is this not a good arrangement which the leaf has to prevent the loss of too much water during dry weather? Sometimes, however, the ground gets so dry that the roots cannot get enough water for the plant. The plants then wilt, and sometimes die.

Leaves help to lift water in the plant. As the water evaporates or transpires from the surface of the leaves more water is drawn up into the leaf to take its place. This work is done by the tiny cells of the leaf. The leaf, then, can help lift water in the plant. This can be well shown by the experiment in Fig. 137. A leafy shoot of coleus, geranium, or other plant is cut, and connected by a short piece of rubber tubing to one end of a bent, or U, tube

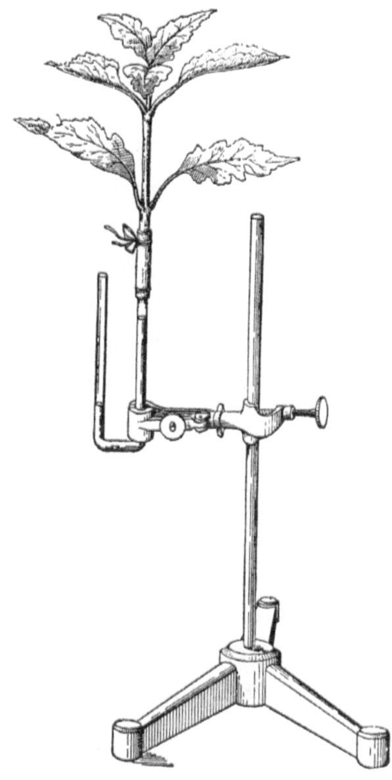

Fig. 137. Showing that the leaf can raise water in the stem as it is given off at the surface.

which has been filled with water so that the end of the cut shoot is in contact with the water. The rubber tube must be tied tightly both to the shoot and to the glass tube, so that air cannot get in. As the water transpires from the leaf it is gradually drawn from the tube so that it lowers in the other arm of the tube. When the water is nearly all out of this arm, mercury may be poured in, and after a time the mercury will be lifted higher in the arm of the tube which is connected with the plant than in the other. Mercury is a great deal heavier than water, so the leaves can do some pretty hard work in lifting.

Can the roots take the water into the plant faster than the leaves can give it off? Here is a pretty experiment to show the power of root absorption. Young wheat plants growing in a pot will show it clearly if the pot is covered with a fruit jar and the roots are kept warm. Fig. 138 shows how this can be done. If it is not summer time, when the soil in the pot would be quite warm enough, the pot may be set in a broad pan of wet moss or sawdust, and here covered with the fruit jar. A flame from a spirit lamp may be set so that it will warm the edge of the pan, but the soil in the pot must not be allowed to get hot. In a few hours or a day the leaves will appear beaded with the drops of water which are pressed out. There are little holes on the edge of the leaf through which the water escapes. These are *water stomates.*

This condition of things sometimes happens at night when the soil is warm and the air damp and cool, so that the green leaves cannot transpire rapidly. We say, then, that ***root pressure exceeds transpiration.*** *When a plant wilts on a hot, dry day, it is transpiring faster than the roots can lift up water, because there is so little water in the dry soil.* ***Transpiration now exceeds root pressure.***

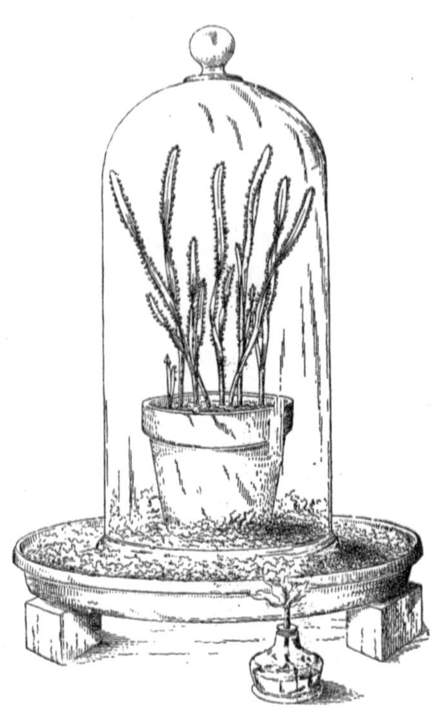

Fig. 138. The roots are lifting more water into the plant than can be given off in the form of water vapor, so it is pressed out in drops.

CHAPTER XIV.

The Water Path in Plants

How to determine the water path. You will be interested to find the paths by which so much water flows through the plant. These may be shown in a very easy way. You may cut some garden-balsam plants, or the wild *Impatiens* or jewel weed, or similar plants. These are very good ones for the purpose. Cut also some shoots of begonia or other plant with white flowers. If there are corn plants or wheat plants half grown at hand, some of these should be used. Use also some good bleached celery leaves cut from a bunch.

Fig. 139. Shoots of garden balsam, begonia, and pea, in colored solution.

Set these shoots in a vessel containing red ink. Or if preferred a red dye can be made by dissolving one of the red "diamond dyes" in water. In a few hours, sometimes, the plants will show the red color in the leaves, or in the white petals. At least in a day they will begin to show the red color.

There are several distinct water paths in the shoot. This shows us in a very clear way that the red dye is taken up along with the water and stains the plant. In the garden balsam or the jewel weed we can sometimes see red streaks in the shoot by looking at the outside. These mark the paths through which the water

Fig. 140. Portion of stem of garden balsam. The colored tracts show through the outside of the stem.

flows. They are better seen if we cut one of these colored shoots in two. In the cut shoot they will show as small round red spots where the colored water has passed. In splitting the stem they would appear as long red streaks or bundles. *In these bundles there are tiny tubes or vessels, through which the water flows. Therefore we call the water paths in plants* **vascular bundles**.

The arrangement of the vascular bundles. In cutting across the shoot of the garden balsam, or coleus, or begonia, you will see that these bundles have a regular arrangement. They are in the form of a ring. These plants are annuals, that is, they live only one year. There is but one ring of bundles in them. If you look at the stump of an oak tree or at the end of a log, you will see many rings. Each year the bundle grows in an outward direction as the tree becomes larger. The vessels formed in the bundle in spring and early summer are larger than those formed in late summer. When cut across in the tree these vessels look like pores. As all the bundles in the tree lie close side by side, the larger pores formed in the spring alternate each year with the smaller ones and form a ring. One ring is usually made each year as the oak tree grows, so that the approximate age of the tree can be told from the number of the rings.

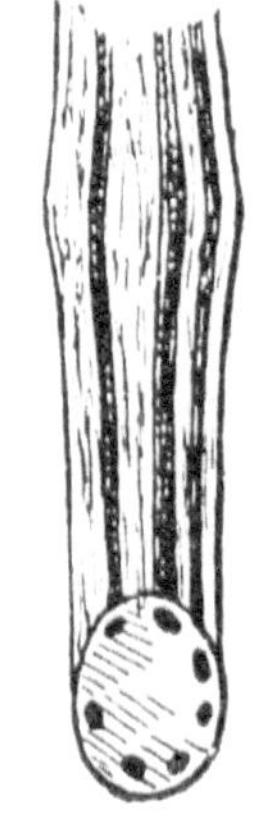

Fig. 141. Cut end of stem showing where the water paths are located.

The vascular bundles in a corn stem. If a young cornstalk was in the red ink, cut it across. The red spots which mark

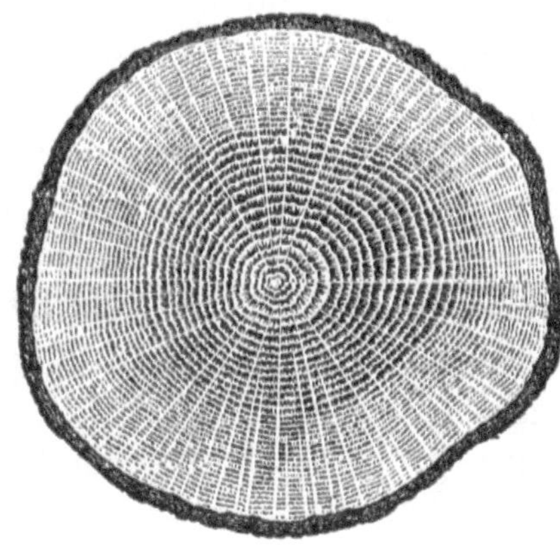

Fig. 142. Cross section of oak, showing annual rings.

the position of the bundles are arranged irregularly. If a fresh-growing cornstalk is not at hand, take an old dried one. With a knife cut around and just through the outer hard layer. Then gently break it, pulling apart the two ends at the same time. As it breaks, the bundles pull out as stiff strings in the pith, and in this way the irregular arrangement is easily seen. A section of the stem of a palm shows that here, also, the vascular bundles are arranged irregularly.

Plants with netted-veined leaves usually have the vascular bundles arranged regularly in rings, while plants with parallel-veined leaves usually have the vascular bundles arranged irregularly. Compare the arrangement of the veins on the leaves of the garden balsam, coleus, begonia, bean, pea, sunflower, oak, etc., with the arrangement of the vascular bundles. The leaves are netted-veined, and the bundles are in regular rings. Compare the veins in a lily leaf or in a blade of corn, wheat, oat, or grass with the arrangement of the bundles. The leaves are parallel-veined, and the bundles are arranged irregularly. You will remember that the bean, pea, oak,

Fig. 143. Vascular bundles of corn stem (where the water paths are located).

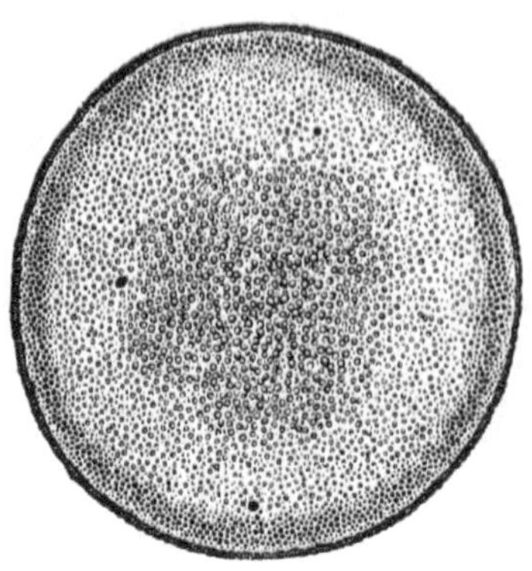

Fig. 144. Cross section of palm stem. There are no annual rings.

etc., have two cotyledons in the seedling, and that the corn has only one.

What kind of venation in the leaves, and what arrangement of the vascular bundles are usually found in plants with two cotyledons? In plants with a single cotyledon? What are these two large groups of plants called?

CHAPTER XV.

The Living Plant Forms Starch

All our starch is formed by plants. Starch is one of the essential foods of man and other animals. It is also employed in many useful processes in the manufacture or dressing of numerous useful articles. It occurs in many vegetables and other plant foods which we eat. Prepared starch, like cornstarch, used for puddings, is nearly or quite pure starch. All this starch is made by plants. The plants use it in a variety of ways for food, and much of it, after being formed, is stored in some part of the plant for future use, as in certain seeds, roots, or tubers. The potato tuber, for instance, is largely composed of starch.

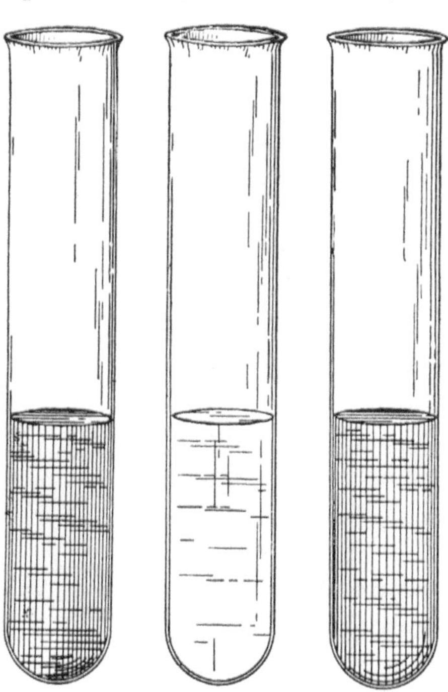

Fig. 145. Cornstarch dissolved in water, and tincture of iodine added. At left the solution is cold, middle one is heated slightly, at right it is cooled.

Tincture of iodine colors starch blue. When starch is wet or moist with water it is colored blue by iodine. A tincture of iodine can be obtained from the drug store, or a few crystals of iodine may be dissolved in alcohol. In a test

Fig. 146. Variegated leaf of grass (white and green)

tube place a small quantity (as much as can be held on the point of a penknife) of corn starch, which can be obtained at the grocery. Pour water into the test tube to a height of two inches. Hold the test tube over a flame for a few minutes to warm the water so that the starch will be well wetted. Now cool it by moving the end of the tube in cold water, or by holding it in running cold water from a hydrant. Add a few drops of the tincture of iodine. The liquid immediately appears blue because the numerous starch grains are colored blue by it. Now hold the end of the tube over the flame again for a few minutes, but do not let it get hot. The blue color disappears, because the warm water extracts the iodine from the starch. Cool the tube again and the blue color reappears.

To test the starch in a potato tuber. Cut a potato (Irish potato) in two, and on the cut surface scrape some of the potato into a pulp with a knife. Apply some of the tincture of iodine to the potato pulp. It becomes blue. The potato, then, is largely made up of starch. Place some of the pulp in water in a test tube, and add a few drops of the

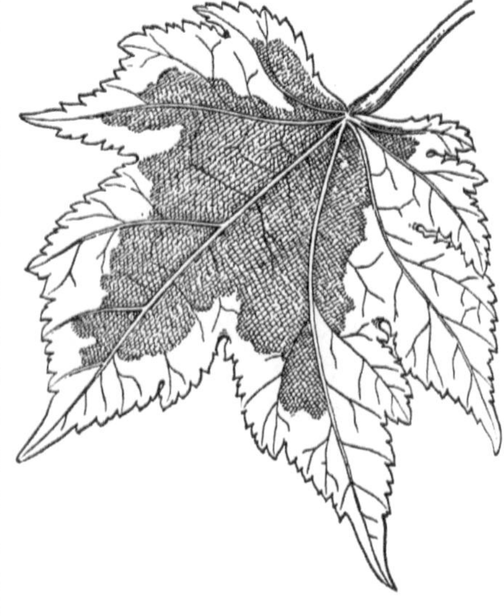

Fig. 147. Variegated leaf of abutilon.

tincture of iodine. Then heat it gently to see if it behaves like the cornstarch.

Test for starch in Indian corn. Split a kernel of Indian corn and scrape out some of the endosperm or meat. Place it in water and test with iodine. What is the result? Test grains of sweet corn[6] in the same way. What is the result? The starch in the sweet corn was changed to sugar and stored in the seed in the form of sugar. The sugar beet is a reservoir for food. It is not stored as starch but as sugar.

Starch formed in green leaves. Take a few green leaves which have been in the sunlight through the day. Immerse them overnight in a strong solution of chloral hydrate in the proportion of five ounces of chloral hydrate[7] to one half a tumbler of water. This will remove the green color and the leaves become pale. Rinse the leaves for a moment in fresh water. Then place them in a tincture of iodine made by dissolving iodine crystals in alcohol. In a few moments the leaves become dark purple-brown in color, sometimes nearly black, with a more or less blue or purplish tinge. This is the color given to starch when it takes up iodine. The experiment shows us that starch is present in the green leaves which have been for some time in the light.

But if we should keep the plant in the dark for a day or two, and then test some of the leaves we should find no starch present.

Where starch is formed in the variegated leaves of the coleus plant. The leaf of the coleus plant is *variegated*, that is, it has different colors. In this one which we are to study, part of the leaf is green and part is white, the green occupying the middle portion and the border, while the white forms a V figure between. We wish to know which part of the leaf forms

6 Chloral hydrate can be obtained at the drug store, ten ounces for about one dollar. More accurately, use eight grams chloral hydrate to 5 c.c. of water.

7 The tincture of iodine can be purchased at the drug store. Or one-quarter ounce of the crystals of iodine may be purchased and a few placed in alcohol as needed.

Fig. 148. Variegated leaf of coleus plant, in fresh condition.

starch. We will immerse some of these variegated leaves in the strong solution of chloral hydrate overnight. Now they are almost entirely white, the chlorophyll having been removed. We will rinse them a moment in water and then place them in the tincture of iodine. Those portions which were green are now quite dark, while the V-shaped figure, or that part which was white, remains white in the iodine or does not take the dark color. *The green part of the leaf, then, forms starch.* We have now learned that the leaf-green as well as sunlight is necessary to make starch. The leaf-green cannot make starch in the dark, nor can the light make starch in portions of a leaf which have no leaf-green.

Starch is formed in the green leaf during the day, but what becomes of it at night? In the afternoon let us cover a part of a leaf in such a way as to shut out the light from that spot. Take two corks, place one on either side of the leaf, covering a small circular portion, and thrust two pins through the edge of one cork to pin it fast to the other. From our former experiments we know that at this time of day all parts of the green leaf contain starch, so that the part covered by the corks, as well as the uncovered portion, now contains starch. On the following day at noon, or in the afternoon, we will take this same leaf, remove the corks, and immerse it overnight in the strong chloral-hydrate solution to remove the green color. Now we will rinse it

Fig. 149. Similar leaf after green color is removed and treated with iodine to show location of starch.

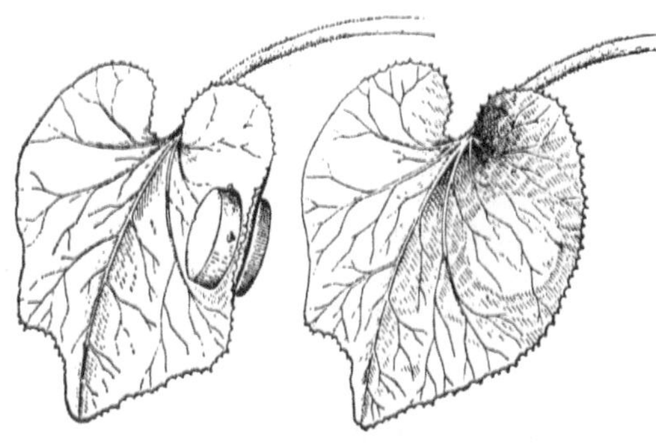

Fig. 150. Pumpkin leaves; at left portion of leaf covered to keep out sunlight; at right same leaf treated with iodine, no starch where leaf was covered.

and place it in the tincture of iodine. *The part of the leaf which was covered by the corks does not show the starch reaction, while the other parts of the leaf do.* So it must be that the starch disappeared from the leaf at night, that new starch was made in the parts exposed to the light, and that no starch was formed in the part covered from the light.

When the starch disappears from the leaf where does it go? Is it found in other parts of the plant not exposed to the light? How does it get there, and where does it come from? For what purpose is the starch stored up in reservoirs?

CHAPTER XVI.

The Work Done by Plants in Making Starch

Plants do work. It seems strange that plants work; yet it is quite true. Some plants do a great deal of work, and hard work too. Plants work when they make starch, though, as we have seen, they cannot do this work without the help of light. But light, without the leaf-green and the living plant, cannot make starch. We cannot see the work which the green plant does, but it is easy to see some of the signs which tell that the work is going on. We must learn to read the sign language.

How water plants tell of this work. Let us select some water weeds, or leafy plants which grow in ponds, lakes, or streams. A very good plant for this purpose is the *elodea*, but when this cannot be found others may be obtained which will serve quite as well. The plants may be brought to the room and placed in a bottle of water which is set in the window, so that they will get the sunlight, or the brightest light which may be had if the day is cloudy. In a very short time bubbles of gas collect on the leaves, small ones at first, but increasing in size until they are freed. Then they rise to the surface of the water. Some of the plants should be placed in an inverted position in the bottle so that the cut end of the shoot will be below the surface. From this cut end of the shoot bubbles of the gas come out more rapidly than from the leaves. Most of the gas, it is true, came from the leaves, but there are air spaces all through the plant between the cells, so that the gas which is formed in the leaves can pass out not only at tiny openings in the leaf, but also through the connecting spaces in the stems.

The more light there is the faster the work goes on. If the

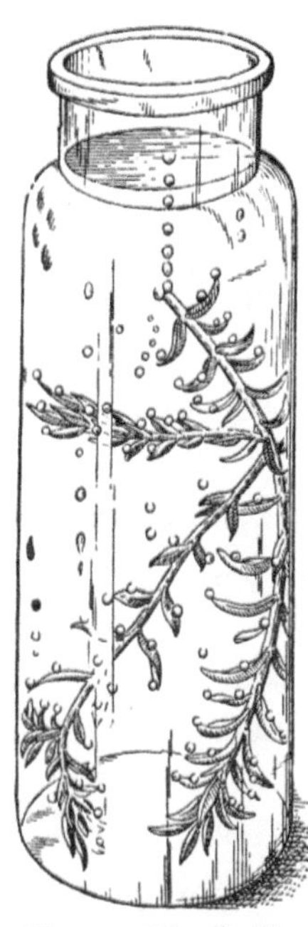
Fig. 151. The "tell-tales", bubbles rising from a water plant.

bottles containing these water plants are kept in the window for several days, and there is cloudy weather as well as sunshine, you will notice that the bubbles of gas come out more rapidly on a sunshiny day than on a cloudy one. The more light there is, then, the more work the plant can do. This can be told in another way. Remove the bottle from the window and put it in a poorly lighted corner of the room. The gas is given off more slowly. Cover the bottle with dark cloth to shut out all light. In ten or fifteen minutes uncover it. The escape of the gas has ceased. Now place it in the brightly lighted window again. The bubbles soon start up afresh.

Do the "pond scums" do the same kind of work? Many of you have seen the green-looking "scum," as some people call it, which floats on the surface of ponds or on the water of ditches, and which is so abundant in the spring and autumn. This pond scum deserves a better name, for it is really made up of beautiful tiny plants, often consisting of silk-like threads, which we can see by lifting a bit of it from the water. To see that it does the same kind of work as the leafy water plant, place some in a bottle of water and set it in the window by the side of the other plants. The tell-tale bubbles show themselves here also. Now you have perhaps noticed that this pond scum, as it floats on the

Fig. 152. Bubbles rising from pond scum in sunlight.

water, has a great many bubbles in it, caught in the tangle of threads. If you take up some of this tangle, rinse it in the water to remove all the bubbles, and then replace it in the water; it does not float well, but tends to sink to the bottom. But when the bubbles of gas begin to form again and are caught in the meshes of the tangle, they are so much lighter than water that they buoy up the plant and lift it once more to the surface of the water. Here the plant can get more light, more air, and so do more work of various kinds.

The leaves of garden herbs and shrubs, trees, and other land plants do the same kind of work. But since they do not grow in water they do not show the signs of this work as water plants do. At least, we cannot see the signs of it because the gas is so much like the air in its nature. Perhaps you have put a lettuce leaf or a leaf of some other land plant under water, and have been told that the bubbles which rise from the leaf in the water are a sign that the leaf is doing work in starch-making. But this brings the land plant into an unfavorable environment, and it soon dies. Not all the bubbles given off are of the same kind of gas as that given off by the water plant, so that this must be regarded as a misleading experiment. [8]

What use the plant makes of starch. Since starch is so necessary to plants, we ought to know some of the uses which the plant makes of it. It helps to make new life substance in the

8 When the leaf of a land plant is placed in water there is always a thin layer of air over the surface of the leaf. If the water is exposed to the sunlight, there is a rise in the temperature which causes the air around the leaf to expand, and some of it rises in the form of bubbles. This may continue for a considerable time. Some of the air inside the leaf is also crowded out because of the change in temperature. This air that is rising from the leaf because of the change in temperature is not the same kind of gas that rises from the water plant or from the pond scum. We cannot distinguish between the two kinds of gas as they rise together from the land plant in the water. Therefore it is no sign that the plant is doing the work, but only an evidence that a change in temperature is going on which expands the air and causes some of it to be freed from the surface of the leaf. The same thing can be seen if we place a piece of broken crockery or a dry piece of wood in water, and then set the vessel in the light. To show clearly that land plants do the same kind of work which the water plants indicate by the bubble sign would be too difficult an experiment for young persons.

plant. This is necessary, not only because more life substance is needed as the plant becomes larger, but because, in one kind of work which the plant does, some of the life substance is consumed. We must understand that when the starch helps to form new life substance it no longer exists as starch but is assimilated along with other foods which the root takes up. *The making of starch* **is not the making of the life substance.** *It must be assimilated with the other food substances taken up by the root from the soil, or by the water plant from the water, before living material is made.*

When we eat solid food substances they are acted on by certain juices of the mouth, stomach, and other organs. A part of the food is thus digested and dissolved. These food solutions are then absorbed through the surface of the large intestine, where they enter the blood. In the blood vessels they are finally carried to all parts of the body, where they come in contact with the living matter. The digested food is now assimilated and helps to make new living matter to replace that which has been used up in growth or work.

The case with the plants is somewhat similar, though their structure, of course, is very different. The starch made in the green leaf is the solid food, though it is not taken in by the plant in that form. It must be digested and changed to a form of sugar by the action of a juice (a ferment) in the life substance. Here it meets other food substances absorbed by the roots. Then by a process of assimilation similar to that which takes place in our own bodies, new living material is made.

So while plants and animals get their food by different methods, and in different forms, it is finally made into living material in the same way. The life substance of plants is the same as the life substance of animals.

CHAPTER XVII.

THE KIND OF GAS WHICH PLANTS GIVE OFF WHILE MAKING STARCH

How to catch this gas in a tube. We are interested to learn more of this gas, and to know, if possible, what it is. We can catch some of it in a tube in the following way. We will take the *elodea* or some other suitable water plant. Place it in a tall, wide jar and invert a funnel over it so that the small end of the funnel will be under the surface of the water. Sink a test tube in the water, and then, without bringing the open end of the tube out of the water, invert it and lower it over the end of the funnel as shown in Fig. 153. Set the jar in the sunlight and leave it there for several days, arranging something to hold down the tube in case it becomes full of the buoyant gas.

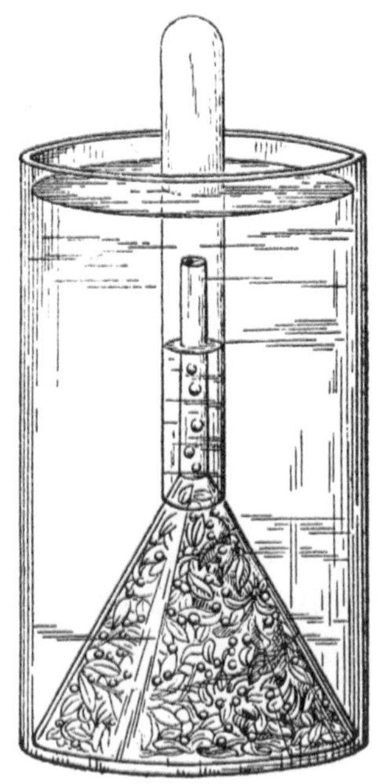

Fig. 153. Catching the bubbles of gas in a test tube.

The gas now, as it is given off from the water plant, rises through the funnel and into the test tube where it accumulates in the upper end and gradually displaces the water. In several days so much gas has accumulated that perhaps the tube is full of it and empty of water. We are now ready to test for the kind of gas.

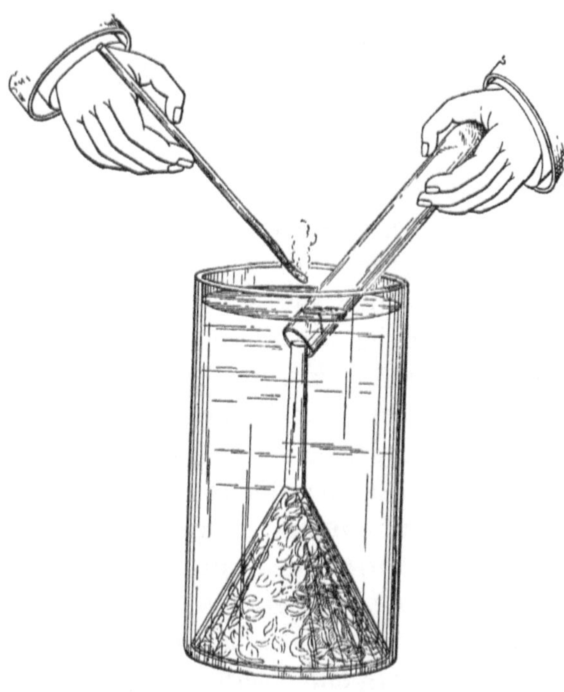

Fig. 154. Ready to see what the gas is.

How to test for the gas. We wish now to bring a glowing splinter into the end of the test tube before the gas escapes, and without wetting the splinter in water. We light a long, soft pine splinter and hold it in one hand, while with the other we grasp the upper end of the test tube, which should be freed if it was tied down. Blow out the flame on the splinter, leaving the coal glowing. Quickly lift the tube from the water and thrust the glowing end of the splinter into the test tube. It flames again! The gas, then, is oxygen, for we know that the oxygen of the air is necessary in making a fire so that it will consume the wood, or coal, or other material.

The reason the glowing splinter does not flame in the air is because the proportion of oxygen is not great enough to ignite it. But there is so much oxygen caught in the test tube from the plant that the glowing coal readily flames again.

Fig. 155. The splinter lights again in the presence of oxygen gas.

How is the gas formed? It is difficult to show here just how this gas is formed, for a considerable knowledge of chemistry is necessary to understand it thoroughly. But perhaps you have learned about some of the chemical compounds, as they are called, and how they sometimes change their combinations and associations. First let us boil some water. When it is cool, put a water plant in it and set it in the sunlight. No gas is given off. This is queer behavior, you may say. But it shows us that something was in the water which the boiling drove off, and which is necessary for the plant in order that the oxygen may be set free. This was air and carbonic acid.[9] If we introduce air and carbon dioxide into the water, oxygen will soon be given off again by the plant, since it can now absorb carbonic acid.

How this takes place in land plants. In the case of land plants, the leaves of which are surrounded with air, not water, the plant absorbs carbon dioxide. You perhaps have been told that the air consists of about *twenty-one parts of oxygen gas, seventy-nine parts of nitrogen gas, and a very small fraction of carbon-dioxide gas.* The carbon-dioxide constituent is a chemical compound; that is, it is composed of two elements united. There is *one part of carbon* and there are *two parts of oxygen*, and it is written thus, CO_2. The carbons and oxygens hold on to each other very tightly, but so soon as they come in contact with water they quickly take up some of it and form carbonic acid. This explains how the carbon dioxide in the air for the land plants becomes carbonic acid in the water for water plants.

Water is a compound composed of *hydrogen, two parts*, and *oxygen, one part*, and its symbol is written thus, H_2O. As soon, however, as the carbon dioxide of the air is absorbed by the leaves of the land plants it comes into direct contact with the water in their cells, and forms immediately carbonic acid, just as it does when it dissolves in the water which surrounds water plants. The symbol of the carbonic acid then is CH_2O_3, since in

9 The carbon dioxide is here in the form of carbonic acid, since it is in water.

the united compounds there is one part of carbon to every two parts of hydrogen and three parts of oxygen.

Now the carbon, hydrogen, and oxygen in the carbonic acid do not hold on to each other very tightly. When they get into the green of the leaf and the sunlight flashes in, it drives them apart very easily, and they hurry to form new associations or compounds which the sunlight cannot break. Perhaps it is because they hurry so, that the new associations they make are not permanent; at all events these are soon broken and others formed, until finally the elements unite in such a way as to form sugar in the leaf. The symbol for this sugar is $C_6 H_{12} O_6$. To get this it was necessary for six parts of the carbonic acid to combine. This would take all of the carbon and all of the hydrogen, but there would be twelve parts of oxygen left over. This oxygen is then set free. From the great amount of carbonic acid which is broken up in the leaf under these conditions, a considerable amount of oxygen would be left over and set free from the plant. After the sugar is formed, one part of water ($H_2 O$) goes out of it, leaving $C_6 H_{10} O_5$, which is the symbol for starch.

CHAPTER XVIII.

How Plants Breathe

Do plants breathe? Yes. But if plants do not have lungs as we do, how can they breathe? There are many animals which do not have lungs, as the starfish, the oyster, the worm, etc., and yet they breathe. Breathing in animals we call *respiration. So in plants breathing is respiration.*

Respiration in germinating seeds. Soak a handful of peas for twenty-four hours in water. Remove them from the water and put them in a bottle or a fruit jar. Cork tightly or cover with a piece of glass, the underside of which is cemented to the mouth of the jar with vaseline to make it air-tight. Keep it in a moderately warm room for twenty-four hours. Keep an empty bottle covered in the same way. Light a taper or a splinter, and as the cover is removed from the jar thrust the lighted end into the jar. The flame is extinguished. Now light the taper again, uncover the empty bottle and thrust the lighted end of the taper into it. The flame is not extinguished. A suffocating gas, carbon dioxide, was in the first jar. This gas is given off by the germinating peas. Being confined the jar, so much of it accumulated that it smothered the flame.

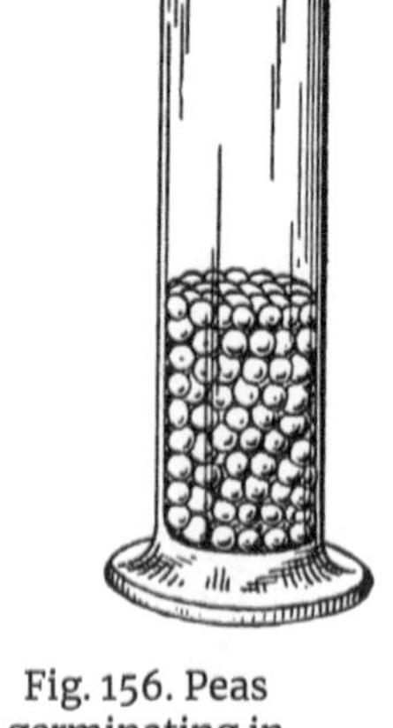

Fig. 156. Peas germinating in a closed jar.

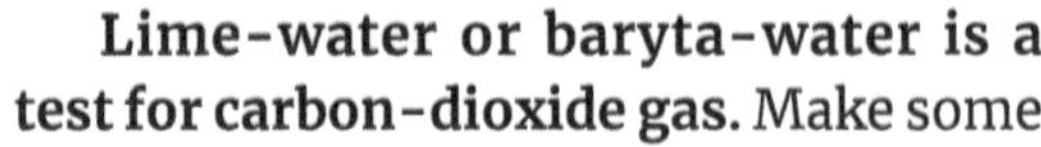

Lime-water or baryta-water is a test for carbon-dioxide gas. Make some

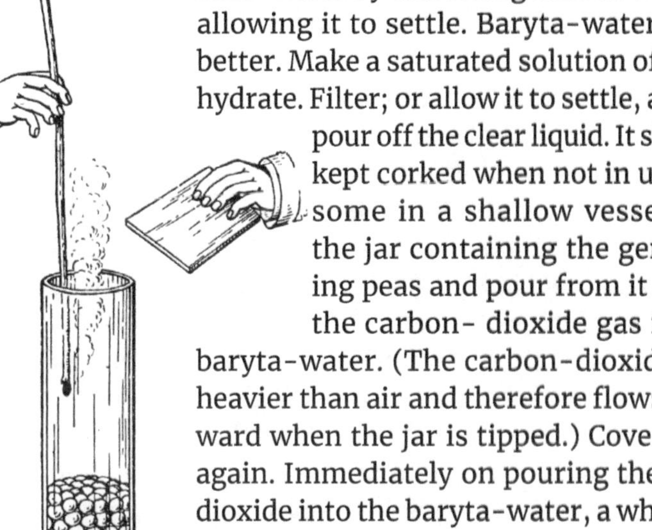

Fig. 157. The light is smothered in the gas given off by germinating peas.

lime-water by dissolving lime in water and allowing it to settle. Baryta-water is even better. Make a saturated solution of barium hydrate. Filter; or allow it to settle, and then pour off the clear liquid. It should be kept corked when not in use. Take some in a shallow vessel. Open the jar containing the germinating peas and pour from it some of the carbon- dioxide gas into the baryta-water. (The carbon-dioxide gas is heavier than air and therefore flows downward when the jar is tipped.) Cover the jar again. Immediately on pouring the carbon dioxide into the baryta-water, a white substance[10] is formed. Chemists tell us that this white substance is formed by the union of carbon dioxide and baryta-water. Pour some of the baryta-water down the sides of the jar and on the peas. Notice the white substance which is formed.

Carbon dioxide from our breath. Take some of the fresh lime-water or baryta-water and breathe upon it. This same white precipitate is formed, because there is a quantity of the carbon dioxide exhaled from our lungs as we breathe. It is interesting to show this close agreement between plant life and animal life.

Plants take in oxygen gas while they breathe. Plants require oxygen in the process of respiration just as animals do. So far as the movement of the gases is concerned, respiration consists

10 Barium carbonate, if baryta-water is used, or calcium carbonate, if lime-water is used. Lime-water is easier to obtain, but the results are not so striking as with baryta-water. To make lime-water, take a lump of lime twice the size of a hen's egg and put it in a quart of water. Allow it to settle and in a day or two pour off the clear liquid; cork in a bottle before using. The white substance formed when lime-water is used is due to the union of the lime-water and the carbon dioxide.

in the taking in of oxygen gas into the plant or animal body, and the giving off of carbon dioxide.

To show that oxygen from the air is used up while plants breathe. Soak some wheat for twenty-four hours in water. Remove it from the water and place it in the folds of damp cloth or paper in a moist vessel. Let it remain until it begins to germinate. Fill the bulb of a thistle tube with the germinating wheat. By the aid of a stand and clamp, support the tube upright, as shown in Fig. 158. Let the small end of the tube rest in a strong solution of caustic potash (one stick caustic potash in two-thirds tumbler of water) to which red ink has been added to give a deep red color. Place a small glass plate over the rim of the bulb and seal it air-tight with an abundance of vaseline. Two tubes can be set up in one vessel, or a second one can be set up in strong baryta-water colored in the same way.

The result. You will see that the solution of caustic potash rises slowly in the tube. The baryta-water will also, if that is used. The solution is colored so that you can plainly see it rise in the tube, even if you are at a little distance from it. In the experiment the solution in six hours had risen to the height shown in Fig. 158. In twenty-four hours it had risen to the height shown in Fig. 159.

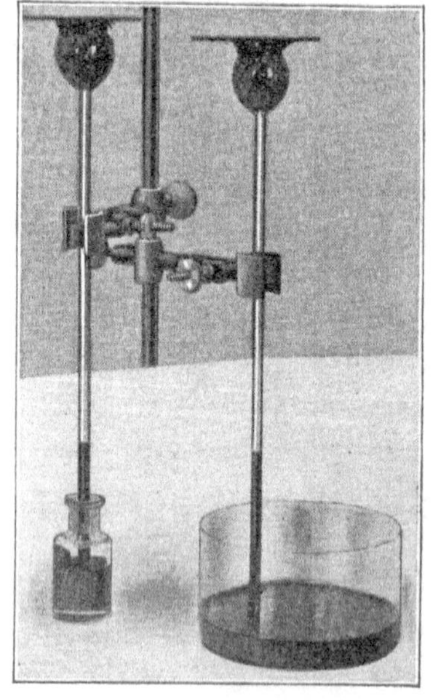

Fig. 158. Apparatus to show "breathing" of germinating wheat.

Why the solution of caustic potash rises in the tube. Since no air can get into the thistle tube from above or below, it must be that some part of the air which is inside the tube is used up while the wheat is germinating. From our study of germinating peas

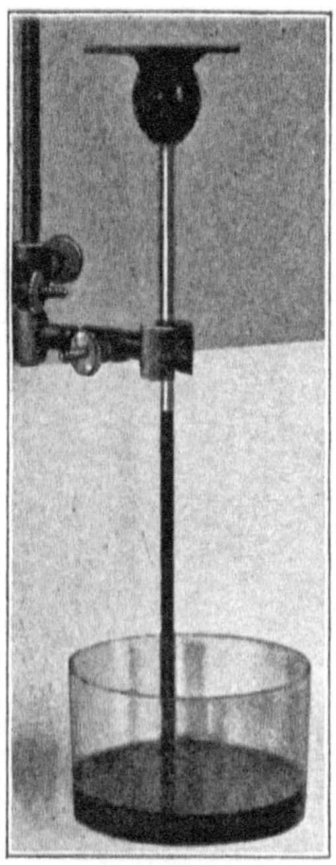

Fig. 159. The same later.

we know that a suffocating gas, carbon dioxide, is given off while they breathe. The caustic potash solution or the baryta-water, whichever is used, absorbs the carbon dioxide. The carbon dioxide is heavier than air, and so settles down in the tube, where it can be absorbed.

Where does the carbon dioxide come from? We know it comes from the breathing, growing seedlings. You will remember that the symbol for carbon dioxide is CO_2. The carbon comes from the plant, because there is not enough in the air. The nitrogen of the air could not join with the carbon to make CO_2; so it must be that some of the oxygen of the air joins with the carbon of the plant. Yes, it does; but the oxygen is first absorbed by the plant. When it gets into the living plant substance, some of the carbon breaks away from its association with the living substance and hurries to join the oxygen, and together they escape into the air.

When plants breathe fast they are doing more work. From what we have just learned we see that some of the living plant substance is used up or consumed while the plant breathes. When a fire burns, oxygen is taken from the air and joins with carbon in the wood or in the coal, and carbon dioxide is set free. This joining of oxygen and carbon is called *oxidation*. In the living plant the joining of the oxygen from the air with the carbon in the plant takes place slowly, so that no flame or fire is made, but it is still oxidation. Oxidation takes place slowly in animals in the same way when they are breathing. But while the plant is being partly oxidized or consumed as it breathes, this very thing enables it to do more work, in growth and in other ways. When you run or play hard, you breathe faster. A part of your body must be oxidized to get power or energy to play; or to work either, for play is one kind of work.

The carbon dioxide which is given off is one form of the waste from your body, or from the plant's body, while work of this kind is going on. To take the place of this waste you must eat, and you know how hungry you are when you are growing and playing. You need a great deal of food to make new living materials to take the place of the waste, and to supply what is needed for growth. So it is with plants; they need food for growth, and to repair waste.

PART III.

THE BEHAVIOR OF PLANTS

CHAPTER XIX.

The Sensitive Plant

ONE of the most interesting manifestations of life in plants is the rapid movement of the leaves in the so-called sensitive plant (*Mimosa pudica*). The plant may be easily grown from

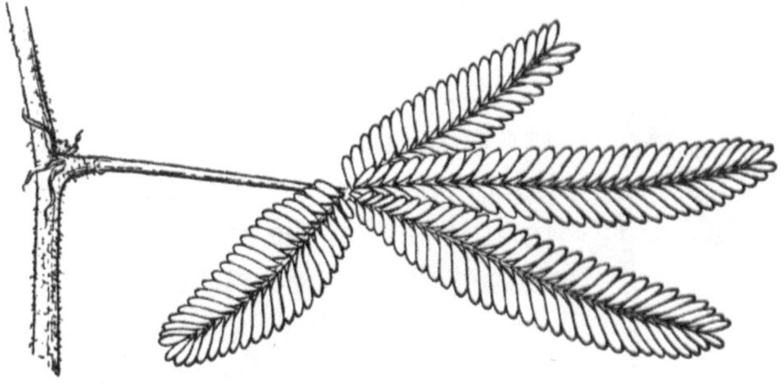

Fig. 160. Leaf of sensitive plant.

the seed in pots, either in a greenhouse or in the window of a room, if it is protected from the hot rays of the sun. The seed planted in late spring will bring forth good plants ready for use in late summer or during the autumn.

Appearance of the sensitive plant. The leaves of the sensitive plant are rather large. A leaf is composed of a large number of leaflets (*pinnæ*) arranged in pairs along four different axes, which are joined to a stalk (the *petiole* of the leaf) somewhat as the toes of a bird are joined at the foot. A single leaf is shown in Fig. 160 attached to the shoot. Imagine a branched shoot with a number of these leaves and you will know how the sensitive plant looks.

Movement of the leaves of the sensitive plant. When you

wish to test the plant, it should be on a bright day, though the plant will work on a cloudy day also if it is not too dark. It must be left undisturbed and quiet for some time before using. We must be careful not to touch or jar it until we are ready.

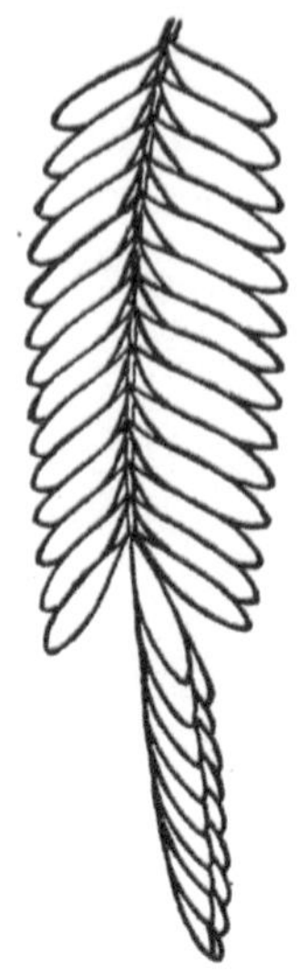

Fig. 161. Movement of the leaflets after pinching one.

Now, with a pair of forceps, or with the fingers, pinch one of the terminal leaflets. Instantly the terminal pair clasp or fold together above the axis. Then the second pair do the same, and the third and fourth pairs follow quite regularly. This movement continues, successive pairs closing up until all on the axis are closed. Then the last pairs on the other three axes fold together, and successive pairs on these close up until all are closed. By this time, probably, the four axes which bear the leaflets are drawn closer together. The stalk of the leaf is also likely to turn downward, and the entire leaf presents the appearance shown in Fig. 162.

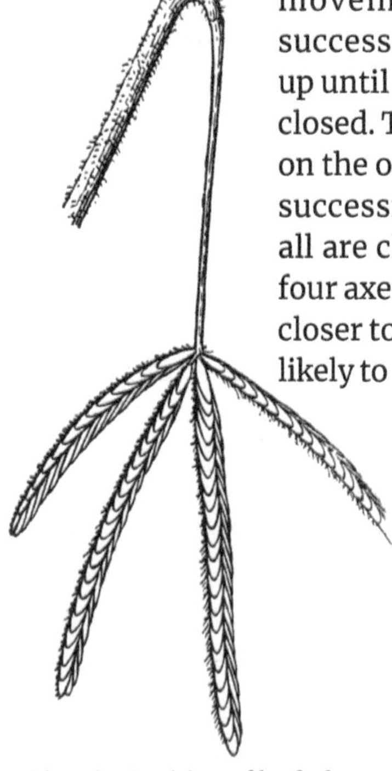

Fig. 162. Position of leaf after movement has ceased.

When we pinched the leaflet, there was given to the leaf what we call a *stimulus*. The stimulus travels all through the leaf, and in response to it the movement takes place. If we jar a sensitive plant suddenly, all the leaves close up and assume a drooping position, as shown in Fig. 163.

Behavior of the leaves at night or on dark days. On a dark day the leaves of the sensitive plant are folded together; or if we take the plant into a poorly lighted room, the leaves will close; then if we bring it out to the light they will open again. So at nightfall the leaves fold together, and the sunlight of the following day is necessary before they will open again. This teaches us one of the influences which light exerts on plants. This plant is very sensitive to contact with other objects or to shock; but we see that it is also sensitive to light, for the leaves will open in a short time when brought into the light. The mimosa is called the sensitive plant because it responds so quickly to contact stimulus or shock. In reality, however, all plants are more or less sensitive, some being more so than others. This we can readily see by observing the relation of other plants to the light.

Fig. 163. The sensitive plant after jarring.

CHAPTER XX.

The Behavior of Plants toward Light

Compare plant stems grown in sunlight with those grown in darkness. When planting seeds of the sunflower, pumpkin, buckwheat, pea, wheat, or corn, etc., place some of the pots under tight boxes to exclude the light. The pots should be covered as soon as the seeds are planted so that no light will reach the young seedlings. They should remain covered for two or three weeks or more. They can be safely uncovered occasionally, for a few moments at a time, to supply the necessary water and to compare them with the seedlings started at the same time, in the light.

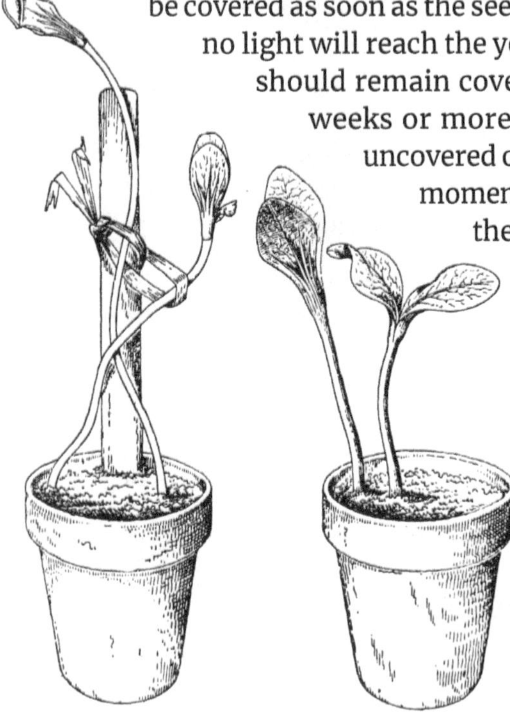

Fig. 164. Pumpkin seedlings: one at left grown in dark, one at right of same grown in light.

Observe the plants about twice each week. Make measurements of the growth; sketch, and keep a record of the observations. Do the stems grow more rapidly in the light or in the dark? Compare the leaves on the plants grown in the dark with those grown in the light. Compare the leaves of the wheat grown in the dark with those grown in the light. How does the wheat differ from the pumpkin, sunflower, or similar plant in this respect?

Fig. 164, left-hand plant, shows a pumpkin seedling grown in the dark. The right-hand plant in the same figure is another of the same age grown in the light. The stem grown in the dark is much longer than the one grown in the light. These plants are about one week old. Fig. 166 represents seedlings of buckwheat grown in the dark; they are longer than those of the same age grown in the light.

Fig. 165. Buckwheat seedlings grown in light.

Are the stems grown in light stouter and firmer? In comparing the seedlings grown in the dark with those grown in the light there is another striking difference between them which we cannot fail to observe. The stems grown in the dark are longer, but they are less firm, and they are not capable of supporting themselves so well as the stems grown in the light. This is well shown even in the week-old seedlings of the buckwheat, as seen in Fig. 166. They cannot

Fig. 166. Buckwheat seedlings of same age, grown in dark.

support their own weight, but fall over and hang down by the side of the pot. This is marked also in Fig. 169, which is a later stage of the pumpkin seedling shown in Fig. 164. It is now three weeks old, and has grown all this time in the dark. To support the stems they were tied to a stake. Those grown in the light are stouter and firmer and are able to support themselves. If we crush these stems with the fingers, we find those grown in the light firmer than those grown in the dark. A more accurate test would be to dry the plants thoroughly and then to weigh them. The plants grown in the light would outweigh those grown in the dark. In other words, they have made more plant substance. It will be remembered that green plants form starch in sunlight. The starch is used, much of it, in making new plant substance, especially cell walls, which constitute the firmer portions of plants. This is the reason, then, why the stems grown in the dark are more slender and less firm than those grown in the light.

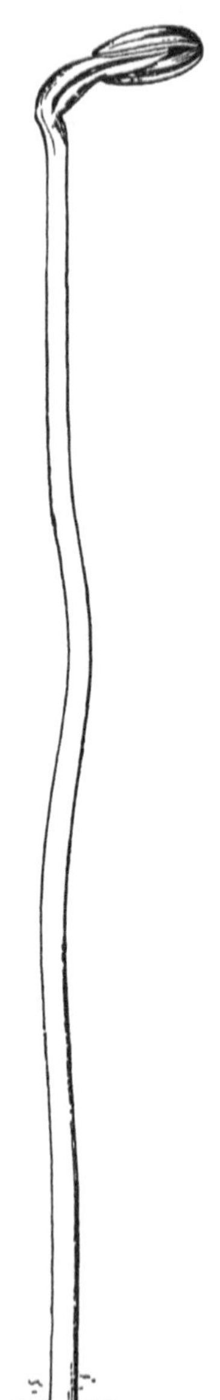

Fig. 167. Sunflower seedling grown in dark. (Nat. size)

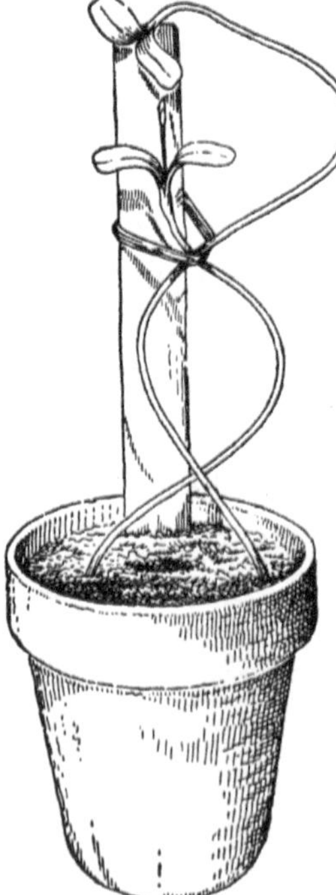

Fig. 168. Sunflower seedlings grown in dark, older than in Fig. 167. (Reduced.)

The leaves on

plants grown in the dark. While stems grow less rapidly in light than in dark, light accelerates the growth of the leaves. Plants grown in the dark have very small or undeveloped leaves. This is well shown in the pumpkin (Fig. 169). Compare the leaves on the plant grown in the dark with those on the plant grown in the light. The plants are of the same age. Light, then, increases the size of the leaves of such plants as the pumpkin, sunflower, buckwheat, etc. How is it with the wheat and similar plants?

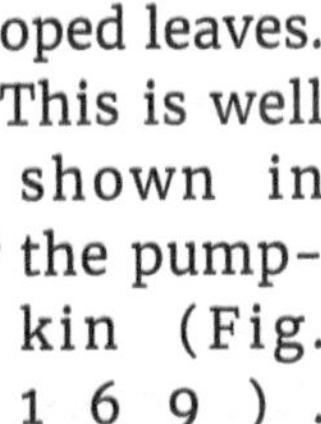

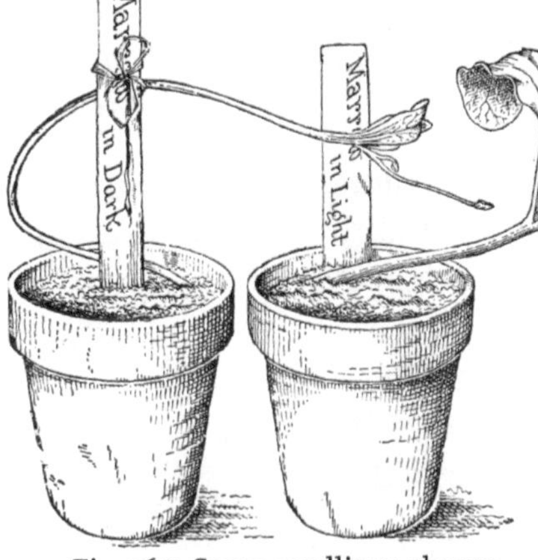

Fig. 169. Same seedlings shown in Fig. 164, but older.

Do the cotyledons of the pumpkin or squash open in the dark? As the cotyledons of the pumpkin slip from the seed coats and are pulled out of the ground by the loop, they are clasped tightly together. But as they are straightening up in the light they spread apart and expand. What causes them to open and expand? Let us cover some pumpkin seedlings which have grown in the light, and in which the cotyledons have just expanded. The box

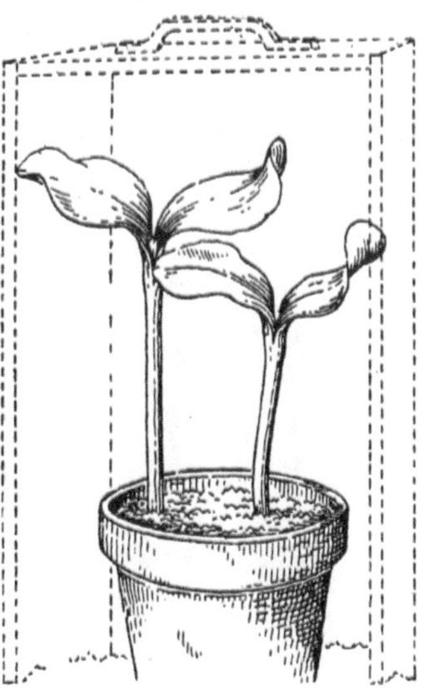

Fig. 170. Sunflower seedlings grown in light, just covered to exclude light.

should be tight so that the seedlings will be kept in the dark. Allow them to remain here a day or two; then remove the box sometime near mid-day. The cotyledons are clasped together and erect, as in Fig. 171. Now leave them uncovered; the cotyledons open again. If we examine them at night when it is dark, we usually find them clasped together and erect. As the morning light comes on they open again. The light, then, must have an influence in spreading the cotyledons apart.

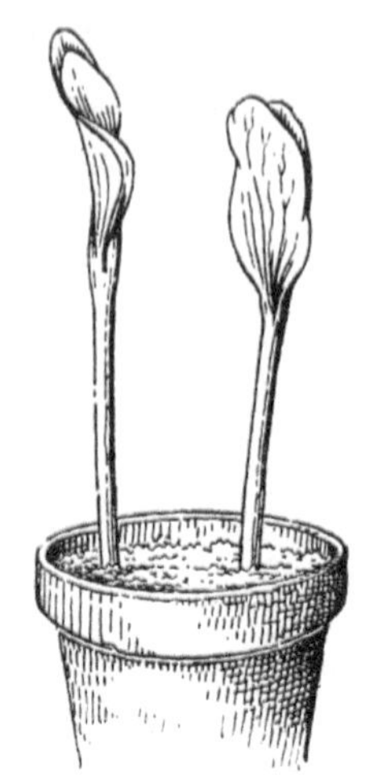

Fig. 171. Same seedlings after being covered two days.

We should now refer to our observations on the squash seedlings, grown in the dark, or if we did not then observe the cotyledons, we should at once examine some seedlings of the pumpkin or squash, grown in the dark, as shown in Fig. 164. The cotyledons remain closed. Fig. 169 is very interesting; the stem as it grows is obliged to push its way out from between the cotyledons at one side, so tightly are they clasped together. These cotyledons have never opened because they have been kept from the light.

Fig. 172. Same seedlings after exposure to light again.

Arrangement of leaves in relation to light. The position of the leaves on plants, whether the plant is small or large, is such as to place the leaf so that it will receive an abundance of light. The relation of the leaves of a given plant to one another is such as to give all the leaves an opportunity to receive light with the least possible interference. Plants of several different types in this respect may be brought into the classroom so that the pupils

Fig. 173. Young sunflower plant; at left in light, at right after being covered two days to shut out light.

may make comparisons; although such observations should be made in fields and gardens whenever possible.

Influence of light on the day position of leaves. Light has great influence on the position of the leaves during the day, just as it has on the position of the pumpkin cotyledons which we have just studied, or on the leaves of the sensitive plant. It acts as a stimulus to adjust the leaf so that the light will fall full upon the upper surface, or nearly so. In some plants this position becomes more or less fixed. But in other plants, like the sunflower, bean, oxalis, and many more, the leaves change their position night and day. The leaves usually occupy a drooping position at night, and on the following morning they are brought by the influence of light into the day position again. This drooping position of leaves at night has been termed the "sleep of plants," but it is not in any sense a sleep. In the "compass" plant the leaves stand vertical and point north and south.

The night position of leaves is due to unequal growth. When the leaves are young and in the bud, they closely overlap

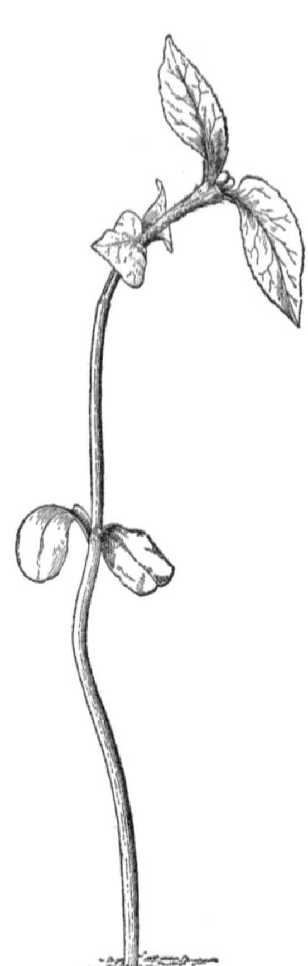

Fig. 174. Young sunflower plant turned toward light from window.

one another. This is due to the fact that growth takes place more rapidly on the under surface of the young leaf. This causes the leaf to curve upward and in, over the end of the stem. But as the leaves become older, growth takes place more rapidly on the upper surface. This causes them to curve outward and later downward so that they occupy a drooping position. This can be demonstrated by covering for several days a bean plant, or by covering an oxalis plant for a day, so that it will be entirely in the dark.

To illustrate it here a sunflower plant grown in a pot was used, the plant being four or five weeks old. It was covered one day, and then at noon on the following day the box was lifted off. The leaves of the sunflower were in the position shown in Fig. 173, the right-hand plant. This shows that if the plant is in darkness the leaves droop, and the drooping has nothing to do with night time, except that the light stimulus

Fig. 175. Sunflower with young head turned toward morning sun.

is then removed. When the plant is exposed to the light, the light draws the leaf up into the day position.

The leaves of many plants turn so as to face the light. From some of the foregoing studies we learn that the leaves of plants are sensitive to the stimulus of light. They stand so that the rays of light fall full upon the upper surface. In the open, the leaves of many plants stand so that the upper surface receives the light directly from above, as the light from this direction in cloudy days is strongest. The leaves of many other plants change their positions through the day if the sun is shining, so that their upper surfaces face the sun directly, or nearly so, at all times of the day.

Fig. 176. Same sunflower plant photographed just at sundown.

Fig. 177. Same plant a little older when the head does not turn, but the stem and leaves do.

Turning of the sunflower plant toward the sun. During the period of growth of the sunflower plant the leaves, as well as the growing part of the stem, are very sensitive to light. On sunny days the leaves on the growing end of the stem are drawn

Fig. 178. The young head follows the sun even though the leaves are cut away.

somewhat together so that they form a rosette. They also turn so that the rosette faces the sun when it is rising. The growing part of the stem also turns toward the sun; this aids in bringing the upper surfaces of the leaves to face the sun. All through the day, if the sun continues to shine, the rosette of leaves follows it, and at sundown the rosette faces squarely the western horizon. For a week or more the sunflower head will face the sun directly and follow it all day as surely as does the rosette of leaves. At length, a little while before the flowers in the head blossom, the head ceases to turn, but the rosette of leaves and the stem also, to some extent, continue to turn with the sun. When the leaves become mature and cease growing, they also cease to turn. It is not true that the fully opened sunflower head turns with the sun, as is commonly supposed. But I have observed young heads four to five inches in diameter follow the sun all day. The growing end of the stem will also follow the sun, even if all the leaves and the young flower head are cut away.

Fig. 179. Seedling sunflower; at left with light from above, at right turned toward window.

Experiments with sunflowers and other seedlings. The seedlings of many

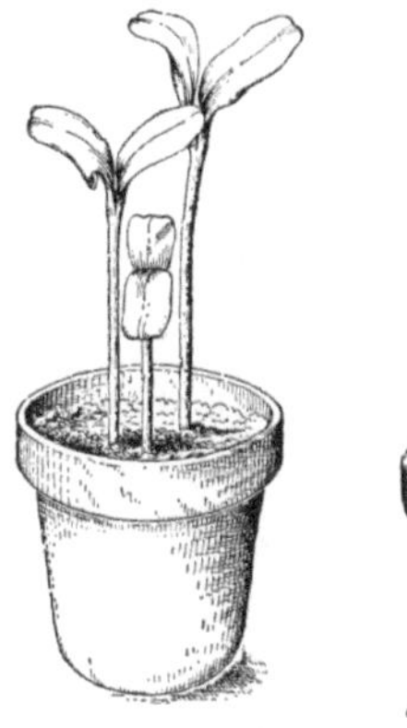

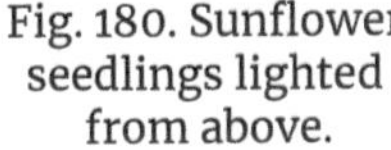

Fig. 180. Sunflower seedlings lighted from above.

Fig. 181. Same seedlings by a window.

plants are so sensitive to the influence of light that they quickly turn if placed near a window where there is a one-sided illumination. The pot of seedlings shown in Fig. 180 was placed near a window. In an hour they had turned so that the cotyledons faced the light coming in from the window. Even when the cotyledons are cut off, the stems will turn toward the light, as shown in Fig. 182. Any of the seedlings which we have studied, or others, will turn to one side where there is a one-sided illumination, but some will turn more quickly than others.

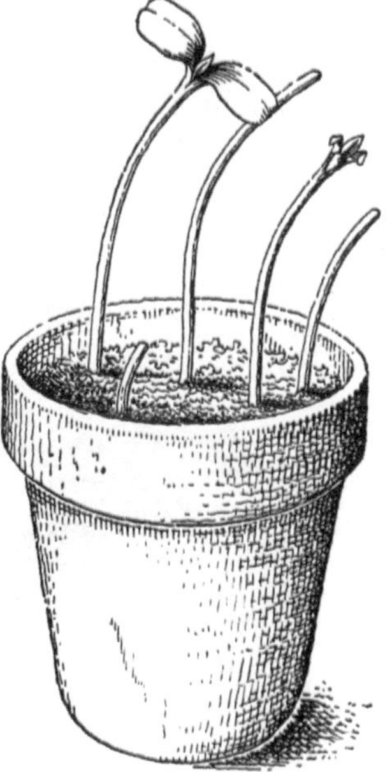

Fig. 182. The seedlings turn even though the cotyledons are cut away, and stem is cut in two.

The influences which light has on the position of leaves, on the growth of the stem, and on the symmetrical or one-sided growth of the branches of a tree, can be seen and observed in any place where plants grow. It will be interesting then, when you come in the presence of plants, for you to endeavor to read from the plants themselves the varied stories which they can tell of the influence which light has on them. Where leaves are crowded together, you will often see that each leaf in the cluster takes a definite place, so that it will

Fig. 183. Cedar of Lebanon, strong light only from one side of tree (Syria).

be in a good position to get the light. This position of the leaf is not taken of itself alone. It is because the light, acting on it, causes it to take up this position. Leaves thus often form what are called pieces of "mosaic," as seen in the Fittonia (Fig. 102) cultivated in greenhouses. In the woods or groves you will have an opportunity of studying many of these "mosaics," and it will be interesting for you to see if there is any difference in the size of any part of the leaf which enables it better to take a favorable position in the "mosaic." Then on

Fig. 184. Spray of leaves of striped maple, showing different lengths of leafstalks.

the edge of the forest or grove you can study many examples of the effect of light on the unequal growth of the branches of trees and shrubs.

What advantage to the plant comes from this power to turn the leaves so as to face the light? What plant food can be formed only in the green leaves in the presence of light? What economy is there in the plants' having broad and thin leaves, instead of having the same amount of tissue in a rounded green mass? Why do trees on the edge of a forest, or of a grove, have more and longer branches on the side away from other trees than on the side next the forest? In leaf clusters on branches why are some of the leafstalks much longer than others (see Fig. 184)?

CHAPTER XXI.

Behavior of Climbing Plants

Different ways of getting up to the light. Plants have different ways of getting into a position where there is light. Trees build tall, stout trunks, which hold their branches and leaves far above other plants. Shrubs and tall herbs build slender trunks to get above their smaller neighbors. Some other plants which have comparatively weak stems have found means of getting up where there is light. Such plants *climb*. Their stems cannot hold

Fig. 185. Coiling stem of morning-glory.

the plants upright. They climb on other plants, or on rocks, fences, houses, etc.

Climbing by coiled stems. A common way for some plants to climb is to coil or twine their stems round other plants. The morning-glory, the climbing bittersweet or waxwork (*celastrus*), and the nightshade are examples. While these plants are growing, watch the stems and see how they coil. The young stems are more or less erect; but the end of the stem is often bent to one side. You may watch the plant in the field, or several shoots may be cut and placed in a vessel of water. Notice now which way the bent ends point. In an hour or so look again. Some of them are pointing in a different direction. If you look at intervals through the day, you will see that the stem swings slowly around in circles.

Fig. 186. Coiling stem of dodder.

The nightshade swings from right to left, or "against the sun." The morning-glory coils in the same direction. Which way does the climbing bittersweet coil? How is it with the "dodder," or "love vine"? Study other vines that you see. If you wind the morning-glory vine or the bittersweet in the opposite way from that in which you find it growing, and fasten it, which way will the young end coil when left to itself?

Climbing by tendrils. The pea vine, the star cucumber,

Fig. 187. Stem of dodder with suckers entering the stem of its victim.

and some other plants climb by tendrils. The squash, pumpkin, cucumbers, and melons also have tendrils, but rarely climb, as they are usually cultivated where there is no opportunity. But these plants are good ones for the study of tendrils, as they grasp other plants near them. Their tendrils are long and slender. Before they have caught hold of a support the end is curved to one side and the tendril swings, somewhat as the stem of the morning-glory does, until it touches some object. The end of the tendril now coils round the object if it is not too large. If you watch a tendril from day to day after it has caught hold, you will see that it finally curls up into a beautiful coiled spring. Consult Fig. 122 to see how you can imitate the action of a tendril with a strip of dandelion stem.

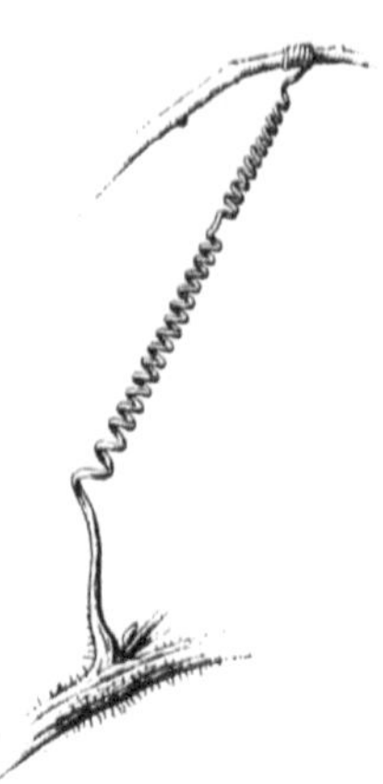

Fig. 188. Coiling tendril of bryony.

Fig. 189. Tendril of star cucumber grasping edge of leaf of nightshade.

Tendrils often grasp the edge of a leaf and coil

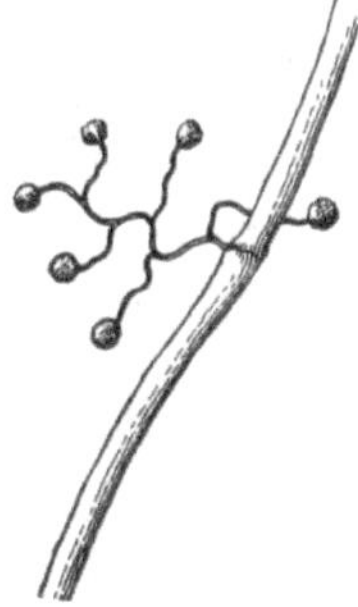
Fig. 190. Tendril of Japanese ivy.

on both sides of the leaf. The tendrils of the star cucumber do this frequently. The end of the tendril can take hold of the flat surface of a leaf and hold on by tiny suckers or root-like processes, which it sends out to penetrate the leaf. These suckers grow out from the surface of the coiled tendril and strike into the object much as the suckers of the dodder strike into its host.

The Japanese ivy, or Boston ivy, as it is sometimes called, climbs by tendrils. It is often used to train on the walls of houses. Where the ends of the tendrils strike against the hard wall of the house, they flatten out into little disks, which cling very firmly and hold up the large and heavy vines.

Fig. 191. Vine of *ampelopsis* (American creeper) clambering over a dead tree trunk.

The clematis, or virgin's bower, climbs in a peculiar way. The petiole, or midrib of the leaf, acts like a tendril and coils round an object for support.

Root climbers. Poison ivy is a plant which some persons should avoid. Others can handle it without becoming poisoned. One form of the plant grows in the shape of a vine which climbs up the trunks of tall trees. It may be known from other vines in the woods by the shape of its leaves. But especially can one tell it in the woods by the numerous climbing roots which cover the side toward the tree, and which take hold in crevices in the bark and hold the vine up.

There is a shrubby form of poison ivy which does not climb. One should learn to know the plant by the leaves. See Fig. 84.

The climbing poison ivy sometimes forms a very large vine, which reaches to the top of tall trees and nearly smothers them with its dense foliage. The English ivy, sometimes trained on the sides of houses, is a root climber.

Some plants climb by leaning on others for support. As they grow upward, being too weak to support themselves alone, they fall against other plants and grow over and between their branches. Such plants are sometimes called scramblers, because they scramble over others.

CHAPTER XXII.

The Behavior of Flowers

THE BUTTERCUP FLOWER

Buttercups. Before we read stories on the behavior of flowers we must know the parts of the flower. This is because the different parts of the flower have different kinds of work to do, and therefore behave differently. Buttercups, no doubt, are known to all who have been in the fields and woods in the spring.

The petals. The bright yellow parts which give the cup shape and the yellow color to the flower are *petals*, as perhaps all of you know. There are usually five of these petals. All together they are called the *corolla.*

The sepals. When you have removed the petals you will see, just below where they were seated, a crown of small scale-like bodies. Each one of these is a *sepal.* There are usually five of these, and together they are called the *calyx.*

Fig. 192. Flower of buttercup, sepals below, petals next, then stamens and pistils in center.

The stamens and pistils. If you look now at the remaining parts of the flower, you will see that there are two kinds. Next to the petals are a goodly number of small stalked bodies called *stamens.* If the little cases on the ends of the stalks have not already opened, prick one open with a pin. The cases crack open of themselves, and a yellow dust-like powder comes out. This is *pollen*, each tiny dust-like particle being a *pollen grain.* The cases on the ends of the stalks are *pollen cases.* Right in the center of the flower are a number of stouter bodies which have tapering points. These are called *pistils.*

What the parts of the flower do. If you look at the young flower bud, you will see that the parts are all wrapped up snugly and covered over by the sepals. The work of the sepals here is to protect the other parts of the flower while they are young. The petals are bright colored, large, and showy. They are the parts of the flower which attract us. They attract bees and other insects. Did you ever see the bees visiting the flowers, going from one blossom to another? They reach down and lap up the bit of honey that is in a claw-like pocket at the bottom of each petal. In doing this their legs drag on the pollen cases. The bees scatter the pollen grains all around as they visit one flower after another. As they crawl over the flowers some of the pollen clinging to the hairs on their legs is left on the pointed ends of the pistils.

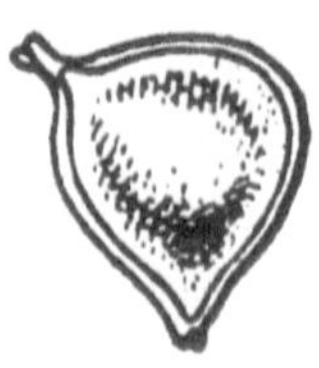

Fig. 193. Seed, or akene, of buttercup.

Where the seed is formed. If you keep watch of some flowers day after day, you can read the story of where the seed is formed. You can read it all on the same day if you have plants on which are flowers of different ages. You should begin with the younger ones and read up through the older ones. You will read that the sepals fall away; the petals wither and fall; the stamens wither, but the pistils grow larger. After a time they will ripen and you can find the seed. The story of just how the seed is formed is a hard one to read, and I am afraid it would be hard for you to understand if I should tell it. But I have attempted to tell it in Chapter XXV. I may tell you, though, that unless each part of the flower did its work faithfully, the seed could not be formed.

BEHAVIOR OF THE PUMPKIN FLOWER

The petals. If you cannot find a pumpkin flower, certainly you can see a squash flower in some garden. The story of the squash flower is very much like that of the pumpkin flower. I do not need to tell you that the flower is very different from that of the buttercup. You can see that. Where are the petals? I believe you can read in the flower that the large, yellow, showy, urn-shaped part just inside the calyx is the corolla. How many points are there on the rim of the urn-shaped corolla? Five, you say, and you have read that each one of these represents a petal, and that all the petals are joined together by their edges.

The sepals. Below the corolla you see five green pointed leaf-like parts arranged in the form of a crown. What does each one of these parts represent?

The stamens and pistils. Now look down in the bottom of the flower for the stamens. All the flowers are not alike, you see. There is a column in the center of each. On some of these there is pollen. These columns in some of the flowers are different from the columns in others. Are the flowers all alike on the outside? No! Those with the three blunt projections on the end of the column have a round enlargement on the flower stalk. In the other flowers there is no enlargement on the flower stalk, and the column of these bears pollen grains. So these columns

Fig. 194. Pumpkin vine with pistil flower.

Fig. 195. Stamen flower closed.

must be stamens joined together. The columns in the others form the upper part of the pistils joined together, while the enlargement in the flower stalk is the lower part of the joined pistils. The point on the pistil where the pollen lodges we call the *stigma.*

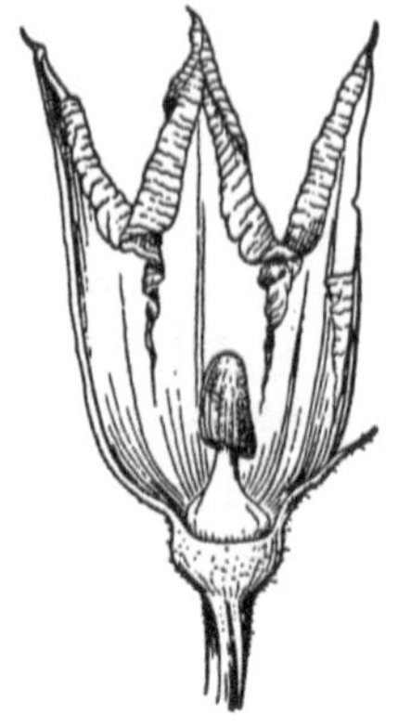

Fig. 196. Stamen flower front cut away, showing stamens grown together in center.

Bees and other insects go from one flower to another. How otherwise could the pollen be taken from the stamen flower and be placed on the end of the pistil in the pistil flower? So the bees are a great help to the flower in making its seed, and the flower gives the bee honey to pay for its labor. If you can get a pumpkin in the autumn, cut one in two, cross-wise. You see what a great number of seeds there are. Can you tell how many parts are joined in this compound pistil which finally makes the pumpkin?

Fig. 197. Pistil flower with front cut away.

THE SUNFLOWER

The flower head. We have already seen how the sunflower plant behaves toward light. We are now interested in observing the behavior of the flowers. You should learn, first of all, that the large, showy blossom is not a single flower. It is made up of a great many flowers. It is a "head" of flowers. There are

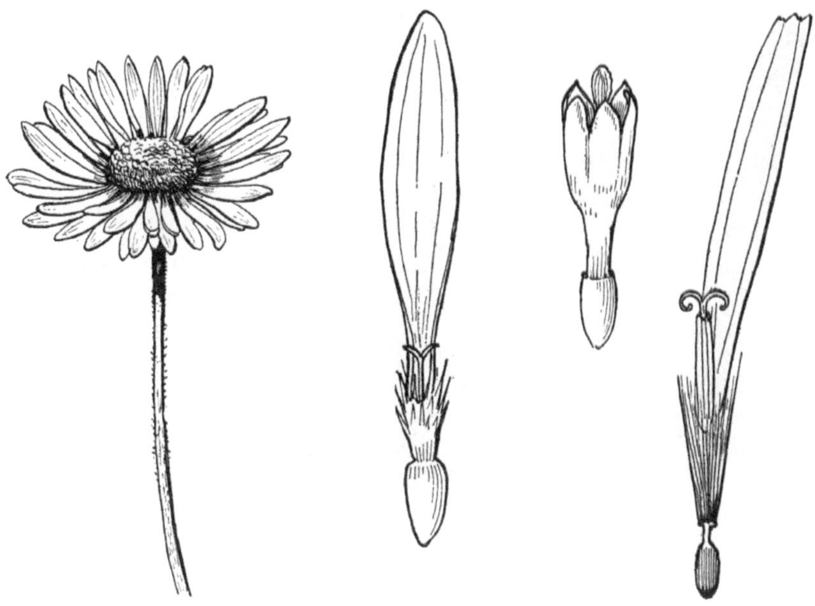

Fig. 198. Squash vine with flowers and young squash.

two kinds of flowers in a head. I am sure you can tell the two kinds apart. The most showy ones are on the edge or margin of the head. They stand out like rays of the sun; so we call them *ray flowers*. The most prominent part is like a strap. The other flowers are more numerous. They are shaped somewhat like a tube, and have been called *tubular flowers*. Because they form a large disk in the center of the flower head they are also called *disk flowers*. Each one of the little ray and disk flowers is called a *floret*.

The behavior of the florets in flowering. If you will read from several sunflower heads, or read from one day by day, you will learn an interesting story. You can cut off a head and put the stem in a vessel of water in the room where you can see it from day to day. It will behave very well for several days. You do not need to pick the flowers to pieces. Just look now and then at the disk florets.

First, in those next the ray flowers, the pollen is pushed

Fig. 199. Sunflower head.

out from the pollen cases and lifted above the corolla tube, so that the pollen grains can be scattered. It is the growing pistil in each floret which pushes the pollen out. Then in a few more rings next these and nearer the center the same thing happens; and so on toward the center of the disk, each day the ring of opening florets approaching nearer the center. Finally the pistil pushes up its style so that it stands above the end of the corolla tube. The style is divided into two slender parts which at first are closed up so the pollen cannot touch the stigma on the inner surface. Later the parts curve outward. When the head has partly blossomed you can see a broad ring of disk flowers, next the rays, with the pistils projecting above the corolla tube.

Fig. 200. Heads of fuller's teasel in different stages of flowering.

Fig. 201. A group of jacks.

Next there is a broad ring of disk flowers with the pollen projecting above the corolla tube, and in the center of the head are disk flowers not yet opened.

If you observe the flowers in the garden, you will see that bees and other insects are crawling over them. The bees drag the pollen from the open florets where the pistil is closed to the open pistils. Since the pistils and stamens of each floret do not ripen at the same time, the pollen from one floret must go to the pistil of another floret, and cannot get to its own. This is a good thing for the plant, for it makes the new life in the seed more vigorous. This taking of the pollen from one flower to another is *cross pollination*. If you study the behavior of flowers in this respect, you will find that insects visit a great many different kinds and cross pollinate them.

Fig. 202. Jack in his pulpit.

If you find a daisy, golden-rod, aster, or black-eyed Susan, read it to see how it compares with the sunflower.

THE TEASEL

The behavior of the teasel in flowering. Do you know the teasel? It is worth your while to learn where it grows, that you may see its interesting way of flowering. The plant grows

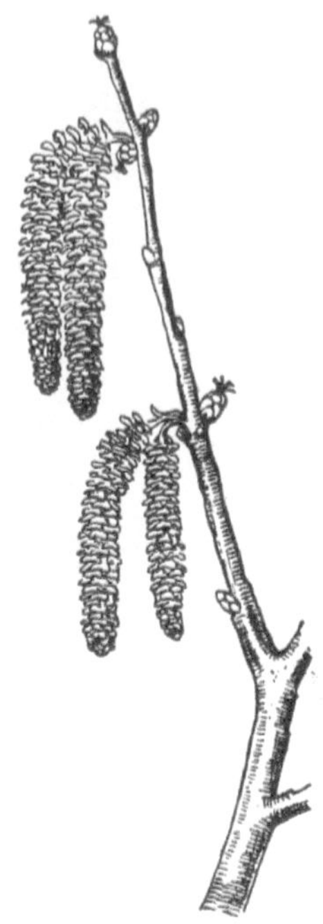

Fig. 203. Jack out of his pulpit; the two upper ones with pistil flowers, the two lower ones with stamen flowers.

Fig. 204. Flower of skunk cabbage with front cut away.

in waste places, along roadsides, and in some places is cultivated as fuller's teasel. The flowers are in heads. I am going to show you a photograph of several heads, with the blossoming of the plants in different stages and let you read the story (see Fig. 200).

Jack-in-the pulpit flower. You are all interested in the Jack-in-the pulpit. The "jack" is tall, and his head reaches up so that we can see it in the pulpit. If you examine them, you will see that some jacks are covered below with stamen

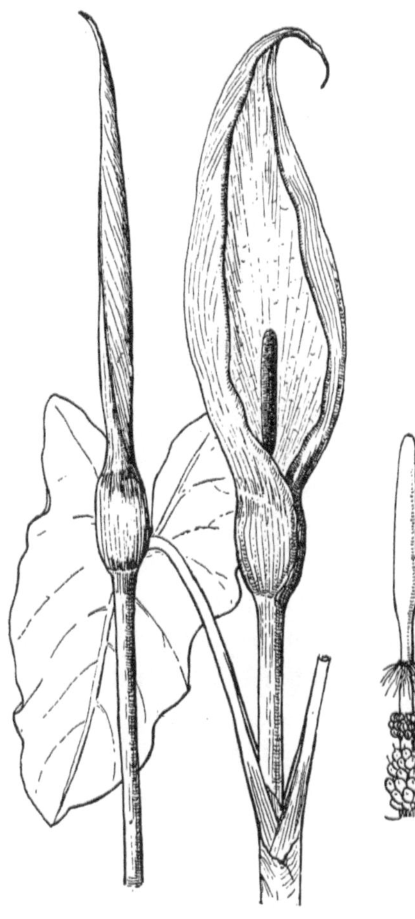

flowers, while other jacks are covered below with pistil flowers. How does the pollen get from one jack to the other (Figs. 201-203)?

The skunk cabbage. In this plant the stamens and pistils are both in the same flower. Can you read their story (Figs. 204, 205)?

The wind helps to cross pollinate many flowers. In many plants no provision is made for using insects to carry the pollen. For many of these plants the wind carries the pollen. The oak, corn, wheat, grasses, etc., are examples of wind-pollinated flowers.

Fig. 205. Another flower of skunk cabbage.

CHAPTER XXIII.

How Fruits Are Formed

The fruit contrasted with the seed. The fruit comes after the flower. As the fruit ripens, the seed matures. Is the fruit the same as the seed? In Fig. 25 is shown a fruit of the sunflower. It is usually called a seed. It is formed from a single flower in the head. Since there are many flowers in a sunflower head, there are also many fruits. The entire fruit, however, is not, strictly speaking, the seed. The seed is inside. The wall of the seed is so firmly joined to the wall of the pistil that it does not separate from it, and the meat (embryo plant) is inside. So we cannot say with accuracy that the fruit and seed are the same. [11]

NOTE.—The matter of this chapter is not particularly concerned with the behavior of plants. But the fruit is best studied after the flower, if we wish to get any idea of the parts entering into the fruit. Its study is also closely connected with the dispersal of seed. For this reason the chapter on fruits is introduced here. If the teacher prefers, the matter of the flower, fruit, and of seed dispersal may quite as well be introduced after Chapter X, in connection with a study of the plant and its parts.

The a-kene'. The seed or fruit of the sunflower is called an *a-kene'*. The beggar needles, seeds of the golden-rod, etc., are also akenes. In the buttercup it is difficult for us to say just what is the fruit. The collection of seeds in the

11 In the gingko tree, and in cycas, the fruit is the same as the seed, though sometimes the embryo is not formed in the fruit. The word "fruit" has a very indefinite significance, as can be seen from its general application to widely different structures or combinations. We even speak of the fruit of ferns, meaning the spore cases and spores, where no seeds at all are formed.

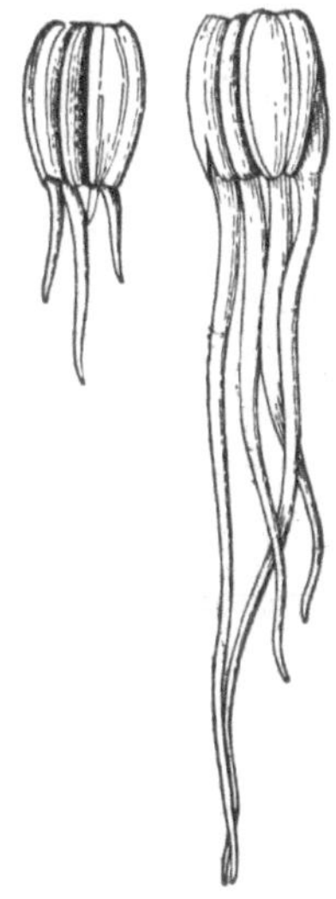
Fig. 206. An akene or fruit of sunflower with four embryos in one seed coat, germinating.

ripe or old flower is probably a fruit, since they are all formed from a single flower. Each part, however, is an akene (Fig. 210) and is generally called a seed, though the wall of the seed is united with the wall of the pistil. An akene, then, is a dry unopening fruit, with a single seed the wall of which is joined with the wall of the pistil.

Fig. 207. An older stage of Fig. 206.

The pod. The pea pod is a good example of one kind of fruit. It is a capsule fruit which has only one chamber, or *locule*. It opens into halves by splitting along the two edges. You can see the seeds inside, and that they are attached at one point to the wall of the pod. The silkweed or milkweed has a fruit which is an example of another kind of pod, which opens only along one edge. The morning-glory has a pod, or capsule fruit, with three chambers or locules, each one representing a part of the pistil. Can you name and describe other pods? How should you describe a pod or capsule fruit?

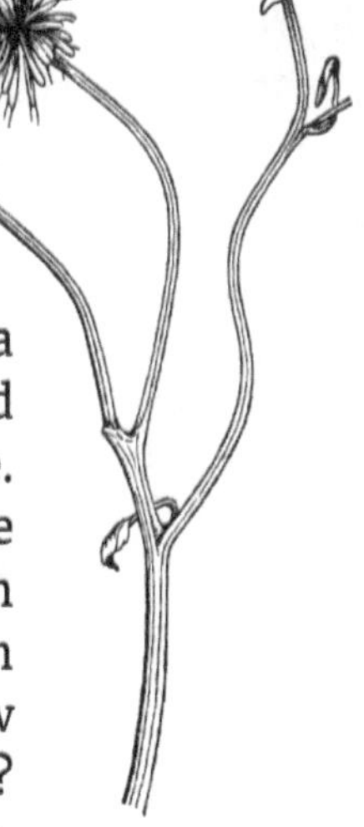
Fig. 208. Fruit of bur marigold, or beggar needles.

Drupes or stone fruits. The cherry, peach, plum, and other fleshy fruits of this kind are called *drupes* or *stone fruits*. The outer part of

Fig. 209. An akene of bur marigold, the "bootjack."

the wall of the pistil becomes fleshy, and the inner part hard and stony, and contains the meat or seed inside.

The strawberry. When you next have some berries you will find it interesting to learn what parts of the flower make the edible portion of the fruit. In the strawberry you can see the tiny seeds, each resting in a tiny depression, as if they were stuck all over the outer part of the pulp or soft part of the strawberry. They are not covered with any soft substance. Each seed is a ripened pistil. There were many pistils in the strawberry flower. If you go into a strawberry patch when the berries are ripening, you can see how the fleshy part of the strawberry is formed, by reading the stories from the flower through the green strawberries up to the ripe ones. You will see that the part of the flower to which the pistils are joined grows larger and thicker, and finally forms the fleshy part of the strawberry, raising the seeds up as it grows bigger. This part of a flower, to which the pistils and usually the other parts are joined, is called the *re-cep'ta-cle* or *to'rus. The fleshy part of the strawberry, then, is the* **receptacle**. The strawberry is not, strictly speaking, a berry. *A berry is a fleshy fruit with several seeds inside,* as the snowberry, gooseberry, grape, tomato, etc.

Fig. 210. Akene of buttercup.

The blackberry. How is it with the blackberry fruit? You can read the story in the same way as you did in the strawberry, when you have a chance. The receptacle becomes larger and longer, and forms the inside of the blackberry which we eat, though it is not a very juicy part. Where are the seeds? They are enclosed in a fleshy substance. This fleshy substance around each seed is the outside of the pistil.

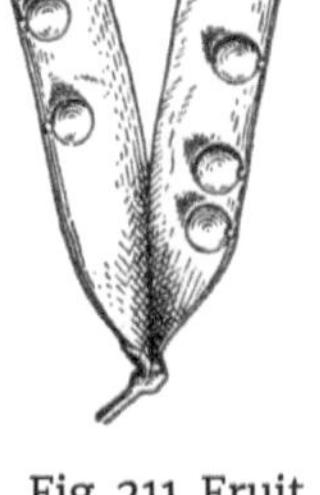
Fig. 211. Fruit of pea: a pod split open.

How different it is from the strawberry!

The raspberry. Compare the raspberry fruit with that of the strawberry and blackberry. Read the story and see if you can tell what part of the flower makes the fruit. You should go to a raspberry patch, or have some stems with ripe raspberries and, if possible, flowers on them.

The raspberry and blackberry are not, strictly speaking, berries. They are collections of tiny stone fruits. In the flowers the pistils are separate, but as the fruit forms, the outer fleshy parts unite to form a collection of little drupes.

Fig. 212. Pods of milkweed.

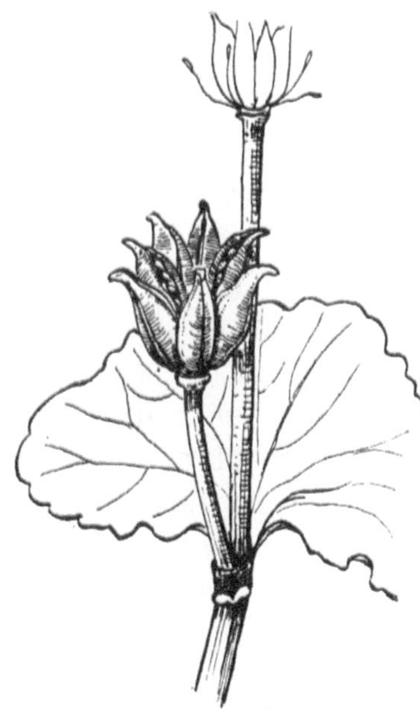

Fig. 213. Fruit cluster of morning-glory.

The apple is an interesting fruit. It would be difficult for you to read the entire story, because older students are not sure that they know just what

Fig. 214. Single pod with three locules of morning-glory.

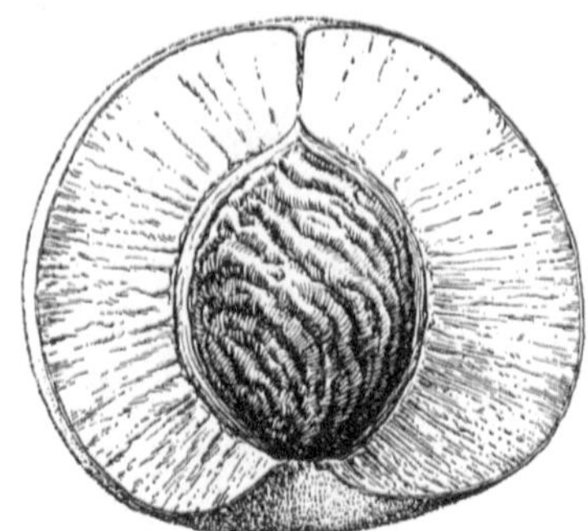

Fig. 215. Drupe or stone fruit of peach.

parts are united in the apple fruit. Cut an apple crosswise. You see the seeds inside. How many chambers, or locules, are there for seeds? What does each one of these locules represent? I shall not ask you what the fleshy part of the apple represents, for we are not sure that we know. It was once thought to be the calyx grown very thick and fleshy. You see at the small end of the apple the dried ends of the sepals. But perhaps these sepals only rested on the edge of the receptacle which is joined to the outer part of the compound pistil. If this is so, then the receptacle grows very large and fleshy and forms the fleshy part of the apple. This is most likely. Compare the receptacle of the rose flower. The rose flower is a near relative of the apple flower, and we should expect the flowers to be somewhat alike, though not entirely so. An apple fruit is sometimes called a *pome*. If you will compare it with the true berries, like the snowberry, gooseberry, etc., you will see that it is very much like a berry.

Fig. 216. Fruit of strawberry and raspberry.

The squash, pumpkin, cucumber, and other fruits of this kind form what is called a *pepo*. The outer part is supposed to be formed from the receptacle of the flower which here is united with the three parts of the compound pistil. You will remember that in the flower (Fig. 194) the calyx and corolla were seated on the end of the young pumpkin, which suggests that the receptacle here encloses and is joined to the pistil. How many chambers, or locules, are there in the pumpkin?

Acorn fruits. The fruit of the oaks is interesting to us all.

Every one knows the acorns and the cups in which they rest. Well, the cup is a very singular part of the fruit. It perhaps represents a crown of tiny leaves around the base of the young flower. As the acorn was forming, these tiny leaves grew larger and were all joined closely together, so that they formed a cup which partly enclosed the acorn (see Fig. 245).

In the hazelnut, chestnut, and beechnut a similar crown of leaves (*in-vo-lu'cre*) around the base of the flower forms the husk or bur in which the nuts are enclosed, and from which they are shelled when ripe.

There are many other fruits which will be interesting to study. Some of these are treated of in the following chapter, since in many cases it is difficult to distinguish between a fruit and a seed. In the study of fruits you should see if you can tell of what use they are to the plant, and how these fruits may be the means of helping the plants to scatter their seeds.

NOTE.— In the walnut, butternut, and hickory nut the fruit is different from that of the hazelnuts, oaks, etc. The "hull" or "shuck" probably consists partly of calyx and partly of involucral bracts consolidated, but very likely there is more of calyx than of involucre. The walnut and butternut are more often called drupes or stone fruits, but the fleshy part of the fruit is evidently not of the same origin as in the case of the true drupes, like the cherry, peach, plum, and others.

CHAPTER XXIV.

How Plants Scatter Their Seed

The touch-me-not. Did you ever see or handle a pod of a "touch-me-not"? The plant is sometimes known as garden balsam. It is well worth while to grow it in any flower garden. The flowers are pretty, but the pods are still more interesting. When you touch them, or throw them on the floor or against the wall, they burst suddenly and scatter their seeds all around. The wild *Impatiens*, or jewel weed, has smaller pods, which burst in the same way. Find some of the plants in a garden during the autumn and try the pods, or look for the wild *Impatiens*, or jewel weed, along streams and in damp, shady places.

Fig. 217. Spray of leaves and flowers and fruit of jewel weed, or wild *Impatiens*.

The witch hazel. The witch hazel is known by its beautiful yellow flowers with slender curled petals, which come out late in autumn, after the leaves have fallen. At the same time the fruit pods are matured from flowers of the previous year. On dry days, when the fruit is ripe, one can hear the snapping of the pods as they burst, and the seeds are thrown with force several feet away.

Fig. 218. Seeds of milkweed ready to scatter from the pods.

Pods which burst and scatter their seeds are called *explosive fruits.* Other examples are to be found in the vetch, locust, violet, oxalis, etc.

The milkweed or silkweed. The milkweed is known by its peculiar flowers and the abundance of white milky substance which flows from wounds in the plant, and gives a disagreeable sticky feeling to the hands when it comes in contact with them. When the flowers go, a few little boat-shaped pods are seen on the flower stalk. These grow larger and larger. When they are ripe the pods split open. A great mass of flat seeds is crowded out by the pushing of great tufts of white silky threads attached to one end of each seed. They are so light and feathery that the wind lifts them easily and sometimes bears them miles away.

Did you ever see these pods bursting and emptying out the great white feathery cloud? Take a pod before it has opened. Split it open and see how beautifully the seeds are packed away in it. Separate some of the seeds to see the soft, silky tuft of hairs on the end. Blow the seeds into the air to see how easily they float away on the "wings of the wind."

Fig. 219. Dandelion seeds.

The dandelion. The dandelion is so common that few persons admire the really beautiful flower. They would rather get rid of it. If the dandelion would only grow in out-of-the-way places, it would not be so unwelcome. But it is an intruder. You dig the plants, root and branch, out of your yard, and in a few years they are there again, or new ones, rather. It makes a great many seeds. But how beautifully they sail through the air like tiny balloons!

Did you ever try to blow all the seeds off the head with one long whiff? There is a mark left where each one stood. How they go sailing away! Watch them! Some are coming down to the ground like a man clinging to a parachute. The seed

Fig. 220. Dandelion fruit in shade (after Macmillan)

is the heaviest part and is below. On the end of the long stalk above is the crown of soft white hairs which forms the float. Down, down, the seed slowly comes and soon is ready to wriggle its way into the ground. Here it germinates and makes a new dandelion in the lawn.

Fig. 221. Dandelion flower and fruit. Flower open at night, old flowers closed and stems elongating at left, ripe seed raised up higher and ready to scatter (after Miyake).

The leaves form a deep-green rosette resting on the grass. The flower stem comes up, and the flower head opens, showing a beautiful cluster of yellow flowers. This head closes at night and opens in the day, closes again at night and opens with the day, and so on, unless the day is a dark one, when all the dandelions may remain closed.

By and by the head stops opening. We can see the tips of the flowers. They wither and die. A white cottony mass begins to appear. Its silky hairs spread apart, the head opens again, and the crown of narrow leaves (the *involucre*) recurves and gives room for the spreading crown on the tips of all the seeds. This forms a great white ball on the end of the stem. The seeds are now in a position where the wind easily catches them.

Did you ever notice that where the lawn is mowed many of the dandelions have such short stems that the flower head is below the lawn mower? Then see how these same short stems will grow much longer just as the seeds are ready to be scattered, so that they are lifted above the grass where the wind may catch hold of them easily. Put a stake by some flowers and measure the stems. Then measure them every day while the seeds are ripening. Along the roadsides or in undisturbed places the flower stems are often longer than those on the lawn. Do these long stems lengthen as the seeds ripen?

The wild lettuce and prickly lettuce, so common in old fields and along the roadsides, have seeds very much like those of the dandelion.

The virgin's bower, or clematis. The clematis, or virgin's bower, is quite as attractive in appearance in the autumn as in the summer when it is in flower. The great masses of foliage and vines clambering over fences and shrubs, and often hiding them entirely, show numerous white puffs of feathery seeds where the flower once was. Each of the seeds is like an arrow-headed plume. Blow or scatter some of them to the wind and see them scudding off to the ground in curious spiral courses.

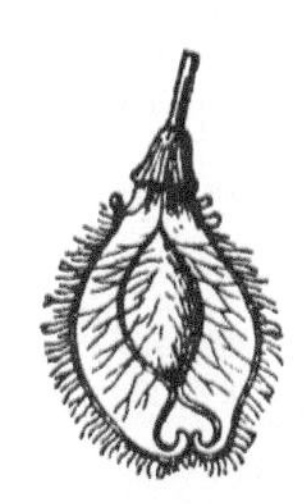

Fig. 222. Fruit (seed) of elm, a samara.

Winged seeds. Some seeds have wing-like expansions on the side and are called *winged seeds.* They, too, are carried by the wind, but they are not quite so buoyant as the seeds of the milkweed and dandelion. The elm seed has two wings. It is sometimes called a *samara*, which means "seed of the elm." The maples and pines also have winged seeds. Do you know any other plants which have winged seeds?

Fig. 223. Winged fruit of maple, two seeds.

The bur marigold. The bur marigold, sometimes called "beggar needles" or "devil's bootjack," is a very common weed with yellow flower heads. The seeds are also in a head, and the cluster bristles all over with the barbed awns. "Bootjack" is not a bad name for the seed, so far as the shape is concerned. At least a boy brought up in the country, who used to pull off his boots at night with the old wooden bootjack, thinks so.

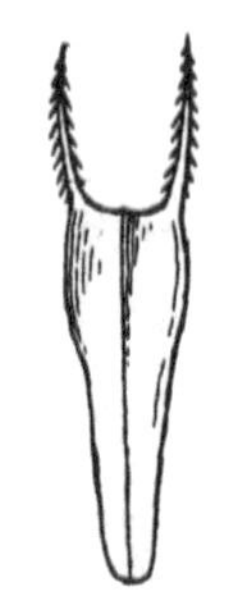

Fig. 224. Seed of bur marigold, "bootjack."

When tramping through the fields, or sometimes in the garden, if you brush against one of these plants, the awns will pierce your clothing immediately. The barbs hold on tight, and soon there may be hundreds of these seeds clinging to you.

The cocklebur, burdock, stick-tights, etc. The bur marigold is not the only seed or fruit ready to "catch on" for a "free ride." There are also cocklebur, burdock, stick-tight, and "what not," and it does not help matters to "crack behind," either. They hold on until they are pulled off, and then they leave in the cloth countless tiny hooks, which are even harder to remove.

If you wish to know more about these "dead-beats" who ride all over the country and never pay a cent of fare, go out for a tramp in the autumn in old neglected fields or in low waste ground. You can carry some home for study. Examine them to see the different kinds of seeds, and how the barbs, hooks, and other hold-fasts are formed. What animals do you think would be of service to the plant in dispersing such seeds? You may wish, also, to visit the same places in summer to see the plants in flower.

Fig. 225. Fruit of cocklebur with hooked appendages.

Have you seen any other seeds than these described here which have means for dispersal? Do seeds ever float on the water and become scattered in this way? How is it with the cocoanut palm? Do seeds of grasses or weeds float in the water of lakes, ponds, rivers, and small streams?

PART IV.

LIFE STORIES OF PLANTS

CHAPTER XXV.

Life Story of the Sweet Pea

THE life story of the sweet pea can be easily read from the plant by any one who wishes to grow it, and observe it. The story of the garden pea is similar, and some of you may wish to read it. But the sweet pea has prettier flowers. It can be grown in the garden, or in the plant house, or in the window garden where you can see it every day.

The seedling stage. The seeds of the sweet pea are round, hard, dark grayish brown objects (see Fig. 211). We plant them in the moist soil. They take water from the soil, swell up, and become soft. This moisture and the warmth in the soil start the dormant life in the seed into action. It "awakens," as we say, from its long sleep. In a few days, or a week or so, the young plant rises through the soil. The leaves are now tiny, but as the stem grows and the light has full play on the small leaves they stretch out so that a greater surface may receive light, for light is good for the leaf and plant. As the stem gets longer, the leaves higher up are better formed and more fully developed.

Fig. 226. Sweet pea coming up.

Fig. 227. Sweet-pea vines needing support.

The growth and work period. If there are no sticks or objects for the pea vine to take hold of, it will show you that it needs some means of support. It will soon lie prostrate. But if you put an upright stick within its reach, or train some cord or string near by, the tendrils on the leaf will stretch out and coil round it. In this way the vine can climb up where there is more light and air. The stem branches, and at length a tall and bushy plant is formed. There is a much greater leaf surface.

While the plant has been growing, and lifting up water and food from the soil by the combined work of the roots and leaves and stem, the green leaves have been doing another kind of work, for which we know they need the help of sunlight. They have been making starch. At night the starch is digested and changes to sugar. It flows to all parts of the plant where growth is taking place and new plant substance is wanted. We know that if the pea vine were grown in the dark, all the plant substance it would have to use in growth would be that which was already in the seed. The stem would be for a time long and spindling, the leaves would be small and yellowish, and the framework of the plant would be soft. It would soon die. But in the light the leaves are green. We know that the carbon dioxide of the air gets into the green leaf. The light then helps the leaf to make the starch from which most of the new plant substance comes.

Fig. 228. Sweet-pea vine trained to support.

Flowering time. The plant has now formed a strong working system, and its numerous branches bear many working leaves. It is prepared to flower. Since the flowers do another sort of work than make food, there must be a good force of working leaves to supply the food and energy needed in flowering. These appear first, next come the flower heads, and later the clusters of flowers, the older ones opening out first.

THE FLOWER

The petals. The flower of the sweet pea is beautiful in color and form. Its form is peculiar; that is, it is not so regular in shape as the flower of the lily. Some one has thought the shape of the flower of the pea, and of its cousins or relations, to be like that of a butterfly. The most attractive parts of the flower of the pea are the petals. I think you already know what petals are. If you do not, just look at the pea flower, select the bright-colored parts which are thin and broad. These are the petals. You see they are of different shapes, instead of having the same shape as in the lily or buttercup. This is what gives the peculiar form to the pea flower.

Now all these parts, or the different kinds of petals of the pea flower, have received names. I should not be surprised if, after studying their shapes carefully and their position in the flower, you could name them yourself, especially if you tried to think of things with which you are familiar and which these petals resemble.

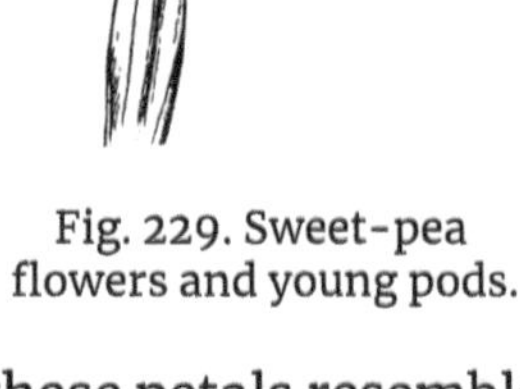

Fig. 229. Sweet-pea flowers and young pods.

Now, first, the large one, held up above, is the *banner*. The two reaching out on the sides are *wings*. Now think hard for the two below, folded up together. Did you ever make or sail a boat? What does the boat have on the underside that cuts through the water? The *keel*. *Banner*, *wings, keel,* —these are the petals of the pea flower and all together we call them the *corolla*.

Now remove the petals from the flower. Place them out in

position and draw the form. The two parts which form the keel are joined in the middle. Is that the case with the keel in the garden pea?

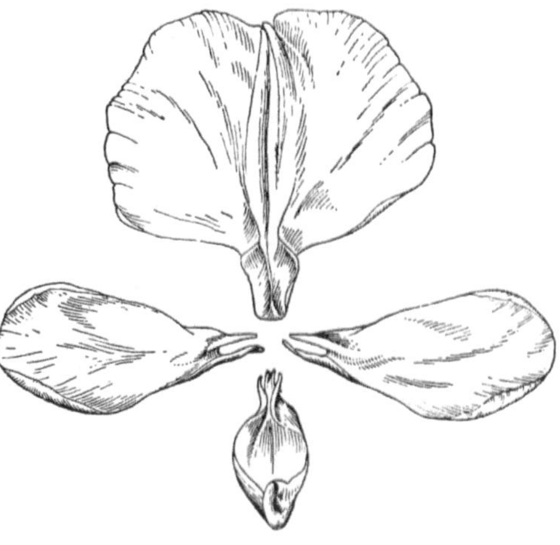

Fig. 230. Petals of sweet pea.

The calyx. The petals are removed from the flower; what remains? Just below where they were joined there is a little crown of five pointed green leaf-like bodies. They are very different in form from the real pea leaves, but like them are green. These are *sepals*. Together they make the *calyx*. In the bud they covered and protected the other parts of the flower. There are five sepals, the same number as the petals, yet they are very different in form and color.

The stamens and pistil. There are now remaining the parts of the flower around which the keel was folded. Count them. There are ten thread-like bodies, surrounding a tiny boat-shaped body. The thread-like bodies are the stamens. Each one has an enlargement at the curved end. It is a little case containing the powder-like substance, called *pollen*. It is a *pollen case*. See if all the stamens are separate down to the calyx. One is. The nine others are joined toward the base. These nine form *one brotherhood*. The other one is a brotherhood all by itself. The pistil is flat, like a thin boat, and it is hairy. It is almost too tiny in

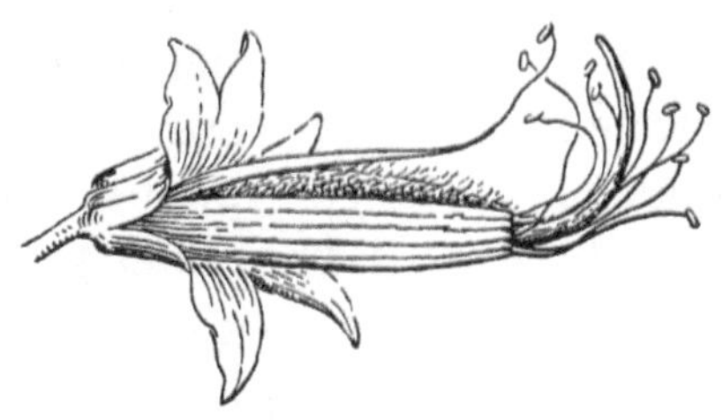

Fig. 231. Flower of sweet pea with petals removed.

Fig. 232. Fruit of sweet pea.

the fresh flower for us to study. We will take one in an older flower.

The old flower. As the flower gets old the petals and stamens wither and die. They either fall away or collapse around the pistil. If the flower has done the work for which it was intended, the pistil does not die. It grows longer and broader and thicker, until we see that it is becoming a pea pod. When it has grown a little, split the young pod open into halves, the same way that you have seen peas or beans shelled. Attached to one edge of the inside of the little pod you will see tiny roundish bodies, in the position in which you find the peas or seeds in the older pods. The pod is a sort of box which contains the seeds. The tiny bodies are cases in which the embryos are formed. They may be called *embryo cases* then. The case and embryo together make the seed. The pistil, or seed box, contains embryo cases in which seeds are formed.

How the seed is formed. You cannot see how the seed is formed. This part of the story has been found out by those who are accustomed to use a powerful microscope. They cut up the growing embryo case (ovule) into very thin layers and search in these with a microscope to see the work that is done here. Thus we read the story of how the seed is formed.

In the first place there is a royal bit of life substance in the very young embryo case, known as the *germ* or *egg*. When the pollen is scattered from the pollen cases some of it falls on the end of the pistil. The pollen grain then starts to grow. It forms a slender tube as fine as a spider's silk. This pollen tube grows down through the pistil, and one enters each embryo case. In each pollen tube there are two bits of royal life substance, called *sperms*.

One sperm escapes from the pollen tube when it has entered the young embryo case and unites with the germ. *The union of these two bits of royal life substance, the sperm and germ, gives a new life to the germ and a new impetus for growth to the embryo case.* The new germ grows to form the embryo plant in the seed, while the new growth of the embryo case around it makes the seed coat. The pea seed is then formed. This completes the life story of the pea.

CHAPTER XXVI.

Life Story of the Oak

The white oak. In the autumn, when the leaves begin to fall, the acorns fall, too, from the oaks. They nestle in the grass or roll down into the furrow or ditch, or strike on the leaf floor of the forest, according to where the tree happens to be. The rains beat on the soil, and some of the acorns become partly buried in the ground. Some are eaten by insects, others are carried away by squirrels and other animals. Some are left to grow.

As we have seen in our study of the germination of the acorn, the root and stem parts of the embryo back out of the shell at the pointed end. The great fleshy cotyledons remain inside. The root pushes its way further down into the ground. The young stem grows out from between the cotyledon stalks. This often begins in the autumn. It continues in the spring among those seedlings which survive the cold of the winter. Or, if the acorn did not germinate in the autumn, it may in the spring. During the first few years the tiny oak makes little growth. A few leaves on a slender stem appear. It is not high enough to be seen above the grass. Of the many which start, but few rise up to saplings. Many, many years the oak grows. It gets a foot or so higher each year. It is making root, trunk, branches,

Fig. 233. While oak in autumn.

and each year a greater number of leaves. The leaves make the plant substance for the new and continued growth.

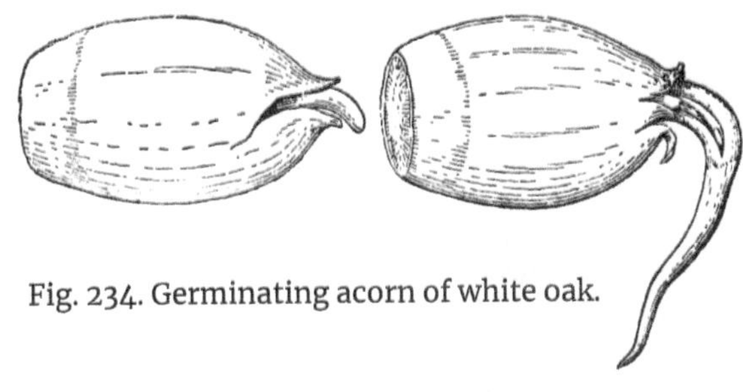

Fig. 234. Germinating acorn of white oak.

The bark on the trunk is smooth at first. As the sapling gets older the bark begins to crack open in long and irregular fissures, making the gray bark more prominent. If you should start when you are very young to read the life of an oak tree, from its beginning as an acorn, I am afraid you would never be able to read the whole story. By the time oak trees are very old, they have lived many more years than we do. So how shall we read the life story of the oak? Read it in a large number of trees,

Fig. 235. Oak trees getting a start. (Photographed in winter.)

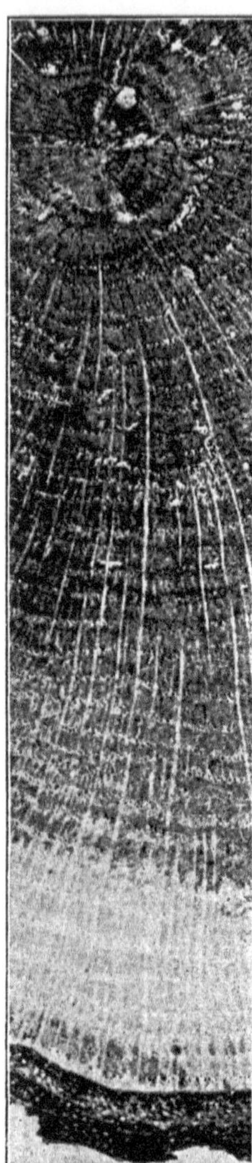

Fig. 236. How old was the tree from which this wood was taken?

from young ones to middle-aged ones, and very old oaks. If you happen to find an oak tree which has been cut down, you know you can tell its age within a few years by counting the annual rings. During the first few years of the seedling, so little growth in diameter took place each year that the rings are not well marked.

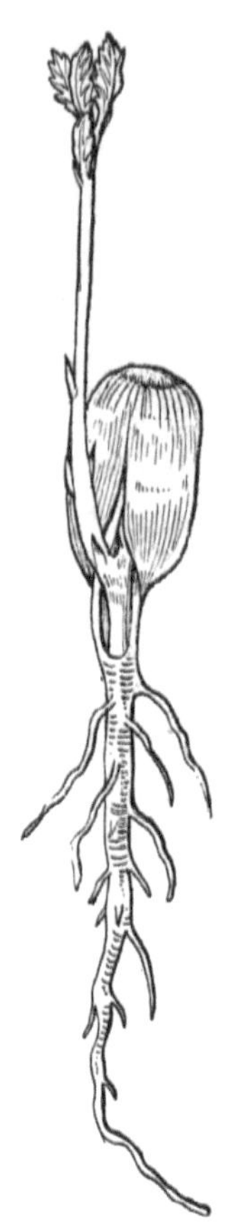

Fig. 237. Scarlet oak, spray of leaves and stamen clusters.

The oak flower. It is many years before the oak comes to flower. Not until it has become quite a tree are the flowers seen. They appear in early spring, before the leaves show themselves. Have you seen the long, slender, graceful clusters hanging on the branches of the middle-aged or old oak in the spring, when the limbs are yet bare? Gather some of these and place them on paper overnight. Next morning there will probably be piles of a fine yellowish powder. What is this? Pollen dust, you say. Yes. Then where does it come from? From the pollen cases. Then these tresses, called catkins, are flower clusters. But there are no pistils here. These flowers, then, are the stamen flowers. Where are the pistil flowers? Look above the stamen flowers for

Fig. 238. Spray of leaves and flowers of red oak, pistil flowers small above, stamen flowers in long clusters.

little urn-shaped bodies, one or two or three together. They stand upright, not hanging down in catkins.

The fruit. After the leaves come and the pollen has been scattered, the stamen flowers, or catkins, fall. But if everything has gone well with the pistil flower it begins to grow, because new life has been put into it by the sperm from the pollen tube joining with the germ in the embryo case. All through the summer it grows slowly. It does not ripen so soon as the pea pod. In the autumn there are the acorns, seated snugly in their little cups. This is the fruit. The acorn ripens and falls; but the tree does not die. Its life goes on for years, and it bears many other crops of acorns.

We love the oak. We think of it as a strong and sturdy tree. We like to play with the acorns and cups, and sometimes to eat the meat inside, especially that of the white oak, after the acorn has been roasted in the hot ashes of a fire. We like to rest under the shade of its branches and to climb to its top when the branches are near the ground.

Fig. 239. Stamen flower of red oak

Fig. 240. Pistil flower of red oak.

The white oak forms its acorns in one season. The red oak and the

Fig. 241. Spray of white-oak leaves and fruit.

scarlet oak take two seasons to form their acorns. Can you tell the red and the scarlet oaks apart by the shape of their leaves? Can you tell the white oak from both the red and the scarlet oaks by the shape of the leaves and the character of the bark? If you were given three acorns in their cups, one of the red oak, one of the scarlet oak, and one of the white oak, could you tell them apart and then name them?

Fig. 242. Leaves and fruit of scarlet oak.

Fig. 243. Leaf of red oak.

Do you know the acorn of the "moss-cup," or "over-cup," oak? Why is it called by these names? (See Fig. 246.)

oak or moss-covered oak.

The winter condition of the oak. The falling of the leaves from trees and shrubs on the approach of winter is a constant habit. We are accustomed, perhaps, to look upon it merely as one of the signs of autumn. It is always interesting to watch the leaves falling from the tree and to observe how the movement of the air aids in freeing them from the limb. A gust of wind knocks off troops of them, and sends them scurrying over the field or rolls them in great drifts.

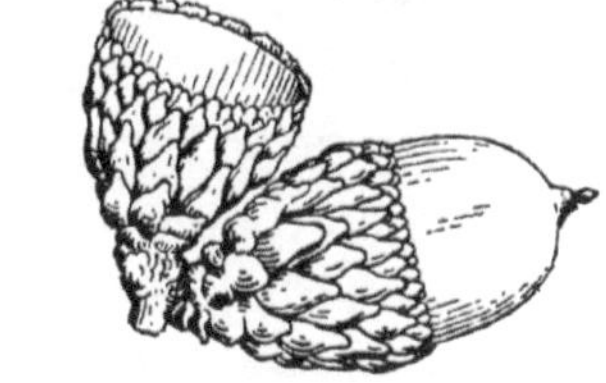

Fig. 244. Fruit of scarlet oak.

Did you ever think what this shedding of the leaves in the autumn means to the leaf and to the tree? It is the death of the leaf. But we know that the tree is not dead, for with the on-coming of spring new leaves appear as the warmth of

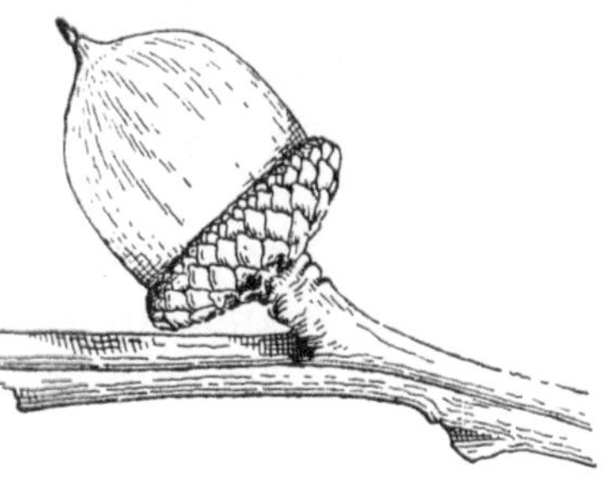

Fig. 245. Fruit of red oak.

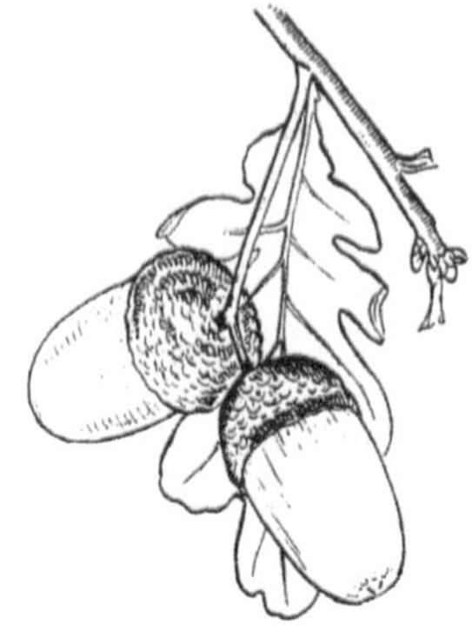

Frig. 246. Fruit of over-cup

the season moves the life into greater activity again.

The leaf is only an organ of the tree for summer work, to make starch food, to dispose of the great currents of water that are taken up by the roots, and to do other work in the preparation of foods and in getting rid of waste matter. When the leaf is cast in the autumn, the tree is only dropping a member for which it has no use during the period of winter rest. Someone may ask why the tree does not keep its leaves during the winter and save the growing of new ones in the spring. It would be fatal to most of the broad-leaved trees to keep their green leaves through the winter. We know that the leaves give off quantities of water from the tree. During the winter, while the ground is frozen or cold, the roots can take up very little water, not nearly so much as the leaves can give off. The tree has thus acquired a remarkably good habit in laying aside its leaves during the winter, when they would be of little service, and would even endanger its life if they were retained.

Some trees keep their green leaves through the winter. The pines, spruces, cedars, and other evergreens do. Why is it not dangerous for them to do so? The leaves of the pines, spruces, and cedars are small and needle-like, or awl shaped, with a thick, hard covering, so that these trees do

Fig. 247. "Needle" leaves and stamen flowers of pitch pine.

not lose water so rapidly as the broad-leaved trees do. Then, too, a change takes place in the condition and work of the leaves of such evergreens, so that they lose less water in the winter than during the summer. Some of the broad-leaved trees and shrubs are also evergreen and retain their leaves during the winter. Like the pines and spruces, they cast a crop of leaves after it has been on the tree for two or more years, a new crop being grown each year. The live oak, the rhododendrons, and the mountain laurel are examples of broad-leaved evergreen trees and shrubs. These leaves, though they are broad, are thick and have a hard covering, so that they do not give off so much water in the winter as thinner and softer leaves would.

Fig. 248. Leaves of American yew, evergreen.

CHAPTER XXVII.

Life Story of Ferns

The fern plant. There are no plants which mean more to us in our home life than ferns. There are no plants which are more generally loved. The refining influence of their presence is constantly felt. Their graceful forms, the beautiful shapes of their leaves, and the restful green of their abundant foliage

Fig. 249. Bank of ferns (after Macmillan).

Fig. 250. Christmas fern.

interest us and satisfy us whenever we see them. If we could only get the maidenhair to grow in our yards as abundantly and easily as the dandelion does, how charming it would be! Many of us would willingly part with some of the dandelions if we could have the maidenhair or Christmas fern in their place.

As we found on p62 (see Fig. 93), the stems of most of our native ferns are either very short, as in the shield fern, or they are underground stems, as in the bracken fern or sensitive fern. In the polypod, at the north, the stem runs under the leaves or grass, while one in the south runs on the surface of rocks. The climbing fern is found in some parts of New York state, but it is rare. Tree ferns with tall trunks, and other tropical ferns which grow high up on forest trees, may be seen in some large greenhouses.

Fruit dots, spore cases, and spores of ferns. If you take a polypod fern or a Christmas fern (some of the "shield" ferns in the greenhouse will do) and look on the underside of the leaves, you will perhaps see them covered with little dark brown spots. Some people take these for bugs, and scrape them off the fern leaf, for fear they will hurt the fern! But you can teach them better than that.

Pick a leaf which has these on it, when the brown dots look shiny. Place it on a piece of white paper in a dry room. In a few minutes or an hour you may perhaps see a sprinkling of tiny dust-like bodies on the white paper. You can brush them off with your hand. What are they? They are what we call *spores*. There is a hard brown wall, and inside a bit of living fern substance. These spores come out of a great many spore cases which are packed together in the fruit dots. So these dark bodies on the

Fig. 251. Little spleenwort fern.

underside of the leaf, instead of being bugs which are harmful to plants, are fruit dots with spore cases and spores in them. If the fern plant is making so many of these tiny spores, each containing a little bit of living fern substance, we would better not scrape them off, for they must be for some good purpose in the life of the fern. If you examine a bracken fern, maidenhair fern, and some other kinds, you will find that the fruit dots are of different shapes, and that some of them are under a flap at the edge of the leaf.

Does the fern plant have flowers? The fern plant does not

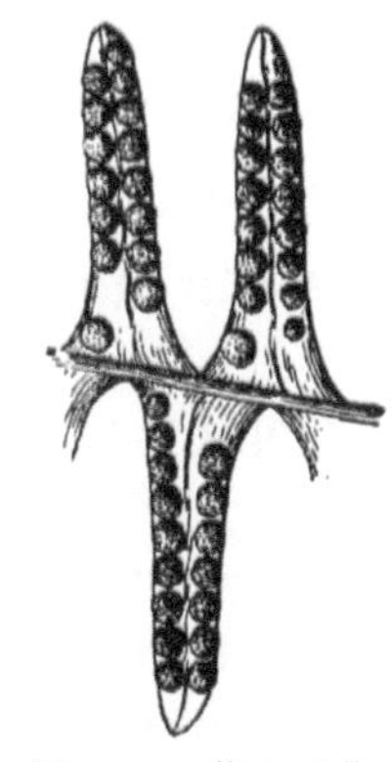
Fig. 252. "Fruit" dots of the common polypody fern.

have flowers as the flowering plants do. Nor does the fern plant have seeds. It will be interesting to know, then, how new fern plants are formed.

How new fern plants are formed. We have already learned that most ferns bear "fruit dots" or lines on the underside of certain leaves. We also know that many tiny spores are in the rounded spore cases which are packed together to form the fruit dots. When these spores are ripe and have been scattered, some of them fall in damp places on the ground, or on a rotting log in the woods. Here this tiny bit of living fern substance begins to grow, and the living matter inside the hard brown coat pushes its way out through a split in the wall; in a few weeks it has grown into a tiny heart-shaped bit of plant tissue no bigger round than a radish seed, or a small pea, and as thin and delicate as fine tissue paper. This little object, shown in

Fig. 253. "Fruit" dots of the maidenhair fern.

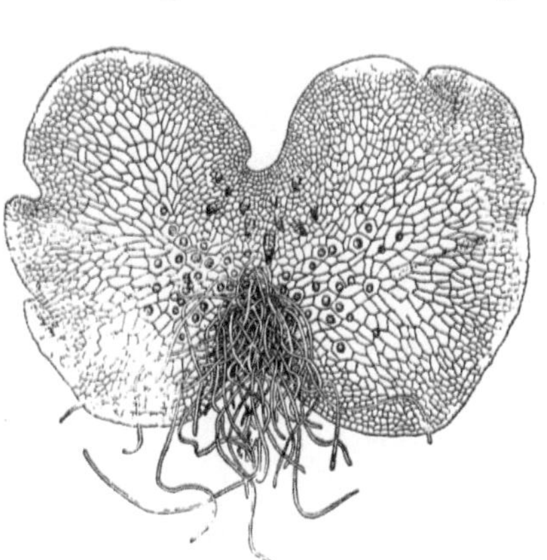
Fig. 254. Prothallium of fern, bearing the germ and sperm pockets. This is a view from the underside, and shows the rootlets also.

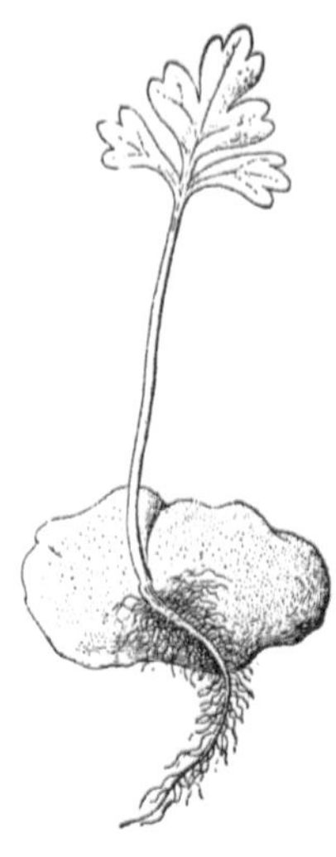

Fig. 255. Embryo fern still attached to the prothallium.

Fig. 254, is a *fern prothallium* (*pro-thal'li-um*). On the underside are numbers of rootlets, like root hairs, and two kinds of tiny pockets. This little prothallium now gives birth to the embryo fern plant.

How the embryo of the fern plant starts. The germ cell is in one of the large pockets near the deep notch in the prothallium, and the sperms are in the round pockets. One of the sperms swims into the germ pocket, unites with the germ, and then the germ grows into the embryo fern plant.

The fern prothallium and embryo compared to a seed. The fern prothallium, with the young embryo fern attached, might be compared to a seed of one of the higher plants, where the embryo is surrounded by a food tissue known as the endosperm, as in the corn. *This endosperm is in fact a prothallium of the higher plant.* In the corn seed it is shown as in Fig. 44. Some of it is still left inside the embryo case. But in the pea, bean, and acorn it is all used up as food by the embryo and stored in the cotyledons. The only way in which the prothallium with the embryo of the fern differs from the seed of the corn or bean is in the fact that the prothallium is green (with chlorophyll), that it has been shed from the spore case, and has been developed as an independent individual. If the fern prothallium were not green,

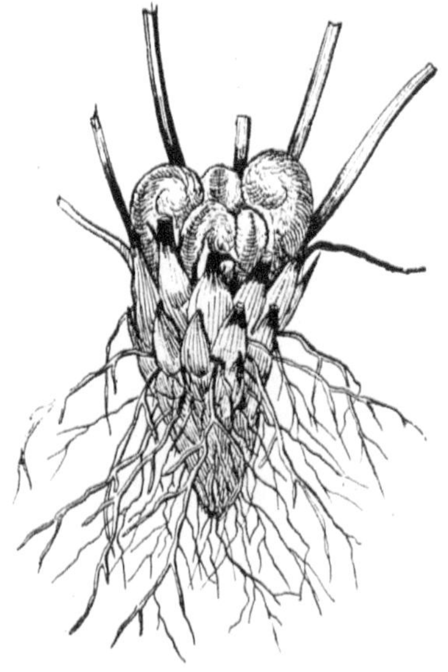

Fig. 256. The walking fern, taking steps down a hillside.

Fig. 257. The bracken fern in company with the "sturdy" oak (after Macmillan).

but were wrapped around the embryo and still in the spore case, it would be a seed. When the young embryo fern grows large enough to burst out of the prothallium, when the root strikes into the soil and the cotyledon or first leaf rises upward, as shown in Fig. 255, it is doing precisely the same thing that a seed does when it germinates, strikes root, and lifts its leaves and stem upward to the light.

The generations of the fern. The life story of the fern reveals to us *two generations*, the *prothallium* and the *fern plant*. They can live independent of each other. Each one can take water and food from the soil. With the leaf-green each one can make its own starch food. The prothallium starts from the spore on the fern plant, and the fern plant starts from the germ in the prothallium. The two generations therefore alternate with each other, as it were. In the corn, the bean, and other plants of this kind there seems to be only one generation. This is because one part of it, the prothallium generation, is packed away and hidden in the embryo case as endosperm, while the other part is hidden in the pollen and pollen tube. Most plants, then, have two generations in their lives. It is only in the ferns, however, and their near relatives that the two generations can exist independently. In the flowering plants the prothallium generation is dependent, and hidden away in the embryo case.

CHAPTER XXVIII.

The Life Story of the Moss

Mossy banks and trees. Those who live near the woods, or who have a chance to go to the woods or mountains in summer, delight in finding a carpet of moss on the ground or on some shady bank. The slender, short stems covered with delicate leaves make a velvety cushion of green. We know that these tiny plants love the cool shade, for, except in the cold arctic or alpine regions, we find them growing freely only in or near the woods. The tree trunks, too, in moist, cool, shady places are often covered with moss. There are sometimes tiny tufts and mats on the ground in open fields, by roadsides and streets, even in cities, and in the cracks of old stone walls. But the mosses do not attract us much in these places because they are so scattered and small.

Fig. 258. Moss-covered trunk.

The pigeon-wheat moss. Who knows the pigeon-wheat moss? Well, here is a picture of a clump of it. In the open wood, or near the woods on damp ground, you may see it in clumps or in large patches.

Fig. 259. Clump of "pigeon-wheat" moss.

The moss is more interesting to study when it is in fruit, because then one can read more of its life story. The moss in Fig. 259 is in fruit. There are little stalks that rise out from the ends of the leafy stem with a little capsule on the end of each stalk. Sometimes this capsule is covered with a large, pointed, woolly hood, and perhaps the appearance of numbers of these suggested tiny wheat stalks and heads. Lift the hood off. There is the capsule with a little lid on the end. You can remove this lid with a pin. There is the mouth of the capsule with a fringe of tiny teeth that you can just see with your sharp eyes. If you thrust the pin into the capsule, you will bring out a dusty powder, like pollen, or like fern spores. These are moss spores; the moss capsule, then, is the spore case.

You should understand that the beautiful red, brown, and green plants so common along the ocean shore, and called popularly "sea mosses," are not true mosses. They are *algæ*. The pond scums are algæ also. Then the "hanging moss," or Florida moss, which is so common in the Southern States, is

Fig. 260. Branched plant of "pigeon-wheat" moss, showing "hood" on spore case at left.

not a true moss. It is a flowering plant. It bears true flowers and also forms seeds. The true mosses do not have flowers, nor do they form true seeds. The spores of the moss form a green thread-like growth on the soil or rotten wood, which resembles some of the "pond scums." From this thread-like growth the leafy moss stem arises.

CHAPTER XXIX.

Life History of Mushrooms

Mushrooms, too, have a story to tell. They live out of sight most of the time. When they show themselves they do so only for a short time. They seem to come up in a single night, and many of them do. But others may be several days in coming up. They keep hidden most of the time in the form of cords, or strings, until they have spread themselves out in reach of a great feast of food in the ground or in wood. Then the mushroom part can grow very fast, and spring out from its hiding place into the light.

Fig. 261. The common mushroom showing stem, cap, ring, gills.

So if you wish to read the story of mushrooms you must be quick about it, for they do not stay long. The common mushroom, like many others, is shaped like an umbrella; it has a handle, a ring, rays on the underside, and a cover. The handle is the *stem*, the ring is called a *ring* or *collar*, the rays are called the *gills* of the mushroom, and the cover is the *cap.*

The spores. Cut off the stem of the common mushroom, a specimen just expanded. Lay the cap, gills down, on white paper for several hours or overnight. The paper underneath the cap becomes covered with a very fine dark brown powder.

Fig. 262. A spore print of the common mushroom.

These are spores, not seeds, for the mushroom has no seeds. The spores take the place of seed. They can start new points of growth for the mushroom.

Spawn of mushrooms. Where the common mushroom is growing in the field, dig some up with a trowel and search in the soil for delicate white cords. If a bed where mushrooms are grown is near, you will find more of these white cords in the soil. This the gardeners call *spawn*. We call it *mycelium*. Gardeners take this spawn and sow it in new beds. It spreads and increases, and makes more mushrooms, after it has feasted on the food in the bed. So in the field or woods this spawn spreads through the earth. It takes up water and food from the soil as roots do, and yet the spawn is not a root.

The beginning of the mushroom. If you can get a quantity of this spawn of the common mushroom, wash out the soil. Look on the cords for very small round bodies. You will find some very small, perhaps no larger than a mustard seed. You may find others as large as a marble. These are the buttons, the beginning of

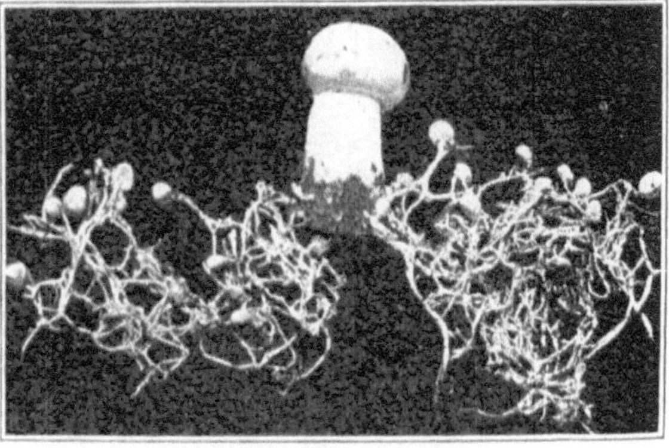

Fig. 263. Spawn and young buttons of the mushroom.

Fig. 264. Buttons of the common mushroom just coming through the sod.

the mushroom. In the ones as large as marbles the upper end is enlarged. This is the beginning of the cap. When it reaches this size the mushroom grows very fast. But the spawn may grow several months, or a year, feeding on decaying plant material in the ground before any mushrooms appear.

Fig. 265. A deadly poisonous mushroom with a "bag" over the base of the stem. (Deadly amanita.)

The common mushroom, which grows in the fields and is cultivated in mushroom houses, has pink gills when young, and dark brown gills when old. It has a white or brownish cap, a stem and a ring.

Other mushrooms. There are many kinds of mushrooms; many are good to eat, and some are very poisonous. No one should gather mushrooms to eat unless he knows very well the kind he picks. Some of

Fig. 266. A toadstool good to eat, with a "bag" on the base of the stem (Royal agaric.)

the poisonous ones have a cup or bag around the lower end of the stem. But some which have this bag or cup are good to eat. So you would better read their stories, and not pick them for eating until you know the kinds as well as you know the faces of your playmates.

Fig. 267. A poisonous mushroom, or toadstool, whichever you choose to call it, with no true "bag" on the stem, only scales which represent one. (The fly amanita.)

Fig. 268. The ink cap.

If you should pick a basket full of different kinds in the woods, and place the caps down on white paper, you would catch the spores. You would probably find that the spores in some cases are black, in others brown, yellow, rose-colored, or white.

Fig. 269. The ink cap turning to ink.

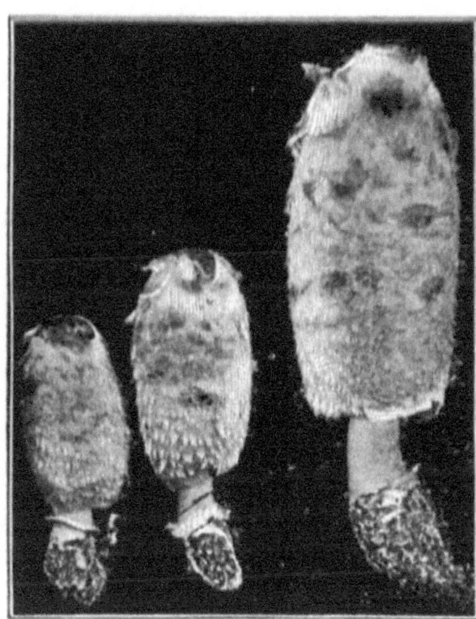

Fig. 270. The shaggy mane, or horse-tail mushroom. Also an ink mushroom.

The ink mushrooms. These are curious and interesting. Soon after they come up, the gills and much of the cap turn to a black, inky fluid which you could write with. One kind is called "ink cap," another is called the "shaggy mane," or "horse-tail." These are good to eat before they turn to ink.

Puffballs and earth stars. Did you ever see puffballs, and pinch one to see the cloud of dust which flies out? Some people call them "devil's snuff-box." They grow from spawn in the ground and in rotten wood too. The cloud of dust is full of spores, which start more spawn to make more puffballs, and so the life story keeps spinning round and round. You have heard of the starfish; did you ever hear of the star fungus or star mushroom? We call it earth star, a pretty name, because it is shaped like a star and grows on the ground. It is a near relative of the puffball.

Fig. 271. The puffball, or devil's snuffbox.

Some will tell you that such interesting plants as the ferns, mosses, mushrooms, and puffballs are *cryptogams*, and

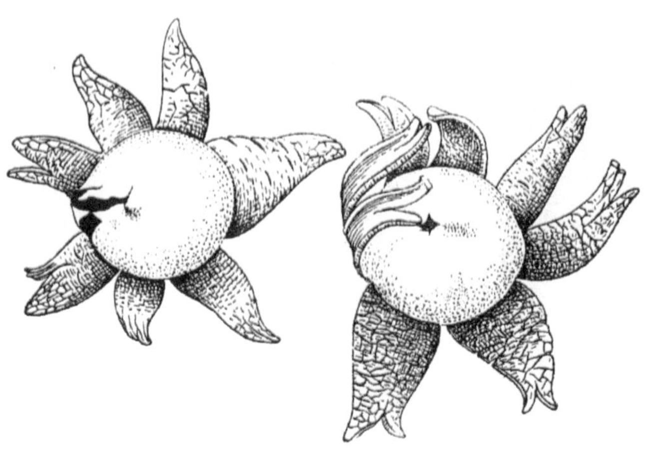

Fig. 272. The earth star.

that therefore you should not try to read the stories they have to tell. But why call them cryptogams? That is a terrible word that ought to be blotted out of the English language. Why not call them plants, as they are? They are just as much God's creatures as the dandelion and thistle and smartweed are. They are just as interesting, too, and mean as much in our lives as they do.

PART V.

BATTLES OF PLANTS IN THE WORLD

CHAPTER XXX.

The Struggles of A White Pine

Many seeds but few trees. If all the seeds of the white pine which fall year after year from the trees in the forest and from individual trees in the fields should grow and form trees, the world could not contain them. For every seed ripened the chances of becoming a tree are very few. It seems a great waste of energy on the part of the tree to form so many seeds when so few can ever hope to become trees. But it is a very fortunate provision of Nature that a single plant should ripen so many seeds where we know the chances for life are so small. Many

Fig. 273. Young and nearly mature fruits of white pine.

Fig. 274. Stamen flowers of the white pine.

trees bear thousands and thousands of seeds, but where are the young pines? Often there are none to be seen in the neighborhood of very prolific trees.

The struggle for a start. From some of the trees the seeds fall on cultivated ground, and if the seedlings start they are plowed under while the crops are being tended. Others may fall on the hard meadow or grass land. The seed cannot bury itself here. If it germinates, the root cannot go deep enough to furnish water and food. In the forest many seeds fall on the thick carpet of

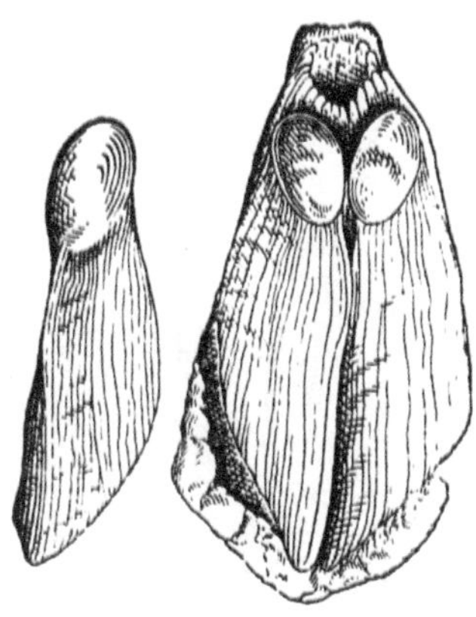

Fig. 275. At left winged seed of white pine, at right a scale with two pine seeds still in position.

dry leaves and are unable to reach the soft, moist humus, or earth below. All these seeds perish. But sometimes a cultivated field may be abandoned for several years and left to grow up to weeds, grass, and bushes. Animals sometimes disturb the leaves in the forest and root up the fresh soil. The woodsman may tear open other places when he drags his logs along the ground. Large trees uprooted by the wind expose an area of moist soil. Seeds which fall in these places have a better chance for life. Some of them become covered in the soil by the beating rains. They are covered at unequal depths. The struggle for a start begins. The good seed which is covered by the soil and moistened by the rains germinates. Before all the roots are fixed deep enough in the soil the sun comes out and several days, perhaps weeks, go by without rain. The surface soil dries. The seedlings which were lightly covered perish. The few which have a good hold in the soil by being buried deeper than the others have plenty of water and food. The crown of leaves is lifted above the soil, and the embryo case is cast off. The seedling has pushed its stem and leaves up to the light, and its roots are spreading in the soil to secure it more firmly.

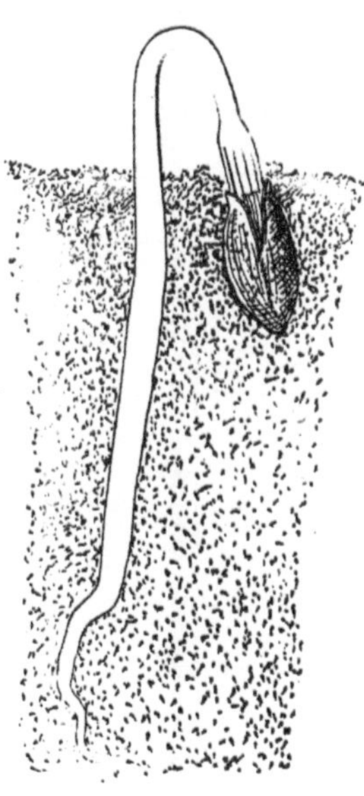

Fig. 276. Seedling of white pine just coming up.

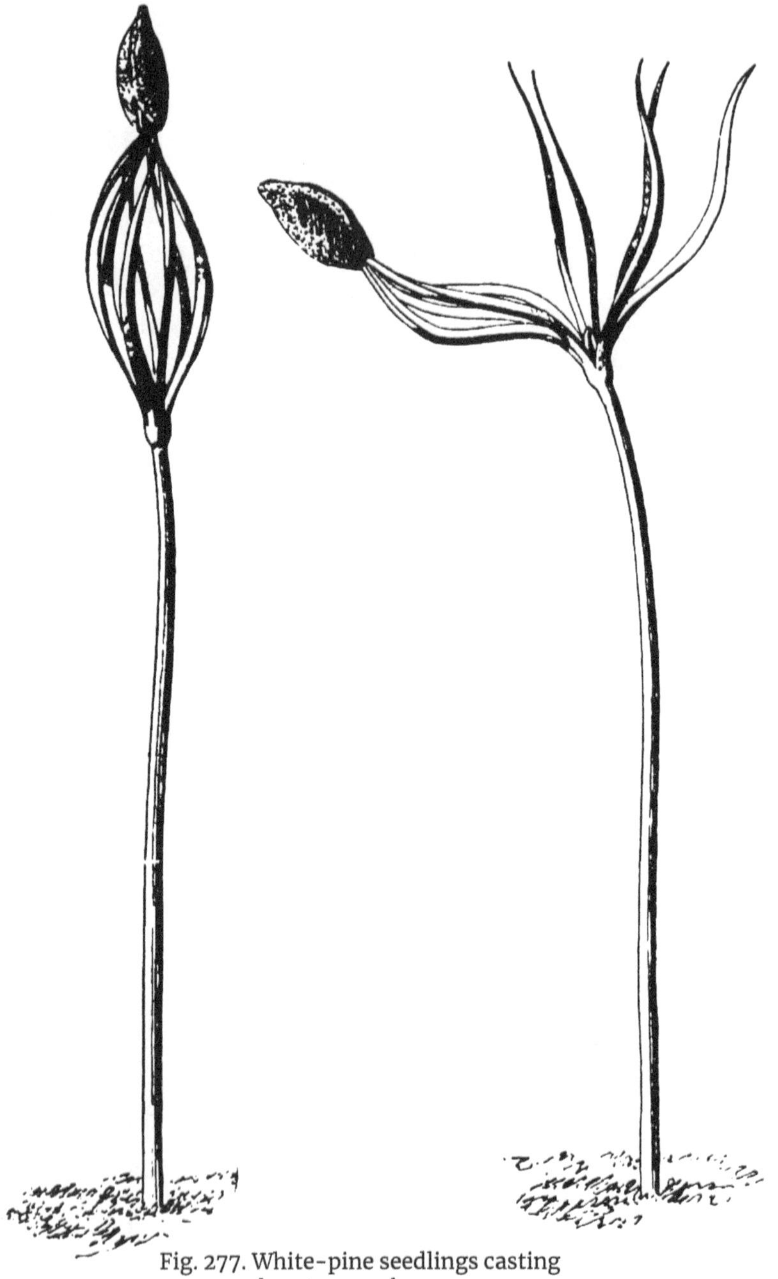

Fig. 277. White-pine seedlings casting seed coats or embryo cases.

Fig. 278. Evergreens and broad-leaved trees just getting above the weeds and grass (Alabama).

There are others around it almost within touch. Troops of these more fortunate creatures are scattered here and there.

The struggle with other vegetation. Now begins a competition among the seedlings and other plants for mastery of the position. Weeds, grasses, vines, perhaps young shrubs and oaks, spring up, for the soil is thick with the seeds of other plants as prolific in seed-bearing as the pine. Many of these grow faster now than the pine seedlings. The weeds and grass soon tower above them and hide them. It looks as if the pine seedlings would be choked out. But they can do fairly well in the shade; better, perhaps, than the weeds think, if they are capable of doing such a thing. The pine seedlings do not hurry. They bide their time. They are making long and useful roots. They are preparing for a long struggle for life.

The score after the first season. In the autumn let us take count of the contest. The weeds raced swiftly and got far ahead. But they have exhausted themselves. They have ripened many seeds, but they die; their leaves wither and dry up. This lets in more light for the tiny pine seedlings. The autumn winds and rain beat on the dead weeds and break many of them down. The snow finishes many more. In the spring, when the

Fig. 279. Young white pines getting a start. Three ages of pine trees are shown (New York).

snow disappears, it looks as if the little seedlings had another chance. If the winter was cold and the ground bare for a part of the time, perhaps some were frozen to death. The second and third seasons come and go. The weeds flourish each year just as before. They hide the tiny pines, but they cannot choke them out. The little trees grow slowly but surely.

Another enemy than weeds to struggle against. Perhaps, in the first season, or the second, or the third, or even later,

Fig. 280. Young "bull pines" getting a start (Colorado).

another foe appears which pursues different tactics from those of the weeds. It is a tiny fungus, or mold, of delicate gossamer-like threads. It is apt to make its attack on the seedlings in wet weather, just at the surface of the ground. The threads of the mold make little holes in the stem and grow inside. They feed on the stem, dissolving so much of it that it shrinks away and becomes thin and soft, and dead at the ground level. The little pine cannot hold itself up. It topples over to the ground and dies. We say it "damps off," because it appears to rot and die on account of the wet ground. But it was the little plant mold that killed it. Though the mold was very much smaller than the pine, it made a successful attack. Many of the seedlings may fall from the attacks of this insidious foe.

The pines get larger. Each year those that remain get higher. They seem to make up in size what they have lost in number. They grow at a more rapid rate now and are beginning to out-strip and shade the weeds. The weeds and grass cannot endure

Fig. 281. Four giant white pines (New York).

the shade as well as the little pines could.

As the pines get higher the branches reach out and nearly cut off the light from the ground. Finally the weeds and grass can no longer grow underneath them. The few pines remaining have overcome the weeds.

Other competitors appear. There were, perhaps, some acorns, or beechnuts, or the seeds of other trees in the ground. A few of these got a start. Some may have started before the pines did. The pines have grown out of the way of the weeds now. In fact, they never feared the weeds. They were grateful for the shade, perhaps, while they were young. Now the young oaks and beeches, elms, etc., are more sturdy and dangerous competitors. They do not die at the end of the season. They grow larger and larger. During the summer their

Fig. 282. Conifers overtopping broad-leaved trees in the forest (New Hampshire).

broad leaves make a great deal more shade than the pine leaves do. Some of the pines get covered and crowded as time goes on. Some of the smaller ones die. This struggle is renewed year after year. One foot, eighteen inches, or two feet, the trees add to their height annually. Their limbs reach out and interlock as if in actual physical struggle. The dense foliage on the upper branches cuts off much light below. The lower branches die away. The tall, smooth trunks of forest trees appear below the rising tops, which get higher and higher. The smaller trees die and fall to the ground. It is a struggle now between the taller and finer pines and the taller and sturdier oaks. It is a battle of giants, a contest for the "survival of the fittest." Here and there between the round tops of the

Fig. 283. An enemy of pines, a shelving "mushroom," growing from a spruce hemlock.

oak are clear views of the sky above. Through these openings the straight shaft, or "leader," of the pine shoots upward in its more rapid growth. Soon the pines begin here and there to tower above the other trees. Their branches reach out and elbow their way above the tops of the oaks. The pines have risen above the other trees of the forest and hold almost undisputed sway. It now becomes a struggle of pine with pine to see which is the stronger.

Enemies of old pines. As the conquered trees have fallen they have crushed down others, or they have broken large limbs and bruised the trunks. The wood and timber enemies, in the shape of the mushroom and bracket fungi, enter the wound by tiny threads and rot the "heart" of the tree, so that it is weakened and hollow. Fires run through the forest, flashing through the leaves and burning longer in the dead logs. Sound trunks are scorched and sometimes killed, which makes other entrance places for their enemies.

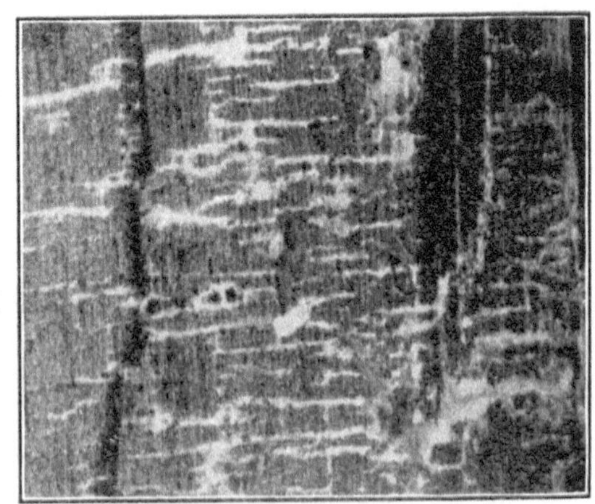

Fig. 284. Spawn of the "mushroom" shown in Fig. 283 as it makes its way through the wood of the tree.

Fig. 285. Effects of fire in forest (New Jersey).

Fig. 286. A bracket "mushroom" growing from a maple.

Insects, in the shape of "borers" and "saw-flies," wound and destroy.

Man sometimes a great enemy of the forest. Then the woodman may come to level the giants with axe and saw. Against him the pines have no means of defense. The finest trees are cut. Here is one which has suffered from a fungus enemy, and so has a hollow trunk. The woodman spares that tree because it is of no value to him. It is left standing alone to tell the tale of the proud pine forest and its grand struggle for mastery.

Fig. 287. Giants of the forest felled by man.

Then man begins his "civilizing influences." The old fallen trunks and the brushwood are burned. The stumps are gradually rooted out. The ground is plowed and planted. Here and there are a few of the remaining giants which man for one reason or another leaves in his cultivated field. One of these is the towering hollow trunk of the pine. It has the look of centuries. It has ceased to advance. Near the top of the tall trunk are great branches. Buildings spring up where once its comrades stood. Many people come to admire this battle-scarred pine. Someone puts a seat near it, and tired travelers rest under this grand old pine. A vine is planted, which climbs up on the great bare trunk and gives it a bit of coloring in summer.

The result of a tussle with a gale. One cold winter day, when the ground was white with the deep snow, a wind came out of the northwest which grew to a gale. A terrific contest came on between the wind and the old pine. Younger elms and oaks, spruces and pines, grown up since the pine's old comrades had disappeared, bent their limbs and trunks with the gale and

Fig. 288. White pine. Result of a tussle with a gale.

rocked to and fro. Now it seemed as if the slender limbs would be torn off. But they were lithe and yielding, and recovered and straightened from each heavy thrust of the gale. The old pine stood proud and fixed, its litheness of limb nearly gone. A fierce gust of the wind snapped off a huge limb like a pipe-stem and dashed it down into the snow bank. Firmly and stiffly did the old pine hold out against each onslaught of the gale, but fiercer came the gusts and half a dozen limbs lay half buried in the snow, and only the stout stubs stood out where once large branches were. Finally the wind subsided, and the old pine still stands, with only its topmost branches left. It is sad to think that the time is near at hand when the old tree must go down.

CHAPTER XXXI.

Struggles against Wind

WHILE the wind is of very great help to many plants in scattering their seed, and thus giving rise to new and young individuals, it is often an enemy against which plants have to contend. Hurricanes and cyclones sometimes sweep down large tracts of forest trees. In some localities there are prevailing winds from one direction. These winds are so frequent and of such force that the tree cannot maintain its normal erect and symmetrical growth. Such prevailing winds often occur along the seacoast or near large lakes, and in mountainous regions, where there are certain well-established and marked differences in temperature and air pressures which tend to create continuous currents in definite directions.

In some places along the seacoast and on mountain heights, especially on the sides of mountains or on elevations in mountain passes, the strong winds are nearly all from one direction and of such force that the entire tree leans with the wind; or the trunk may grow erect while all the branches are on the leeward side. The young lithe branches which come out on the windward side are bent around in the opposite direction. The wind keeps them bent in this direction so continuously that the growth and hardening of the wood finally fixes the branch in that position,—a good example of the force of habit. The young branch finds it easier to bend with the wind than to resist it. When it becomes old this habit is fixed, and the bent and gnarled branches could not straighten even if the wind should moderate. Very interesting examples are seen in regions where the trade winds occur. The trade winds are not very strong, but they blow

Fig. 289. Effects of wind on forest (New Hampshire).

Fig. 290. Tree permanently bent by wind (coast of New Jersey).

Fig. 291. Old cypress trees, permanently bent by wind (Monterey, coast of California).

Fig. 292. Main trunk straight, branches all bent and fixed to one side by wind from one direction (Rocky Mountain).

Fig. 293. Tree permanently bend by trade wind (Nassau).

Fig. 294. Banyan tree spreading equally on all sides from a central trunk where the tree started, and taking root as it spreads to give support (photograph, Rau, No. 6109).

Fig. 295. Banyan tree moved in one direction by trade wind. The older portion of the tree is at the right.

constantly in one direction. Fig. 293 represents a silk-cotton tree on the island of Nassau, in the Atlantic Ocean. The tree is inclined as a result of the constant wind. Where this tree is exposed to the wind, buttresses (bracing roots) are developed at the base of the trunk. It is said that the silk-cotton tree when growing in the forest, where the wind does not exercise such force on it, has no buttresses. The one-sided development of the banyan tree (Fig. 295), influenced by the trade winds, is interesting to compare with the one shown in Fig. 294, where, in the absence of a constant wind in one direction, a symmetrical development has taken place.

CHAPTER XXXII.

Struggles for Territory

The struggle is going on around us all the time. There are opportunities for all of us to see some of these struggles among the plants themselves, and the struggles of plants with the condition of the soil or weather or other surroundings. Go into woods or fields almost any day and you will see some sign of the warfare going on. A grapevine has covered over several small trees and is smothering and weighing them down. The

Fig. 296. Sycamores, grasses, and weeds, having a hard time starting on a rock bed.

Fig. 297. Island with perpendicular sides in Lake Massawiepie, Adirondacks.

grass has stopped growing under trees which branch and produce dense foliage near the ground. When the water is drained from a marshy piece of ground, plants from the drier ground rush in, and soon the character of the vegetation is changed. Did you ever observe how much quicker the grass or cultivated plants wither in dry weather near large trees? The tree takes water from the soil. It cuts off the water supply of other plants. It takes their food also. There is often a struggle among the branches of a tree to see which one shall get most of the light and thus outlive its competitors.

Certain soils are congenial to certain plants. If all plants could grow in all situations, we should have fewer kinds of plants because there would be so many competitors for every foot of ground. But some plants have found one kind of soil congenial to them, and other plants prefer another kind of soil. So, many plants leave certain territory undisputed and only enter into a contest if some favorable changes take place in those localities, provided, of course, their seeds get in there. We do sometimes find a few plants struggling in a very uncongenial

Fig. 298. Island in Raquette River, Adirondacks, with sloping sides and providing different kinds of territory.

soil, but they never become real competitors with the plants which like to grow there. They are struggling only with the physical forces of nature, not with other plants.

Struggles of plants on border territory. The different territories which are congenial to different plants border on one another. Sometimes the border is very abrupt, so that there is no struggle on the part of the plants in one territory to cross over into the other. But in a great many cases the change from one territory to another is gradual. In these cases the border line becomes the seat of a fierce struggle for occupation between the plants of the two adjoining areas.

Fig. 299. Border of lake with sloping shore. Cocklebur on the right fighting with the grasses on the left (Ithaca, N.Y.).

Fig. 300. Plants drawn in battle array on shore line of lake (Ithaca, N.Y.).

These struggles are very commonly seen along the borders of lakes, ponds, or streams, where the ground slopes gradually down to the water edge and out into deep water. So, also, on the borders of marshes or where there is a gradual difference in elevation from a moist soil up to one which is drier. Here we often see various kinds of plants drawn up in battle array defending and holding their ground. The arrow-leaf likes to grow in soil covered with water on the borders of lakes and ponds, where the water is not too deep. The cat-tail flag prefers a little less depth of water, and it contends for the ground nearer the shore, where the water is very shallow. The Joe-Pye weed and boneset like very moist soil near the water.

In this picture (Fig. 300) you see such a contest going on, and the lines of battle sharply drawn. Near this place you could see an army of rushes occupying the same kind of territory that the arrow-leaf occupies here, because the same conditions were congenial to it and the rush drove the arrow-leaf out. So, on such disputed grounds, struggles for possession go on between the kinds of plants which like that territory, and the weaker ones are often crowded out of existence.

CHAPTER XXXIII.

Plant Societies

Plant associations. Plants which have congenial dispositions often grow together in harmony on the same territory. There is room for several different kinds, just as there is room for many small stones in the spaces between large stones in a pile. Moreover, several kinds of plants of the same size may have congenial dispositions toward each other, so that they can live peaceably together. No one of these kinds tries to cover all the ground. They are content with a spot here and there. At least they have not very pugnacious dispositions, nor are they so forward as to crowd themselves in and push out the others. Plants which live together peaceably in this way form societies. They are really social in their dispositions, and often several kinds in one society are dependent on the others. They could not live alone. They need something to cling to, or they need protection from the great light and heat of the sun.

Even where the rushes, and cat-tails, and arrow-leaf, and

Fig. 301. Peat-bog formation with heaths, cranberries, sedges, etc. growing on it, and all advancing to fill in the pond. This is a plant "atoll."

Joe-Pye weed seem to occupy the ground, there are many other kinds of plants which are not so large that fit in between the tall ones or cling to them, or float in the water.

Peculiar societies of peat bogs. When you visit the peat bogs or sphagnum moors, where the peat moss or sphagnum grows, you will find a society of peculiar plants. These plants like cold water and other singular surroundings for their stems and roots. Their disposition is so unusual in this respect that none of the common plants you are familiar with in the fields and woods would go into their society or live in their territory, unless after many years the character of the territory should change so that it would be more congenial.

Growing along with the peat moss you will often find cranberries, Labrador tea, the curious pitcher plant, and many other plants with thick leaves which are retentive of moisture. The

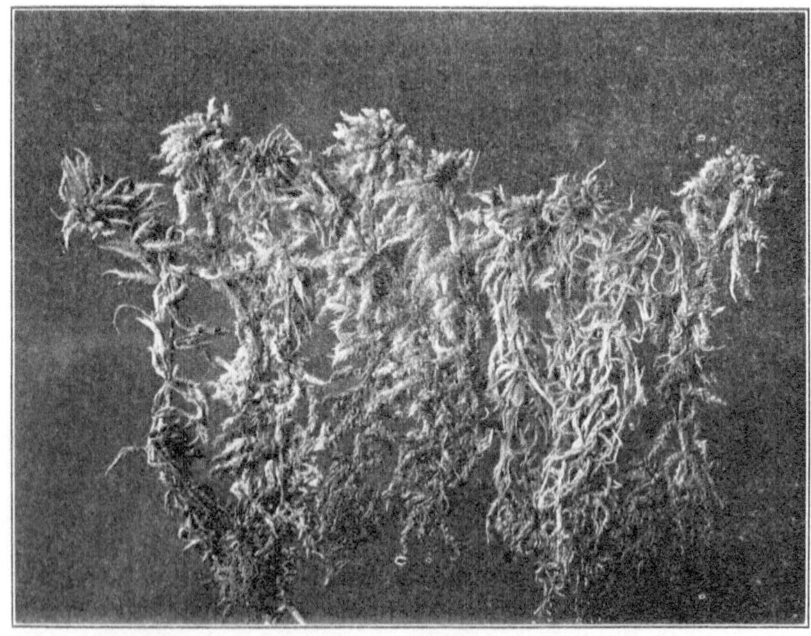

Fig. 302. Plants marching into the sea. They have advanced from the trees at the let in about two hundred years.

plants that associate with the peat moss must be those which give off water into the air slowly, since the cold water and certain acids about their roots in the dead peat below the surface prevent the roots from taking up water rapidly.

The vegetation on the margin of the peat bog. On the margin of the peat bog, where the ground is drier and contains more soil, you may see the plants drawn up in battle array. The societies are struggling among themselves, and are also pushing their way slowly out into the peat. The story of the advance is plainly told by the size and age of the vegetation, as well as by its difference in character.

Many of the peat bogs were once small ponds or lakes. The peat moss and other plants which find shallow water a congenial place to grow in begin marching out from the edge of the water toward the center of the pond. The stems of the peat die below and grow above. So in this way they build up a floor or platform in the water. The dead peat now in the water below does not thoroughly rot, as the leaves do in the moist ground of the forest, because the water shuts out the air. The partly dead stems of the moss pile up quite fast in making the platform, which sometimes is entirely composed of peat. Other plants may grow along with the peat. Their dead bodies also help to build up this floor beneath.

The army of peat and other water plants continues to march out toward the center of the pond, though slowly. Finally, in many cases the line around the shore meets in the center and the pond is filled up, the floor having been extended entirely across. But they keep on adding each year to the floor, raising it higher and higher, until it is high enough and dry enough for the marching armies of the dry land grasses, shrubs, and trees. At length a forest comes to stand on the floor built across the pond by the peat moss and the other members of its society.

Forest societies. There are many kinds of forest societies, just as there are of herbaceous plants. These depend on the elevation, the action of the climate, soil, etc., as well as on the

Fig. 303. Vegetation on border of marsh.

kinds of trees. Forests in the arctic regions are different from those of the temperate zones, and these are different from the forests of the tropics. The society may be at first mixed, cone-bearing, and evergreen trees, with broad-leaved trees. In the end of the struggle some of these are likely to be crowded out. Where the forest growth is even and the leafy tops cut off much of the light, the forest floor will be covered with leaves; there will be an absence of shrubs and herbs, except the shade-loving ones, and the wood will be open below and free from "undergrowth."

When the forest is open above because of the unequal growth of the trees, or because of the destruction of some of the larger trees, light will enter and encourage a greater or less development of undergrowth,—young trees, shrubs, flowers, grass, etc. Then, too, you observe in the forests the great numbers of mushrooms, singular but beautiful and important members of a

Fig. 304. Coniferous forest society, white pine.

Fig. 305. Edge of broad-leaved forest society in winter.

forest society. Some of them, however, become enemies of trees, entering at wounds and rotting out the heart. Others attack the leaves, and by injuring or destroying these food-getting organs weaken the life of the tree. Others attack branches and deform or blight them.

Mosses and lichens, in the temperate and arctic forests, greatly influence the character of the tree trunk which they cover and color. Those hanging on branches give a grotesque appearance and sometimes do injury. In sub-tropical and tropical forests there is a tendency to a change of position of the smaller members of the society from the forest floor to the tree tops, where hanging moss and tree-dwelling orchids and ferns abound.

Desert societies. The oddest looking of plant societies are

Fig. 306. Desert society chiefly cactus (Arizona).

Fig. 307. Desert society, chiefly yucca.

desert societies,—the great trunks of different kinds of cactus, with no leaves on them, or the sprawling *opuntias*, many of the cacti covered with spines. These large fleshy trunks do not lose water so rapidly as thin leaves do; so these plants are well suited to grow in the dry climate of the desert, where the soil is often parched and little water can be found by the plants. This character of the vegetation is the result of ages of warfare with uncongenial conditions. All plants not suited to grow here either have been driven out or have not been able to enter. Those which could take on these forms of the cacti, or of the yuccas, etc., bore trunks with a few hard-skinned leaves at the tops, survived, and now find these conditions quite congenial to them.

Fence-corner and roadside societies. Not every one of you can go to the desert to see the desert societies, or to see the arctic or tropical societies. You must be content with pictures of them. But nearly every one can see plant societies near at hand that are interesting if looked at in the right way. Some of you,

Fig. 308. A roadside society in low ground. Jewel weed attacked by dodder.

in large cities, perhaps do not often see fence corners (though there are some in the heart of New York city) or country roads. But you surely get an outing into the country once in a while. If you don't, you ought to, that's all. Then you can study fence-corner societies, roadside societies, field and forest societies, the brambles, weeds, berries, golden-rod, and asters, and the new-mown hay.

Garden societies. Most of you can have, at least, a garden society; a little plot of ground where you can plant seeds or see the flowers grow, and in the corner of the garden a place where the wild flowers and weeds may struggle.

Plant societies in windows. Here, I am sure, all can have a plant society for observation. Fasten on a window ledge a long box, with broken bits of crockery in the bottom and garden soil on top. There should be an outlet in one end to drain off the surplus water. Here you can grow peas, beans, and other plants to see them struggle with each other and turn toward the light. In another box, or in pots, you can raise some flowers,— geraniums, primroses, and other suitable ones.

You can also have a water-plant society by fitting up an aquarium in a well-lighted window. This can be made by using a large glass vessel, or perhaps some small ones can be made by using fruit jars or broad pans. Put some garden soil in the bottom to supply some of the food. Then nearly fill the vessel with water. In these aquaria you can place *elodea*, the pond scum, and other water plants; but do not have them too crowded. With several of these aquaria and the window gardens you will have an opportunity of learning some interesting habits of plants.

While you can learn many interesting things about plants from window-garden societies, you should not be content with these mere glimpses of the habits and social life of plants. The best place to study plants is in their own homes; so improve every opportunity to visit the fields and woods, become acquainted with some of the flowers and trees, and especially to study their behavior under different conditions and at different seasons of the year. When the fields and woods cannot be visited, the parks and gardens will furnish many subjects from which you can read most interesting stories if you will only try to interpret the sign language by means of which the trees and flowers express to us their lives and work.

www.ingramcontent.com/pod-product-compliance
Lightning Source LLC
Chambersburg PA
CBHW030608310726
48979CB00003B/623